한국현대인형극본 선집

The Anthology of Modern
Korean Puppet Theatre Scripts

한국현대인형극본 선집

The Anthology of Modern
Korean Puppet Theatre Scripts

선욱현 엮음 • 유니마 코리아 번역

평민사

한국현대인형극본 선집

The Anthology of Modern
Korean Puppet Theatre Scripts

초판 1쇄 인쇄일 2025년 5월 9일
초반 1쇄 발행일 2025년 5월 19일

지은이   조현산·문재현·배근영·정승진·기태인
번 역   유니마 코리아
번역 감수   김주연
서 평   오판진
엮은이   선욱현
기획·제작   사단법인 유니마 코리아
만든이   이정옥
만든곳   평민사
            서울시 은평구 수색로 340 〈202호〉
            전화 : 02) 375-8571
            팩스 : 02) 375-8573
            http://blog.naver.com/pyung1976
            이메일: pyung1976@naver.com
등록번호   25100-2015-000102호
 ISBN   987-89-7115-877-7   03800
 정가   17,000원

이 책은 예술경영지원센터의 장르별 시장 거점화 지원사업으로 출간되었습니다.

— 차례 —

한국인형극, 세계를 향한 새로운 전환점

최준호

유니마 코리아 이사장 | 춘천인형극제 예술감독

인형극의 창작은 단순한 연극적 요소를 넘어, 여러 장르를 넘나드는 복합적인 접근을 고려해야 합니다. 다양한 형태의 인형, 대본, 무대 연출, 그리고 그 안에서 일어나는 감정적 교감까지 모든 요소가 유기적으로 결합하여야 하기에, 이를 실현하는 데 드는 노력과 시간은 상상할 수 없이 많습니다. 그런데도 인형극인들은 기존의 전통적인 형태에 얽매이지 않고, 현대적인 감각을 더하며 새로운 길을 개척해 왔습니다. 그래서 〈한국현대인형극본 선집〉이 지닌 의미는 단순히 작품을 모아둔 희곡집이 아니라, 한국인형극의 발전을 위해 지난 수십 년간 끊임없이 노력해 온 인형극인들의 헌신과 열정에 대한 기록입니다.

인형극은 그 특유의 감각적 요소와 표현 방식으로 관객과 깊은 교감을 만들어 내는 예술 장르입니다. 그러나 이 장르를 발전시키기까지의 과정은 절대 쉽지 않았습니다. 인형극인들은 수많은 실험과 훈련을 통해 작품을 만들어왔으며, 그들이 겪은 고뇌와 노력 없이 오늘날 한국인형극이 이만큼 성장할 수 없었을 것입니다. 틀을 넘어서는 새로운 시도와 창의적인 접근을 통해 한국인형극의 발전을 이끌어낸 창작자들의 혁신적이고 도전적인 노력의 결실이 이 책에 담겨있습니다.

이번 희곡집의 발간은 단순히 책 한 권을 출간하는 것을 넘어, 한국인형극의 발전을 알리고 그 중요성을 재조명하는 데 큰 의의를 두고 있습니다. 한국인형극은 오랜 시간 동안 어린이들만을 위한 예술로 여겨졌지만, 이제는 다양한 연령과 사회적 배경을 가진 사람들에게도 깊은 감동과 메시지를 전달할 수 있는 장르로 자리매김했습니다. 이 책은 바로 그 변화와 발전의 과정이 기록된 중요한 자료로서, 한국인형극이 가진 가능성을 널리 알리는 초석이 될 것입니다.

이번 책에 실린 다섯 개의 작품 '달래 이야기', '구름이와 욜', '소금인형', '이야기 쏙! 이야기야', '이야기 하루' 는 각기 다른 형식과 접근 방식으로 현대 한국인형극의 다양한 모습을 보여줍니다. 특히, 각 작품이 다루고 있는 철학적이고 심오한 주제들은 관객들에게 단순한 오락을 넘어서 깊은 성찰을 안겨 줍니다. 작품들은 기존의 인형극이 가진 단순함을 넘어서, 복잡하고 다층적인 메시지를 전달하며, 다양한 연령층과 사회적 배경을 가진 관객들과 교감할 수 있는 능력을 지니고 있습니다.

이 책을 통해 우리는 한국인형극이 어느새 세계와 소통할 수 있는 예술 장르로 성장했음을 알 수 있습니다. 이 책에 실린 작품들은 현재 진행형인 한국인형극의 모습을 보여줄 뿐만 아니라, 한국인형극이 앞으로 나아가야 할 방향과 그 가능성을 제시합니다. 이는 한국인형극의 역사적 순간을 기록하는 작업이며, 한국인형극을 더 넓은 세계로 이끌고 갈 전환점의 중요한 자원이 될 것입니다. 이 희곡집이 한국인형극의 가능성과 가치를 새롭게 확인하게 하고, 한국인형극의 지속적인 발전에 필요한 기반의 한 축이 될 수 있기를 희망합니다.

A New Turning Point for Korean Puppet Theatre on the Global Stage

Choe Junho

President of UNIMA Korea
Artistic Director of the Chuncheon Puppet Festival

The creation of puppet theatre goes beyond mere theatrical elements; it requires a multidisciplinary approach that traverses various genres. Every aspect - including different types of puppets, scripts, stage direction, and the emotional interactions that unfold within - must be intricately interwoven. The time and effort required to bring such a performance to life are beyond imagination. Despite these challenges, puppeteers have continually pushed beyond traditional forms, incorporating modern sensibilities to forge new paths. Thus, the Anthology of Modern Korean Puppet Theatre Scripts is more than just a collection of scripts. It stands as a testament to the dedication and passion of puppetry artists who have ceaselessly contributed to the evolution of Korean puppet theatre over the past decades.

Puppetry is an art form that creates deep emotional connections with audiences through its unique sensory elements and expressive techniques. However, the journey towards the development of this genre has been anything but easy. Puppeteers have crafted their works through countless experiments and rigorous training, and without their struggles and dedication, Korean puppetry would not have reached its current level of growth. This book encapsulates the innovative and daring efforts of creators who have driven the evolution of Korean puppetry by pushing boundaries and embracing creative approaches.

The publication of this script collection goes beyond merely releasing a book; it holds great significance in promoting the development of Korean puppetry and re-examining its importance. For a long time, Korean puppetry was regarded solely as an art form for children. However, it has now established itself as a genre capable of delivering profound emotions and messages to people of all ages and social backgrounds. This book serves as a crucial record of that transformation and growth, laying the foundation for raising awareness of the vast potential that Korean puppetry holds.

The works included in this book **- Dallae Story, Guroom and Yol, The Story of Haru, Tale of Tales and The Salt Doll -** each showcase the diverse aspects of contemporary Korean puppetry through different formats and approaches. In particular, the philosophical and profound themes explored in these pieces offer audiences more than just entertainment; they provide deep reflection. These scripts go beyond the simplicity traditionally associated with puppetry, delivering complex and multi-layered messages while possessing the ability to connect with audiences of various ages and social backgrounds.

Through this book, we can recognise that Korean puppetry has grown into an art form capable of communicating with the world. The works included not only reflect the current state of Korean puppetry but also suggest its future direction and potential. This publication serves as a record of a historic moment for Korean puppetry and as an important resource that will help propel it onto a broader global stage. We hope that this collection reaffirms the potential and value of Korean puppetry and becomes a foundational pillar for its continued growth and development.

소중한 첫 시작

선욱현

극작가 | 춘천인형극제 예술감독(2019~2024)

우연한 기회로, 1989년에 시작하여 한국에서 가장 오랜 역사를 가진 인형극축제, 춘천인형극제와 인연을 맺었다. 청년기 이후 극작가, 배우, 연출 등 연극만 했던 필자는 2019년 1월에 춘천인형극제 예술감독으로 일을 시작하여 2024년 12월까지, 만 6년을 인형극과 만났다. 매년 축제 참가작 결정을 위해 평균 200여 편의 국내, 국외 작품을 심사했다. 그리고 프랑스 샤를르빌 축제, 캐나다 몬트리올 카스텔리에 축제, 스페인 예이다 축제, 핀란드 투르크 TIP 페스티벌, 루마니아 PUCK 페스티벌, 일본 오키나와 리카리카 페스티벌, 카자흐스탄 알마티 오르테케 인형극제 등 해외 인형극 축제를 다니며 해외인형극을 만났다. 우연한 인연으로 정말 많은 인형극을 만났다. 그리고 인형극을 새롭게 이해하게 되는 시간을 갖게 되었다. 대부분의 한국인은 인형극을 '아이들이 보는 극' 정도로 생각한다. 필자도 70년대 중후반, 초등학생 시절, TV를 통해 인형극을 보며 자랐다. 성인이 되어 다시 만난 인형극은 달랐다. 지금도 물론 많은 어린이들이 인형극을 본다. 하지만 인형극은 아이들만의 것이 아니고 전 연령층을 대상으로 하며 그 포용성이 아주 크다. 기본적으로 동심을 바탕으로 하는 까닭에 그 순수함과 보

11

편성이 많은 연령층과 계층을 끌어안게 된다. 연극, 뮤지컬, 오페라는 대중적이라 하기에는 일부 마니아층의 선호도가 강하다. 하지만 인형극은 기존의 극을 보지 않던 이들에게도 쉽게 다가가고 스며든다. 그게 인형극의 차별성이자 더 대중적으로 확장될 수 있는 장점이라고 생각한다. 춘천인형극제 재직 기간 동안 기존의 인형극을 하던 인형인들, 그리고 대중적이지 않지만, 자신만의 인형극을 창작하는 이들, 그리고 청년들이 보여주는 새로운 물결도 보았다. 연극영화과를 나온 젊은이들이 인형극이라는 장르를 새롭게 배우고 적용했다. 연극, 뮤지컬, 마임, 마술, 서커스, 국악, 무용을 했던 청년들이 인형극이라는 새로운 아이템을 장착하고 장르를 혼합한, 이른바 콜라보레이션 인형극을 선보였다. 기존의 인형극인들에게는 최근의 이런 현상이 조금 혼란스러울 수도 있다. 이게 인형극인가? 이런 극까지 인형극으로 수용해야 하는가? 하지만 이미 세계의 인형극들은 경계를 넘어서고 있다. 아니 심지어 경계의 구분도 모호하고 불필요하게 느껴지기도 한다. 필자는 한국의 인형극이 변화와 확장의 시대를 통과하는 그 길 가운데 서 있었다. 한국의 인형극은 이미 변화를 맞고 있고 할 수 있다면 새로운 시기를 앞당겨야 한다. 이 책 또한 그 일의 하나였음 한다.

  춘천인형극제 예술감독 일을 하면서 필자는 자연스럽게 숙제 하나를 갖게 되었다. 극작가로서 1995년 등단한 이후 올해 30주년을 맞았고 희곡집을 다섯 권이나 낸 경험에서 자연스럽게 인형극본집을 생각하게 되었다. 한국은 오랜 역사 속에 꼭두각시놀음, 그림자극, 발탈, 탈춤과 같은 가면극 등 전통적인 인형극이 있었고 1960년대 이후 활발하게 전개되는 현대 인형극의 시기도 존재한다. 그런데 그 역사의 기록이나 인형극 관련 출판 활동은 많지 않았다. 인형극본집 또한 마찬가지였다. 그래서 지금의 시기야말로 꼭 필요한 책이라는 생각을 했다. 인형극본이지만 이건 곧 한국 현대 인형극의 현재이며, 이 기록으로 인해 다른 많은 일이 생겨나는 확장이 있었으면 한다.

수록된 희곡 5편은 필자가 재직했던 시기에 만난 작품 중에서 우선으로 선택했다. 인형극도 대사극, 오브제극, 비언어극 등 다양하고 대상층 또한 어린아이부터 성인을 대상으로 한 인형극들도 있다. 그래서 다양한 작품들을 선택하고자 했다.

〈달래 이야기〉는 비언어극으로 한국뿐 아니라 세계 여러 나라에서 호평을 받은 작품이다. 한국전쟁을 배경으로 한 까닭에 한국적이며 세계 보편적인 주제까지도 담아냈다. 그래서 확장성이 큰 장점을 가진 작품이다. 〈구름이와 욜〉은 동화를 원작으로 각색한 작품이다. 많은 인형극이 기존의 명작 동화를 원작으로 하는 경우도 많다. 필자가 만난 인형극인들은 동화를 어떻게 인형극으로 각색해야 하는지 작법과 관련한 질문들도 많이 했다. 그래서 선택한 작품이 이 작품이고 인형극인의 전문성이 동화를 어떻게 극으로 바꾸어 내는지를 잘 보여주었다. 〈소금인형〉은 철학적 물음을 인형극으로 옮긴 작품이다. 나는 어디서 왔지? 소금인형이 바다를 찾아가는 여정은 철학적이며 시적이다. 어린 관객들에게 그 질문이 다소 어려울 수도 있다. 물론 어떻게 전달하느냐에 따라 다르겠지만. 아무튼 인간이 실존적으로 갖는 질문을 〈소금인형〉은 담고 있고 소금인형이 나중에 바다를 만나고 바닷물에 자신의 몸을 담그는 장면은 감동을 선사한다. 성인관객들이라면 인형극이 아이들만 보는 게 아니구나 라고 느낄 수 있을 것이다. 〈이야기 쏙! 이야기야〉에는 배우들의 재담과 그림자극, 전통적 이야기 소재가 잘 녹아있다. 그리고 그동안의 인형극본을 인형극단 대표들이 직접 쓰고 연출하는 경우가 많았다면 이 작품은 전문 극작가가 대본을 썼다. 동화로 등단한 정승진 작가는 인형극계에서 최근 활발한 활동을 이어가는, 이른바 전문 인형극 작가이다. 연극계에서 활발하게 활동 중인 김민정 극작가 또한 최근 극단 봄과 함께 좋은 인형극본을 선보이고 있다. 전문 작가가 극을 쓰고 인형극인이 연출하는 시대가 이제 시작되고 있는 것이다. 인형극 전문 작가가 늘어난다면 당연히 발전의 속도는 가속화될 것이다. 〈이야기 하루〉는 주인공 할아버지를 배우가 하는데, 그래서 연극성이 강하게 느껴지기도 하지만 인형들이 손인형부터 그림자, 오브제 등 다양한 장르의 인형극들이 모두 등장한다. 바로 그 지점이 현대 인형극의 현재를 보여주고 있다. 장대인형극은 장대인형만 나오고 손인형극은 손인형만 나오는 게 아니라 현대 인형극은 극에 필요한 다양한 표현 방식이 동시에 나온다. 이렇게 다섯 편의 인형극은 〈달래 이야기(2003)〉한 편 외에는 모두 2010년 이후 초연되고 현재까지 공연되고 있는 한국의 현대 인형극들이다.

한국의 인형극은 기록할 역사도 많고 필요한 책도 많다. 외국 서적 중에도 번역 출판된다면 많은 인형극인들, 관계자들이 반길 것이다. 스스로 숙제로 여겼던 이 출판을 선뜻 결정해 주고 추진해 주신 춘천인형극제와 유니마 코리아에 감사드리며 공연 관련 서적을 성심으로 출판해 주시는 도서출판 평민사에도 감사드린다.

A Cherished First Step

Sun Wook-Hyun

Playwright
Artistic Director of the Chuncheon Puppet Festival(2019~2024)

By chance, I became connected with the Chuncheon Puppet Festival, the longest-running puppet festival in Korea, which began in 1989. After transitioning from being a playwright, to actor, to director, who had focused solely on theater, I started working as the artistic director of the Chuncheon Puppet Festival in January 2019. I continued this role for six years, until December 2024, working closely with puppetry. Every year, in order to decide which performances would be included in the festival, I reviewed an average of 200 domestic and international works. I also visited various international puppet festivals, including the Festival Mondial des Théâtres de Marionnettes in France, the Festival International de Casteliers in Montreal (Canada), the Fira de Titelles de Lleida (Puppet Festival of Lleida) in Catalonia (Spain), the Turku International Puppetry Festival (TIP-Fest) in Finland, the PUCK International Puppet Theatre Festival in Romania, the Ricca Ricca Festa in Okinawa (Japan), and the International Puppet

Theater Festival "Orteke" in Kazakhstan. Through these festivals, I encountered numerous puppet performances. It was a fortunate connection that allowed me to experience so many puppet shows and gave me the chance to deeply understand puppetry in a new way. Most Koreans think of puppet theatre as something primarily for children. I also grew up in the late 1970s, watching puppet shows on TV as an elementary school student. The puppet theatre I encountered again as an adult was different. Of course, many children still watch puppet shows today. However, puppet theatre is not just for children; it is for all age groups, and its inclusiveness is vast, because puppetry is fundamentally based on childlike innocence, its purity and universality appeal to a wide range of ages and social groups. Theater, musicals, and opera, while popular, tend to have a strong preference from a specific fanbase. However, puppetry easily reaches and resonates with those who may not typically watch traditional theater. I believe this is the unique quality of puppetry and an advantage that allows it to expand more broadly to a wider audience.

During my time at the Chuncheon Puppet Festival, I witnessed puppeteers who had been doing traditional puppet theatre, those who created their own unique puppet theatre, though not widely popular, and the new wave brought by young people. Young individuals who graduated from theatre and film studies applied the genre of puppet theatre in a fresh way. Young people who had worked in theatre, musicals, mime, magic, circus, traditional Korean music, and dance introduced what is now called "collaborative puppet theatre," mixing genres and adding puppet theatre as a new element. This recent phenomenon may be somewhat confusing to traditional puppeteers. Is this really puppet theatre? Should we accept such performances as puppet theatre? However, puppet theatres around the world have already transcended boundaries. In fact, the distinction between boundaries sometimes feels ambiguous and even unnecessary. I found myself standing at the crossroads of an era where Korean puppet theatre is undergoing change and expansion. Korean puppet theatre is already evolving, and if possible, we should accelerate the arrival of this new era. I hope this book serves as part of that process.

When I was the artistic director of the Chuncheon Puppet Festival, I naturally took on a task. Having debuted as a playwright in 1995, marking the 30th anniversary of my career this year, and having published five volumes of plays, I was naturally led to think about a collection of puppet play scripts. Korea has a long history of traditional puppet theatre, such as puppet plays, shadow puppetry, Bal-tal (foot puppetry with masks – a traditional Korean performance), and mask dances. There has also been a period of active development of modern puppetry since the 1960s. However, there has been a lack of documented history and few publications on puppet theatre. The same applies to puppet script collections. Therefore, I felt that the time had come for such a book to be created. Although these are puppet play scripts, this is also the current state of modern Korean puppetry, and I hope that this record will lead to an expansion that brings about many other developments.

The five plays included were primarily chosen from the works I encountered during my time as an artistic director. Puppet theatre, like dialogue-based theatre, object theatre, and non-verbal theatre, is diverse, and there are puppet shows for audiences ranging from children to adults. Therefore, I aimed to select a variety of works.

"**Dallae Story**" is a non-verbal theatre piece that has received acclaim not only in Korea but also in many countries around the world. Set against the backdrop of the Korean War, it captures both a distinctly Korean and universally relevant theme. This makes it a work with great potential for expansion. "**Guroom and Yol**" is an adaptation of a fairy tale. Many puppet performances are based on classic fairy tales, and during my time with puppeteers, there were often questions about how to adapt fairy tales into puppet theatre. This work was chosen because it shows how the expertise of puppeteers transforms a fairy tale into a theatrical performance. "**The Story of Haru**" features a grandfather as the main character, played by an actor. Although this adds a strong theatrical element, various types of puppetry, including hand puppets, shadow puppets, and object puppets, appear in the performance. This point illustrates the present state of contemporary puppet theatre. While traditional puppet theatre may feature only one type of puppet, such as stilt puppets or hand puppets, modern puppet theatre incorporates various forms of expression that suit the needs of the play.

"Tale of Tales" is also an example of this. It combines the actors' witty dialogue, shadow puppetry, and traditional storytelling themes in a well-blended manner. While many puppet theatre scripts in the past were written and directed by the heads of puppet theatre companies, this work was written by a professional playwright, Jeong Seung-Jin, a playwright who debuted in fairy tales, and is a so-called professional puppet theatre writer who has been actively contributing to the puppet theatre world recently. Similarly, playwright Kim Min-Jeong (Korean), who is active in the theatre world, has also presented excellent puppet plays with the theatre company 'Bom'(meaning 'Spring' in Korean). We are now entering an era where professional playwrights write scripts, and puppet theatre artists direct. If the number of professional puppet writers increases, the speed of development in the field will naturally accelerate.

"**Salt Doll**" is a work that translates philosophical questions into puppet theatre. "Where do I come from?" The Salt Doll's journey to find the sea is both philosophical and poetic. For young audiences, this question may be a bit difficult. Of course, it depends on how it is delivered. In any case, Salt Doll addresses existential human questions, and the scene where the Salt Doll eventually meets the sea and dips its body into the seawater is deeply moving. Adult audiences will likely realize that puppet theatre is not just for children. These five puppet plays, with the exception of Dallae Story(2003), were all first performed after 2010 and are still being performed today as contemporary Korean puppet theatre.

Korean puppet theatre has much history to be recorded and many books that are needed. If foreign books are translated and published, many puppeteers and people involved will welcome it. I would like to express my gratitude to the Chuncheon Puppet Festival and UNIMA Korea for decisively supporting and promoting this publication, which I considered a personal task. I also thank Pyeongminsa Publishing, which sincerely publishes books related to performances.

달래 이야기

극작 조현산

예술무대산

등장인물

아빠

엄마

달래

강아지

1. 이야기의 시작

봄볕이 따사로운 어느 농가의 마당, 아침이 밝아오면 흰 나비 한 마리
가 날아 들어온다.
장대 끝에 잠시 앉았다가 날개를 몇 번 접고 다시 날아간다.

따뜻한 햇볕이 비추면 아낙이 빨래를 광주리에 담아 들고나온다.
날씨가 참 좋다, 달래 치마를 꼭 짜서는 잠시 쳐다보고는 줄에 넌다.
빨래집게가 없다는 걸 알고 집안으로 찾으러 들어간다.

밖에 나갔던 사내가 들어온다, 아낙이 어디 있나 살피고 아낙이 없는걸
확인하고는 뒷춤에 감추었던 꽃신을 꺼내어 보고 흐뭇해한다.
빨래 광주리를 발견하고 무언가 생각났는지 다가가 빨래 광주리 안에
꽃신을 감추고 숨는다.
빨래집게를 가지고 들어온 아낙이 다시 빨래를 널고 사내는 아무 일도
없다는 듯 헛기침을 하며 다시 들어온다.
힘들게 빨래를 짜는 아낙을 보고 달려가 도와주려고 한다.
장난처럼 잠시 실랑이하다 사내가 빨래를 받아 넌다.
숨겨 두었던 꽃신을 발견하는 아낙, 의기양양해하는 사내,
아낙으로부터 꽃신을 받아 들고 정성껏 신을 닦아 신어보라는 듯 바닥
에 내려놓는다.
꽃신에 살짝 발을 넣으려다 차마 신지 못하고 냉큼 집어 들고 좋아한다.

사내도 같이 좋아하다가 눈이 마주치자 묘한 분위기를 느낀다.
입술을 쭈욱 내밀어 보는 사내, 부끄러운 아낙은 빨래로 사내 얼굴을 휙 덮고 도망간다.
혼자 남은 사내는 겸연쩍은 듯 웃음 짓고 남은 빨래를 널고 집안으로 들어간다.

2. 봄

빨랫줄 위로 작은 진달래 동산이 생기고 아낙의 처녀적 모습의 손 인형이 등장, 누군가를 기다리고 있다.
사내 모습의 손인형 등장, 아낙을 발견하고 달려간다.
새침한 아낙과 어수룩하고 어쩔 줄 몰라 하는 사내가 이곳저곳 서로 쫓아다니며 논다.
때때로 인형과 사람으로 번갈아 보이는데 사내와 아낙이 인형 놀이를 하는 듯하다.
결국 서로 입을 맞추며 (인형으로) 빨래 밑으로 사라지면 아이 울음소리가 들리고 초가집이 빨랫줄 위로 생긴다.

금줄을 초가집에 올리며 기뻐하는 사내(사람)와 인형!
아이를 안고 아낙이 배웅하고 지게를 진 사내가 일하러 나간다.
아이를 안은 아낙이 집 안으로 들어가고 걸음마를 하는 달래가 아장아장 걸어 나오면 사내가 달려와서 달래를 안아 올린다.
아내와 같이 집 안으로 들어간다.

3. 여름

(이하 장면들도 빨랫줄 위의 인형극으로 보여진다)

낚싯대를 든 달래와 사내가 집에서 나온다.

낚싯대를 드리우지만, 물고기가 잡히지 않자 사내는 빨랫줄 밑으로
휙 사라진다. (사람으로 바뀐다)

물고기를 달래의 낚싯바늘에 끼워 주지만 놓치고 만다.

커다란 물고기가 나타나 천천히 헤엄치다 달래와 사내를 태우고 사라
진다.

갑자기 천둥이 치고 소나기가 내린다.

급하게 뛰어나와 빨래를 걷고 (사람) 사내가 아낙의 비를 막아주며 집
안으로 들어간다.

4. 가을

빨랫줄 위로 감이 주렁주렁 달린 감나무가 생기고 잠자리 한 마리가 날
아다닌다.

집 안에서 나오던 달래가 잠자리를 발견하고 아빠에게 잡아달라고
한다.

아빠는 잠자리를 잡으려다 잠자리채로 달래를 잡는다.

토라진 달래를 달래려고 감을 따주려 하지만 잘되지 않는다.

아낙이 나오고 달래가 감을 따 달라고 한다.

아낙은 머리로 한 번에 들이받아 감을 따고 그 모습을 보고 놀랐던 달
래와 사내는 금세 좋아하며 같이 집으로 들어간다.

(사람) 아낙이 나와서 빨래를 걷어 들어간다.

5. 겨울

달이 뜨고 눈이 내린다.

달래와 강아지가 나와서 좋아라. 뛰어다닌다.

사내가 나와 달래에게 눈사람을 만들어 준다.

눈을 굴리다 손이 시려하면 달래가 아빠 손을 호호 불어주기도 하고 눈사람에 밀짚모자도 씌워준다.

아낙까지 함께 나와서 다 만든 눈사람을 구경하고 집 안으로 들어간다.

어두워지고 초가집 창호지 문에 가족의 단란한 모습이 그림자로 비친다.

6. 사내 이야기

사이렌 소리와 함께 공습 소리가 들리면 초가집과 빨랫줄은 사라지고 스크린에 그림자로 초가집 울타리와 널린 빨래가 보인다.

탱크가 지나가며 울타리를 부순다.

누군가에게 끌려가는 사내. 아낙이 말려 보지만 소용이 없다.

혼자 남아 울부짖는 아낙.

스크린의 그림자가 겨울 산으로 바뀌고 (사람) 사내가 눈을 맞으며 보초를 서려고 총을 메고 터덜터덜 걸어 나온다.

소복이 쌓여있는 눈을 보다가 허기를 못 이겨 한 움큼 뭉쳐 베어 먹는다.

너무 춥고 시리다.

문득 무언가 생각났는지 눈을 뭉치는 사내, 눈사람을 만든다.

돌을 주워 눈, 코, 입까지 만들고는 뭐가 좋은지 혼자 바보처럼 웃는다.

갑자기 총격전이 시작되고 겁에 질린 사내는 바닥에 납작 엎드려 기어서 도망간다.
총격 소리가 잦아들고 숨을 돌릴 때 그림자로 누군가 나타난다.
얼결에 총을 겨누고 살려달라는 그림자 안의 사람을 보고 놀라 방아쇠를 당긴다.
자신이 사람을 죽였다는 걸 알고는 혼란에 빠져 버린 사내.

스크린에 물고기 한 마리가 보인다. 점점 다가오면 사내도 고개를 들고 물고기 뒤를 쫓는다. 어느 순간 달래가 물고기 등에 타고 있다. 사내와 달래 그리고 물고기가 한데 어우러져 재미나게 논다.

술래잡기를 하는데 달래와 물고기는 더는 보이지 않는다.
하지만 사내의 눈에는 달래가 보이는 것처럼, 달래를 찾아 꼬옥 안아주고 손을 잡고 일어서는데 '쾅' 하는 총소리 들린다.

사내는 현실과 환상의 경계에 있는 듯 달래를 찾아 두리번거린다.
끝까지 현실을 믿지 못하는 사내는 천천히 무너지듯 쓰러진다.

어디선가 날아온 나비 한 마리가 사내의 어깨 위에 잠시 앉았다가 날개를 몇 번 접고 다시 날아간다.
눈이 내리기 시작한다, 무대 위의 나비가 사라지고 스크린에 다시 나비가 나타난다.
나비가 사라지고 무대는 천천히 어두워진다.

7. 아낙의 이야기

공습 소리와 함께 남루한 행색의 (사람) 아낙이 뛰어 들어온다.
공습을 피해 이리저리 뛰다가 소중히 안고 있던 꽃신도 떨어뜨린다.
땅에 머리를 박고 바들바들 떨고 있다.
폭격 소리가 작아지고 겨우 머리를 들어 주위를 살피다, 눈앞의 개울에서 허겁지겁 물을 퍼마신다.
문득 개울에 비친 자기모습을 바라보고는 머리를 쓸어 올린다.
나비 한 마리가 날아 들어와서 아낙을 떨어뜨린 꽃신 쪽으로 이끌어 준다.
떨어뜨린 꽃신을 발견하고 허둥지둥 달려가 줍는다.
꽃신을 소중하게 털고 닦다가 옛일이 생각나는 듯 꽃신을 들고 일어선다.
너무나 소중하고 행복한 기억에 꽃신을 와락 끌어안는다.
진달래 꽃비가 흩날리고 아낙은 춤을 춘다.
마치 사랑하는 사내와 함께 춤을 추는 것 같다.
때론 수줍게 때론 명랑하게, 처음 만나 연애하고 사랑하던 시절로 돌아간 것처럼 즐겁고 행복하게 보인다.

처녀 적으로 다시 돌아가 소중하게 꽃신을 신어보려는 순간, 어디선가 들리는 아이 울음소리, 두리번거리다 자기가 떨어뜨린 보따리를 발견하고는 마치 자기 아기인 양 소중하게 안아 올린다.

보따리를 소중하게 꼭 안아주고는 등 뒤로 업고 일어선다.

너무나 행복한 표정으로 아이를 어르며 무대 앞을 지나 천천히 퇴장
한다.

무대 위에는 꽃신만 남아있다.

8. 달래 이야기

(인형) 달래가 혼자 흙장난하며 놀고 있다.

땅에 그림도 그리고 두꺼비집 놀이도 하고 놀다가 벌떡 일어나 누굴
기다리는 듯, 한곳을 멍하니 바라본다.

혼자 놀다가 지쳐 잠이 든다.

달래가 가지고 놀던 강아지 인형이 살아나 움직인다.

달래를 깨운다.

처음에는 살짝 놀라 경계하던 달래도 금방 친해져 함께 뛰어논다.

함께 뒹굴고 뛰고 하늘을 날기도 한다.

작은 바구니를 들고 엄마가 (아낙) 들어온다. 마치 부엌에라도 있다가 오는 듯하다. 강아지도 엄마에게 다가가 반가운 시늉을 한다.

달래는 잠시 바라보다 달려가 엄마 다리를 꼬옥 안는다.

달래는 엄마 무릎을 베고 누워 강아지와 장난을 치고 엄마는 바느질을 한다.

강아지와 장난을 하다 엄마를 타고 오르기도 하고 엄마가 만들어 준 치마를 입어 보기도 한다. 엄마와의 놀이가 이어지다가, 달래는 엄마 등에 업혀 거닐다 잠이 들고

깨어나서는 엄마에게 '무궁화꽃이 피었습니다' 놀이를 하자고 한다. 놀이 중에 엄마가 사라지고 강아지 인형도 어느 순간 처음처럼 누워 있다.

달래, 널브러진 강아지 인형을 주워 들어보고는 사라진 엄마를 찾아 주위를 둘러보다

그 자리에 주저앉자, 강아지를 꼭 끌어안는다. 그 모습 위로, 나비 두 마리가 날아 들어왔다 사라지고, 달래네 가족의 행복했던 모습이 그림으로 보여지고, 달래 머리 위로 꽃비가 날린다.

〈끝〉

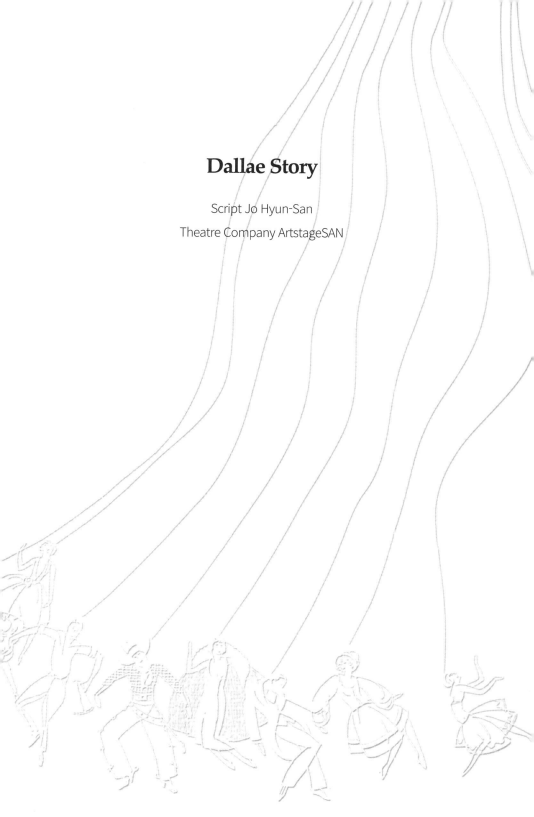

Dallae Story

Script Jo Hyun-San

Theatre Company ArtstageSAN

Characters

Father
Mother
Dallae
Dog

1. The Beginning of the Story

On the yard of a farmhouse, with the warm spring sunlight, a white butterfly flies in as the morning dawns. It briefly sits on the end of a pole, folding its wings a few times, and then flies away again.

When the warm sunlight shines, a woman carries out a basket of laundry.
The weather is really nice. After wringing Dallae's skirt, she briefly looks at it and then hangs it on the line. Realizing she doesn't have any clothes pegs, she goes back inside to find them.

The man who had been outside comes in.
He looks around to see if the woman is there, and after confirming she is not, he takes out a pair of flower shoes he had hidden behind his back and looks at them with pleasure. He notices the laundry basket and, as if having remembered something, approaches it, hides the flower shoes inside, and then hides

The woman comes back with the clothes pegs, hangs up the laundry again, and the man enters as if nothing happened, clearing his throat. Seeing the woman struggling to wring out the laundry, he rushes to help her. They briefly have a playful scuffle, and then the man takes the laundry and hangs it up. The woman finds the flower shoes that had been hidden, and the man looks pleased. He takes the shoes from her, carefully cleans them, and places them on the floor as if inviting her to try them on.

She starts to slip her foot into the silk shoes but hesitates, quickly picks them up, looking pleased. The man is also pleased, and when their eyes meet, a subtle, intriguing tension fills the air. The man pouts his lips, and the embarrassed woman quickly throws the laundry over his face and runs away. Left alone, the man smiles awkwardly, hangs the remaining laundry, and then goes inside the house.

2. Spring

A small azalea hill forms on the laundry line and a hand puppet resembling the woman in her maiden days appears, waiting for someone.
A hand puppet resembling the man appears, sees the woman, and runs towards her.
The coy woman and the clumsy, awkward man play, chasing each other here and there.
Sometimes, they alternate between being puppets and people, making it seem as though the man and woman are playing with the puppets.
Eventually, they kiss each other and, as puppets, disappear under the laundry, followed by the sound of a child crying, then a thatched house appears above the laundry line.

The man(human) and the puppet joyfully raise a golden thread over the thatched house.

The woman, holding the child, sees him off, and the man, carrying a jige[1] on his back, heads out to work.

The woman, still holding the child, goes inside the house. When Dallae, now walking, toddles out, the man runs to her, lifts her up, and enters the house with his wife.

3. Summer

(From here, the scenes continue to be presented as a puppet play on the laundry line.)

Dallae and the man, holding fishing rods, come out of the house.

They lower their fishing rods, but when no fish are caught, the man quickly disappears under the laundry line(changing into a human).

He places a fish on Dallae's fishing hook, but it slips away.

A large fish appears, swimming slowly before carrying Dallae and the man away as it disappears.

Suddenly, thunder strikes, and a downpour begins.

In a hurry, the man rushes out to collect the laundry and, as a human, shields the woman from the rain and guides her into the house.

---

1) A jige is a traditional Korean carrying frame, typically used to carry heavy loads on the back, often with the help of straps

4. Autumn

A persimmon tree, heavy with fruit, appears above the laundry line, and a dragonfly flutters around.

Dallae, coming out of the house, spots the dragonfly and asks her father to catch it.

Her father, trying to catch the dragonfly, accidentally catches Dallae with the butterfly net.

To cheer up the sulking Dallae, he tries to pick persimmons for her, but fails.

The woman comes out, and Dallae asks her to pick persimmons.

The woman, using her head, knocks the persimmons down.

Seeing this, both Dallae and the man are surprised, but soon become happy and go back inside together.

The woman comes out, collects the laundry, and takes it inside.

5. Winter

The moon rises, and snow falls.

Dallae and the dog come out and run around, excited.

The man comes out and makes a snowman for Dallae.

As they roll the snow, when their hands get cold, Dallae blows on her father's hands to warm them, and she even puts a straw hat on the snowman.

The woman comes out too, and they admire the finished

snowman before heading back inside.

As it grows dark, the family's happy image is cast as a shadow on the paper window of the thatched house.

6. A Man's Story

As the siren wails and the sound of an air raid is heard, the thatched house and laundry line disappear. And on the screen, the shadow of the thatched house's fence and the laundry can be seen.

A tank passes by, crushing the fence.

A man is dragged away, and though the woman tries to stop them, it's no use.

The woman is left alone, crying out.

The shadow on the screen shifts to a winter mountain, and the man, with a rifle slung over his shoulder, trudges out, preparing to stand guard in the snow.

He looks at the snow piling up, then, unable to resist his hunger, grabs a handful and eats it.

It's so cold, and his body shivers.

Suddenly, as if remembering something, he starts to make a snowball, forming a snowman.

He picks up stones to make eyes, a nose, and a mouth, and then laughs like a fool, pleased with his creation.

Suddenly, gunfire erupts, and the terrified man flattens himself on the ground, crawling away to escape.

The gunfire dies down, and as he catches his breath, a shadow appears on the screen.

In a daze, he points his gun, and when he sees a person in the shadow begging for his life, he is startled and pulls the trigger.

Realising he has killed someone, the man is thrown into confusion.

On the screen, a fish appears and slowly swims closer, and the man raises his head, chasing after it.

At some point, Dallae is seen riding on the fish's back.

The man and Dallae, and the fish play together, having fun.

They play a game of tag, but Dallae and the fish disappear.

Yet, in the man's eyes, Dallae is still there. He hugs her tightly, grabs her hand, and tries to stand, when a gunshot blasts.

The man, caught between reality and illusion, looks around desperately for Dallae.

Unable to believe reality, he slowly collapses as if he's falling apart.

A butterfly, flying from somewhere, briefly lands on his shoulder, folds its wings a few times, and then flies away.

Snow begins to fall, and the butterfly on stage disappears, while another butterfly appears on the screen.

The butterfly vanishes, and the stage slowly fades to darkness.

7. A Woman's Story

With the sound of an air raid, the woman(human) in shabby clothes runs in.

She runs in panic to avoid the air raid, dropping the flower shoes she had been holding carefully.

She buries her head in the ground, trembling.

As the bombing sound fades, she raises her head and looks around, then hurriedly drinks water from the stream in front of her.

Suddenly, she notices her reflection in the stream and brushes her hair back.

A butterfly flies in, leading her towards the flower shoes she dropped.

She finds the shoes and rushes to pick them up.

Carefully brushing off the dust and wiping them, she stands up, as if recalling old memories, holding the shoes.

Overcome by precious and happy memories, she hugs the shoes tightly.

Azalea petals fall like rain, and the woman dances.

It feels as if she is dancing with her beloved man.

Sometimes shy, sometimes cheerful, she seems to have returned to the days when they first met, fell in love, and were happy.

Just as she tries to put on the shoes again, as if returning to her maiden days, a child's cry is heard.

Looking around, she spots the bundle she dropped and

gently picks it up, holding it as if it were her own child.
She holds the bundle close, lifts it onto her back, and with a joyful expression, she slowly exits the stage.
Only the flower shoes are left on the stage.

8. Dallae's Story

(Puppet) Dallae is playing alone in the dirt.
She draws on the ground and plays a game of building a mushroom house out of sand, then suddenly stands up as if waiting for someone and stares blankly at one spot.
After playing alone, she becomes tired and falls asleep.

The dog puppet Dallae was playing with comes to life and moves.
It wakes Dallae.
At first, Dallae is a little surprised and wary, but soon she becomes friendly and plays with it.
They roll around, run, and even fly in the sky.

Her mother(the woman) enters with a small basket, as if she had just come from the kitchen. The dog also approaches her mother, excitedly greeting her.
Dallae watches for a moment, then runs and hugs her mother's legs tightly.
Dallae lies down with her head on her mother's lap, playing with the dog, while her mother sews. Dallae plays with the

dog, climbs onto her mother's back, and tries on the skirt her mother made. The play with her mother continues, and eventually Dallae falls asleep while being carried on her mother's back. When she wakes up, she asks her mother to play the[2] "Mugunghwa Kkoch-i Pieot-seumnida(a traditional Korean play)." During the game, her mother disappears, and the dog puppet also lies still, just like before.

Dallae picks up the dog puppet, looks around for her mother, then sits down, hugging the dog tightly.
At that moment, two butterflies fly in and disappear and the happy memories of Dallae's family appear like a picture.
Then, flower petals fall gently above Dallae's head.

⟨Curtain Call⟩

---

2) The play "Mugunghwa Kkoch-i Pieot-seumnida" is a traditional Korean folk game, similar to a game of 'red light, green light'. This rhyme became famous after it was used in the first game of Netflix Squid Games.

창작자의 글

역할 : 극작, 연출
이름 : 조현산

    달래 이야기는 달래라는 소녀와 엄마 아빠 이렇게 세 가족의 이야기이다. 세 가족 중에 달래의 이름을 작품의 제목으로 정한 것은 전쟁에 희생되는 이들은 늘 그중에 가장 힘없고 죄 없는 약자라는 의미를 담고 있고 이름이 '달래'인 것은 봄을 알리는 진달래꽃에서 따온 것으로 혹독한 겨울 같은 세상이 지나가고 봄날 같은 세상이 되기를 담았다. 또한 극중 시대에는 흔하게 지었던 자연스럽고 평범한 이름이기도 하다.

    인형과 배우의 움직임에 좀 더 집중하도록 대사가 없는 무언극으로, 무대 표현과 연출도 최대한 간결하고 담백하게 하여 여백을 만들어 내는 방식을 선택하였다. 전쟁이 소재이지만 전쟁에 대한 묘사보다는 우리가 진짜 지켜야 하는 것들이 작고 소박하지만 얼마나 아름답고 소중한 것인지 이야기하는데 중심을 두었다.

달래 이야기는 전쟁을 소재로 한 작품인 "전쟁", "전쟁 2", "진달래 산천", "봄이 오면"에 이어 예술무대산에서 만든 다섯 번째 작품이다. 수년에 걸쳐 작품과 함께 나도 변화를 겪게 되었다. 내가 작품을 통해 무슨 말을 하고 싶은지가 구체적이고 조금 더 명확해졌고 그 것을 전달하기 위해서는 어떠한 이론과 실기가 필요한지 탐구하게 되었다. 그리고 인형극이 무엇인지 인형은 무엇인지 인형극에서 배우는 어떤 존재인지, 배우와 인형은 어떤 관계이고 거리를 유지해야 하는지 등등 무수히 많은 질문을 시작하게 만든 작품이다.

　초연 이후에 17년이 지난 지금에 시선으로 보면 아쉽고 부족한 부분도 많고 지금이라면 좀 다른 방식으로 풀지 않았을까 생각도 들지만 작은 디테일들을 수정한 것 외에는 큰 틀에서 당시의 방식과 장면을 바꾸지 않았다. 조금 더 세련되고 진보된 기술과 연출법, 미술, 장치 등을 담아 새롭게 만들 수도 있겠지만 달래 이야기가 담고 있는 고유성과 작품만이 가진 가치와 미덕을 지키는 것에 대한 고민을 늘 하고 있다.

Creator's Story

Role : Playwright, Director
Name : Jo Hyun-San

⟨Dallae Story⟩ is the story of a family of three, Dallae and her parents. The reason for choosing Dallae's name as the title of the work is to symbolize that those who suffer the most in war are always the weakest and most innocent. The name 'Dallae' is derived from the Korean name of the azalea flower, Jindallae, which heralds the arrival of spring, conveying a hope that the harsh, winter-like world will pass and be replaced by a warm, spring-like one. Furthermore, Dallae was a common name often used during the period in which the story is set.

To encourage the audience to focus more on the movements of the puppets and the actors, the performance is presented as a silent play without dialogue. The stage design and direction are also kept as simple and understated as possible, creating space for interpretation. While the theme of war is present, the focus is not on depicting the war itself, but rather on highlighting the small, humble things in life that we must truly cherish - how beautiful and precious they are despite their simplicity.

Dallae Story is the fifth production by ArtstageSAN, following other war-themed works such as War, War 2, Azalea Mountains, and When Spring Comes. Over the years, as I worked on these productions, I experienced changes as well. My understanding of what I wanted to express through my work became more concrete and clear, leading me to explore the theoretical and practical aspects necessary to convey these ideas. This piece sparked countless questions - what exactly is puppetry? What is a puppet? What role does an actor play in puppetry? What is the relationship between actors and puppets, and what distance should be maintained between them?

Looking back now, 17 years after its premiere, I see areas that feel lacking or that I might approach differently today. However, aside from minor refinements in details, I have not altered the overall framework, methods, or scenes from the original production. While it would be possible to create a new version incorporating more refined, advanced techniques, directing methods, visuals, and stage mechanisms, I constantly deliberate on preserving the unique essence of Dallae Story - its intrinsic value and artistic virtues.

[달래 이야기] 초연기록

· 단체명 : 예술무대산
· 일시/장소 : 2008년 8월 1일(금)~2일(토) 20:00
　　　　　　　남양주북한강야외무대
· 작가/연출 : 조현산
· 출연 : 조현산 유지연 김양희 김승우
· 창작 스태프 : 인형디자인·제작_류지연·예술무대산/ 음악감독_김영준/ 작곡_
　　　　　박인수/ 안무_신미경/ 조명_용선중/ 프로듀서_오정석
· 저작물 이용 문의 : artstagesan@gmail.com

주요 공연 기록

2024.04.24~05.05	키타큐슈예술극장 등 6곳 (일본)
2022.07.30~08.11	나하문화예술극장 등 4곳 (일본)
2021.03.19~20	노원어린이극장
2019.07.26	경기도문화의전당 / 경기인형극제
2018.12.01~04	로마인디아 국립극장 등 2곳 (이탈리아)
2017.08.15~20	예술의전당 자유소극장 / 어린이연극 시리즈
2016.09.16~17	힐튼칼리지 메모리얼홀 / 힐튼아트페스티벌 (남아프리카 공화국)
2012.05.25~06.03	제21회 유니마총회&세계인형극페스티벌 (중국)
2010.05.14~22	달오름극장 / 국립극장 청소년 공연예술제
2009.09.18~25	샤를르빌 국제인형극축제 (프랑스)
2009.07.31~08.02	문화일보홀 / 아시테지여름축제

주요 수상 기록

2012	제24회 춘천인형극제 금코코바우상 대상
2012	세계유니마(인형극협회) 총회 최고 작품상 (Best Play)
2010	국제아동청소년연극협회 아시지연극상
2009	스페인 티티라지이 인형극축제 최고작품상 (Jury's Prize)

2009   국제아동청소년연극협회 미술상
2009   김천가족아동극축제 최우수남자연기상

구름이와 욜

원작 : 오미경 동화 〈꿈꾸는 꼬마 돼지 욜[1]〉

극작 문재현

극단 인형극단 아토

---

1) 원작 〈꿈꾸는 꼬마 돼지 욜〉은 휴먼어린이 출판사에서 출판되었다.

등장인물

해설
욜
돼지
돼지 형제들
구름
토끼
오리
아주머니

무대

시골 마을 작은집
들판
언덕

극이 시작하기 전에

해설   안녕하세요? 저는 … (공연하는 자신을 소개한다)
       지금 이 시간이 여러분들께 선물 같은 시간이 되길 바라며
       공연을 준비했습니다.
       오늘 준비한 공연은 오미경 작가가 쓴 창작동화 '꿈꾸는 꼬
       마 돼지 욜'을 인형극으로 꾸민 〈구름이와 욜〉이에요. 자신
       만의 특별한 소리를 찾고, 자신의 이름을 스스로 지은 조금
       은 엉뚱한 꼬마 돼지 이야기입니다. 그럼 큰 박수와 함께
       시작해 볼게요.

음악 1. 오프닝

해설   여기 시골 마을 이 작은 집에 오리도 살고, 토끼도 살고 돼
       지들도 살고 있어요. 지금은 꿀꿀이들 밥 먹는 시간이에요.
       첫째 꿀꿀이.
돼지   꾸우울… 꾸우울… 꾸꾸꾸울 맛있다. (느릿느릿하고 굵은 소리,
       토실토실 아기 돼지 음으로)
해설   둘째 꿀꿀이.

돼지	꿀꿀! 꿀꿀! 꿀꿀! 맛있다. (조금 신경질적이고 빠른 소리)
해설	막내 꿀꿀이! 막내 꿀꿀이가 보이지 않아요! 아주머니는 막내 꿀꿀이를 찾아 나섭니다.
아주머니	이 녀석이 또 어디를 갔나? 작고 귀여운 우리 막내 꿀꿀이 보았나요?
	(당황해서는 여기저기 막내 돼지를 찾는다. 막내 돼지를 발견)
	꿀꿀아! 어서 밥 먹어야지, 안 그럼 형들이 다 먹어 치운다. 어서 먹어!
율	싫어 싫어, 싫다구요. 꿀꿀이 싫어~~
	첫째 형아도 꿀꿀이, 둘째 형아도 꿀꿀이 난 꿀꿀이 싫어!
돼지 형제들	뭐냐! 저 녀석 또 시작인 거냐?
	또 시작인 거냐?
	꿀꿀이를 꿀꿀이라 부르지 않고 그럼 뭐라 부르라는 거야?
	하여튼 엉뚱하다니까!
	엉뚱하다, 엉뚱해!
해설	막내 돼지는 언젠가부터 꿀꿀이라고 부르는 게 싫었어요. 꿀꿀꿀, 우는 소리도 마음에 들지 않았죠. 그래서 막내 돼지는 자신만의 소리를 찾기로 마음먹었어요.
율	뭐가 좋을까? 쫄쫄쫄쫄! 쫄쫄쫄쫄! 쫄래쫄래 따라다니는 거 같네.
	툴툴툴툴~ 이건 고집불통 같고,
돼지 형제들	막내야, 밥 먹어야지!
율	배고프지 않아.
돼지 형제들	아 그래? 그럼, 우리가 먹을게~

음악 2. 욜 찾기

해설　막내 돼지는 배고픈 줄도 모르고 자신만의 소리 찾기에 매
　　　　달렸어요.
　　　　지치지 않고 계속 소리를 찾고 있습니다.
욜　　룰룰룰룰~ 왠지 가벼워 보여. 쿨쿨쿨쿨~ 잠이 올 것 같잖아.

해설　아직도 소리를 찾고 있어요. 좀처럼 맘에 쏙 드는 소리를
　　　　찾을 수가 없어요.

돼지 형제들 막내야, 밥 먹을 거야?
욜　　안 먹어.
돼지 형제들 앗싸! 또 다 먹어야지. (집 세트가 닫힌다)

해설　(막내 돼지를 들여다보다가) 아! 뭔가 찾았나 보네요?

욜　　욜!욜!욜! 욜욜욜 욜욜욜 아아 기분이 좋아져, 욜욜욜 그래
　　　　욜이다!

욜! 이제부터 내 이름은 욜이야! 욜욜욜 음~~~
쿵쿵쿵! 어디서 나는 냄새지? 쿵쿵! 쿵쿵! 달콤한 냄새가 나!
쿵쿵! 쿵쿵! 아! 정말 향긋해! 쿵쿵쿵! 앗! 저쪽이다!

욜이 퇴장한다.

해설 엄마의 입김처럼 부드러운 바람결에 몸을 맡기고, 욜은 콧
구멍을 벌렁거리며 꽃향기를 따라갔어요.

음악 3. 욜이 언덕 위로

세트 전환.
작은집 세트 위로 올리면,
작은 욜이 들판을 지난다. 언덕길을 따라 올라간다.

욜 너희들이었구나. 너희들 정말 귀엽다.
(객석을 보고) 여기도 꽃, 저기도 꽃! 나는 욜이야! 욜~ 욜욜
욜~~~

구름 넌 누구니? 생긴 건 돼지가 분명한데 그 요상한 소리는 뭐지?

욜 난 욜이라고 해! 왜, 내 소리가 이상했니?

구름 아니! 그건 아니고 네가 다른 돼지들이랑 좀 다른 것 같아서.
욜? 욜! 이쁜 이름이네.

욜 고마워. 넌 이름이 뭐니?

구름 난 구름이야. 내 털이 구름처럼 새하얗다고 엄마 아빠가 지
어주셨어.

욜 구름이? 구름이? 예쁘다! 그런데 구름처럼 하얗다니, 구름
이 뭐니?

구름 뭐? 구…름을 몰라? 저기 하늘에 떠 있는 구름 말이야. 눈처

럼 새하얀 구름!

율　어디? 하늘이 어디 있다는 거니?

구름　고개를 더 들어야지. 자, 나처럼 이렇게 고개를 번쩍 들어 봐.

율　어떻게?

구름　이렇게!

율　어떻게?

구름　어머, 그러고 보니 넌 목이 굳었구나!
넌 목이 굳은 돼지! 난 목이 묶인 염소!
저 하늘의 구름은 말이야. 이리저리 흘러 다니며 이 모양이
되었다 저 모양이 되었다가 온종일 봐도 지루한 법이 없거
든. 구름을 보고 있으면 내가 묶여 있다는 것도 잊게 돼. 그
래서 난 구름이 좋아! 그런데 넌 구름을 모른다니 안됐네!
난 그만 풀이나 뜯어야겠다.

구름이 퇴장한다.

해설　율은 이제껏 살면서 하늘이니 구름이니 하는 소리를 들어
본 적이 없었어요. 한 번도 본 적 없는 하늘과 구름이 바로
위! 율의 머리 위에 있는데 볼 수가 없다니! 율은 조금 슬퍼
졌어요.

율 퇴장한다.

율의 집 세트 등장하고.

해설　구름이를 만나고 온 다음 날 아침. 율은 형제들과 아침밥을
먹고 있어요.

토끼	산토끼 토끼야 어디를 가느냐? 깡총 깡총 뛰어서 소풍을 가려고 하는데, 날씨가 어떤가? 나 빠르지! 진짜 빠르지! 무지 빠르지? 엄청 빠르지? (리듬을 타며 빠른 속도로 관객에게) 음, 좋아, 좋아! 아주 화창하구나! 소풍 가자구!!!
오리	오리는 꽥꽥! 참새 짹짹! 비둘기 구구!! 오늘 물놀이를 가기로 했는데 비 오는 거 아니겠지? 아 좋다! 하늘이 정말 파랗구나! 물놀이 가자구! 오리 꽥꽥!! 참새 짹짹!!

해설	이제 봤더니, 율 주위의 동물 친구들은 모두 하늘을 볼 수 있었어요. 율은 밥을 먹다 말고 언덕 위로 부리나케 달려갑니다.

돼지 형제들	아 배부르다. 밥 먹었으니 우리 이제 끝말잇기 할까? 그래, 그래. 만두, 두부, 부침개, 개떡, 떡볶이, 와! 맛있겠다. 이번엔 노래 부르자! 기기 기자로 끝나는 말은? 백설기, 번데기, 뻥튀기, 쫀드기, 맛있는… 딸기 맛있겠다!!!

집 세트 닫히고 내려감, 언덕 위 종이 판지 세트 세워지고 율 등장.

율	(관객을 보고) 애들아! 우리 돼지들은 손으로 음식을 줄 수 없으니까 밥을 먹을 때면 고개를 숙였지. 그래서 목이 아래로 굳어버린 거 같아. 그래서 하늘도 구름도 볼 수 없었던 거야. 이제부터 고개 드는 운동을 하면 하늘을 볼 수 있지 않을까? 고개 운동 시작! 하나, 둘 셋, 들고 돌리고 올리고, 들고 돌리고 올리고…
구름	(헛기침) 그래서 지금 고개 운동 하는 거니? 그건 좀 아닌 것 같은데!

내가 도와줄까? 자! 이 나뭇잎을 잘 봐! (나뭇잎을 주워 한 손에 들고)

절대로 눈에서 놓치면 안 돼! 알겠지?

(나뭇잎을 입에 물고 조금씩 올려 욜의 시선을 끌어본다)

욜   어, 보여, 보여, (구름이 고개를 들어 욜의 시야에서 없어지자) 아! 없어졌다!

구름   그래? 다시 해 보자. 천천히 할게. (다시 입에 물고 천천히 올린다)

욜   어디 갔지? (두리번거린다)

구름   휴우, 안 되겠다. 기초체력부터 키워야겠어. 고개 들기 열 번!

욜   하나, 둘, 셋… 열… (숨을 몰아쉬고 나서)

         구름아! 그런데

구름   지금 구름은 어떤 모양이냐면……

음악 4. 욜 찾기

구름   지금은 말이야.

         자동차 모양의 구름. 물고기 모양의 구름. 비행기 모양의 구름… 나타났다 사라진다.

욜   와, 정말 예쁘다.

해설   구름이의 설명을 들은 욜은 하늘의 구름이 더 보고 싶어졌어요.

         구름이 자동차, 물고기, 비행기가 되기도 한다니 얼마나 근사할까요?

구름   욜~ 이제 돌아갈 시간이다, 하늘에 노을이 지려 해.

율 노을? 노을은 또 뭐니?

구름 해와 구름이 헤어지면서 아름답게 인사하는 거지. 저녁이 되면 봉숭아, 나리꽃, 도라지꽃 같은 고운 빛깔로 물드는 거야.

율 정말? 참 예쁘겠다! 구름아, 나 내일도 그다음 날도 또 그다음 날도 매일매일 와서 고개 드는 운동을 할 거야. 그래서 너와 같이 꼭 노을을 볼 거야.

율 퇴장 후 구름이도 퇴장.

음악 5. 고향의 봄

해설 율은 그다음 날부터 매일 언덕 위에 올라가 구름이와 함께 운동을 했어요. 백 번, 이백 번 조금씩 횟수를 늘려가면서 열심히 운동을 했죠.
힘들게 고개 드는 운동을 하고 돌아온 율을 엄마는 가만히 안아줍니다. 그러면 율은 낮 동안 구름이에게서 들은 여러 이야기를 가족들에게 하나하나 풀어놓아요. 아름다운 무지개, 쏭~~~별똥별, 번쩍번쩍 번개, 알록달록 꽃밭 같은 노을… 들으면 들을수록 신기하고 재미난 하늘에 관한 이야기!
예쁜 꽃과 나무들에 관한 이야기들을요.
율의 식구들이 모두 잘 준비를 하고 있지만 율은 잠이 오지 않았어요.

율 구름이는 잘 자고 있을까? 구름이는 혼자서 무섭지 않을까?

음악 6. 율의 꿈

해설	(효과 낸다) 똑똑똑!!! 똑똑똑!!!
욜	누구지? (풍선 욜의 모습으로 등장)
구름	(풍선 구름으로 등장) 욜! 어서 나와! 무지개 보러 가자.
욜	어 구름아 어떻게 온 거야?
구름	어서 나와 시간이 없어.
욜	그래! (창문 세트 치워진다)

집에서 나온 풍선 욜과 풍선 구름이. 둘은 음악에 맞추어 하늘을 난다.

음악 7. 빗소리

해설	욜은 비가 오는 날에도 운동을 멈추지 않았어요.

돼지 형제들	앗! 뜨거 뜨거! 코 데일 뻔했네! 앗 뜨거라~ 이 녀석 이번엔 무슨 일이야? 왜 이렇게 몸이 불덩이인 거야?
아주머니	(모자를 둘러쓰고 수건으로 땀을 닦으며 돼지 밥을 주려 한다)

자! 귀여운 꿀꿀이들아 밥 먹자! 많이 먹고 쑥쑥 커라.

응? 웬일로 막내 꿀꿀이가 집에 있네~ 자 밥 먹어라! 응? 왜 이렇게 축 늘어져 있는 거지? 어디가 아픈가? 어? 열이 있는 것 같고. 이그, 제대로 먹지도 않고 매일 밖으로 나돌더만. 쯔쯔쯧!!!

큰일이네! 아무래도 안 되겠다. 이 막내 꿀꿀이 녀석은 다음에 장이 열리면 내다 팔아야겠어.

돼지 형제들	큰일 났다! 막내를 팔아버린대. 팔아버린대. 욜! 어서 일어나! 어서 일어나 욜 정신 차려! 어서! 욜~ 네가 누워있으니 신나지가 않아.

네가 들려주는 바깥세상 이야기 듣고 싶어. 어서 일어나서 들려줘.

막내야~ 전엔 잘 몰랐는데 네가 들려주는 이야기 못 들으니 슬프다. 어서 일어나!

해설 어느새 욜 가족들은 욜이 들려주는 바깥세상 이야기에 귀 기울이고 있었어요. 이제껏 먹는 거 말고는 기다려본 적 없는 욜의 가족들이 욜이 들려주는 이야기를 기다리고 있습니다. 고개를 들어 하늘을 보겠다는 욜의 바람이 가족 모두의 바람이 되었지요.

돼지 형제들 이럴 게 아니라 욜이 기운을 낼 수 있도록 토마토를 구해오자.

해설 욜의 형제들은 처음으로 울타리 밖으로 나섭니다.
얼마 전 막내 꿀꿀이가 맛있게 먹었던 토마토를 따오려고요! 저어~! 울타리 밖! 가시덤불을 건너면 토마토밭이 있다는 말을 아빠에게 들었거든요. 겁은 나지만, 막내 동생을 위해 두 형제는 용기를 냅니다.

음악 8. 토마토를 구해오자

형제들이 토마토를 가져와서 집안으로 옮긴다.

돼지 형제들 토마토다!
해설 일주일 후 욜은 밥을 든든히 먹고 언덕 위로 올라갑니다.

음악 9. 욜이 언덕으로

언덕 무대가 세워지고 중간 크기 욜이 지나간 다음 언덕 무대 다시 내려오고.

해설	구름이는 욜이 오기만을 기다렸어요.

구름이	욜!!! 어서 와 봐! 여기, 여기~ 얼마 전에 비가 많이 왔었잖아. 오랜만에 왔더니 이 웅덩이에 물이 가득 고였지, 뭐야. 자, 이것 봐! 이 웅덩이에 하늘이 있어. 구름도 있고.
욜	(잔뜩 기대에 찬 얼굴로 등장하며) 정말? 와아!~~~~~ 아! 세상에! 저게 구름이라고? 저게 진짜 하늘이란 말이야? 너무 멋있다! 웅덩이에 비친 하늘도 이렇게 멋있는데. 진짜 하늘과 구름은 얼마나 더 근사할까? 나 빨리 고개 운동 해야겠어.
구름이	그래. 내가 도와줄게.

해설	욜은 오랫동안 운동을 쉬어 목이 뻣뻣하게 굳었지만, 천천히 고개 드는 운동을 시작했어요. 언제나처럼 구름이가 숫자세기를 도와줍니다.

구름	욜! 고개 드는 운동 천 번!
욜	알겠어. 하나, 둘, 셋, 넷…열! 백, 이 백, 삼 백…천 번!
구름	이번엔 고개 돌리기 운동 천 번!
욜	알겠어. 알겠어. 하나, 둘, 셋, 넷…열! 백, 이 백, 삼 백…천 번!
구름	제자리 뛰기 천 번
욜	하나 둘 셋… 천 번.
해설	욜은 숨이 차서 가슴이 터질 것 같았어요. 다리도 힘이 풀려서 가만히 서 있는 것도 힘들어 보여요.

구름이	욜~ 이제 그만하자.

욜	아니야. 나 조금만 더 할래. 나 빨리 하늘을 보고 싶단 말이야. 이번엔 저기, 높은 가시덤불을 건너 뛰어볼래.

해설 　 욜의 각오가 대단하네요. 어쩌죠? 구름이는 목이 묶여 멀리 못 가는데… 어쩌면 좋을까? 혹시 친구들이 도와줄 수 있을까요?
손가락으로 가시덤불을 만들어주세요. 아! 안 되겠다. 숫자세기도 해야 하는데, 숫자세기도 할 수 있다고? 좋아요! 그럼, 가시덤불 건너뛰기 천 번! 시~작!

음악 10. 여우야 여우야

해설 　 하나, 둘, 셋, 넷…열! 백, 이 백, 삼 백…구 백, 구백 구십, 구백 구십 구!
마지막 천 번째 가시덤불을 건너뛰려는데 갑자기 눈앞이 노래지고, 다리에 힘이 풀렸어요.

욜 　 악~ (굴러서 테이블 바닥에 떨어진다)
구름 　 욜~ 안돼~

해설 　 욜은 언덕 아래로 마구 굴러 내려가요. 구름이는 아무 생각도 안 나요. 욜이 걱정되는 마음뿐이에요. 구름이는 힘껏 욜에게 달려갑니다. 그저 욜이 무사하기를 바라며, 욜에게 달려가요. (말뚝이 튕겨 나간다)
욜은 정신을 잃었다가 눈을 떴어요. 순간 숨이 막히는 줄 알았죠.
아! 눈부시게 파란 하늘! 욜은 눈이 부셔 눈을 감았다 다시 뜹니다.
꿈에도 그리던 하늘이 눈앞에 끝없이 펼쳐져 있습니다.
이게 꿈은 아니겠지요? 주르륵, 눈물이 흘러내립니다.

구름	욜! 너 괜찮아? 안 다쳤어?
욜	응, 괜찮아! 구름아, 하늘이 보여! 구름은 정말 네 털빛처럼 하얗구나! 내가 하늘을 보게 되다니! 그동안 왜 몰랐을까? 이렇게 벌러덩 누우면 하늘을 볼 수 있다는 걸! 천 번을 뛰어넘지 않았다면 영영 몰랐겠지?
해설	쓰러져 모든 게 다 끝났다고 생각했을 때, 신기하게도 길이 보였습니다. 지금까지 몰랐던 전혀 다른 길.
욜	(일어나며) 구름아! 아! 구름아! 어떻게 된 거야? 네 목에서 피가 나!
구름	말뚝에 메인 줄 때문에 긁힌 것 같아. 고삐가 이렇게 쉽게 뽑히는 줄 몰랐네! 괜찮아!
욜	고마워, 구름아! 네가 없었으면 난 하늘을 보지 못했을 거야. 그런데 난 너와 친구가 된 게 더 기뻐.
구름	나도 그래 욜~ 넌 이제 목이 굳어 슬픈 아기 돼지가 아니야. 언제든 구름을 볼 수 있으니까! 나도 이제 목이 묶여 슬픈 아기 염소가 아니야. 이제 어디든 갈 수 있어.
욜	잘 됐다! 그럼, 우리 저 아래 민들레 꽃밭에 같이 가자!

음악 11. 여행

해설	고개를 들어서 하늘을 볼 수는 없었지만, 욜은 이제 언제든 하늘의 구름을 볼 수 있어요. 벌러덩 드러누우면 하늘을 볼 수 있다는 걸 알았으니까요. 그렇지만 욜은 운동을 멈추지 않을 거예요. 언젠가는 누워서가 아니라 선 채로 고개를 들고 하늘을 꼭 보고 싶거든요. 욜은 구름이와 힘껏 달려 나갑니다. 그러다 지치면 누워서 하늘의 구름을 보겠지요? 그렇게 보고 싶어 하던 저녁노을

도 함께 볼 거예요.

지금까지 욜의 도전을 함께 응원하며 지켜봐 준 친구들 감사해요.

여러분의 꿈도 응원하겠습니다. 구름이와 욜이 함께 응원할게요!

고맙습니다!

〈끝〉

Guroom and Yol

Original : Dreaming Little Pig, Yol[1] by Oh Mi-Kyung

Script Moon Jae-Hyun
Puppet Theatre Company ATTO

1) The original 〈Dreaming Little Pig, Yol〉 was published by Human Children Publishing.

Characters

Narrator
Yol
Pig
Pig Brothers
Guroom
Rabbit
Duck
Aunt

Setting

Small House in a Countryside Village
Fields
Hills

＊Note : the Korean word "Guroom" means "Cloud" in English.

Introduction

| Narrator | Hello! I am··· (introduces themselves as the performer) I hope this performance becomes a special gift for all of you, since I've prepared it with that in mind. Today's performance is Guroom and Yol, a puppet show based on the original story 'Dreaming Little Pig Yol' by Oh Mi-Kyung. It's the story of a little pig on a journey to find his own special sound and the name he gave himself - he's a bit quirky. Now, let's start with a big round of applause! |

Music 1. Opening

Narrator	In a small house in a countryside village, there are ducks, rabbits, and pigs living together. Right now, it's mealtime for the little pigs. The first little pig···
Pig	Oink, oink··· oink, oink··· oink, oink··· so delicious! (Slow, deep voice, mimicking the sound of a chubby piglet)
Narrator	The second little pig···
Pig	Oink! Oink! Oink! So delicious! (A bit annoyed and fast)
Narrator	The youngest pig?! The youngest pig is nowhere to be found! The aunt goes off to look for the youngest pig.
Aunt	Where has this little one gone now? Have you seen our little, cute youngest pig? (Flustered, searching here and there, she finally finds the youngest pig.) Oinky! you have to eat, or your brothers will finish it all! Hurry

	up and eat!
Yol	No, no! I don't want to! I don't like it! First brother oinks, second brother oinks, I don't like oinking!
Pig Brothers	What? Is this happening again? Is this really happening again?
	What's all this nonsense about not wanting to be called or say "Oink"?
	Seriously, this piglet is so strange! So odd!
Narrator	The youngest pig didn't like saying "oink" since long ago. He also did not like oinking while crying either. So, the youngest pig decided to find his own special sound.
Yol	What would be good? Chul chul chul chul! Chul chul chul chul! It sounds like something following me. Tul tul tul~ This one sounds stubborn.
Pig Brothers	Hey, little one, it's time to eat!
Yol	I'm not hungry!
Pig Brothers	Alright then, we'll eat instead!

Music 2. Looking for Yol

Narrator	The youngest pig, not even realizing how hungry he was, kept focusing on finding his own special sound. He continued searching for sounds without tiring.
Yol	Lulululul~ I feel so light, Kulkulkul~ I think I'm getting sleepy.

Narrator	He's still searching for a sound. He hasn't found one that he likes yet.

Pig Brothers	Hey, little one. Don't you eat, really?
Yol	No.
Pig Brothers	Yay! Time to eat it all again. (The house set closes.)

Narrator	(Looking at the youngest pig) Ah! It looks like he's found something!

Yol	Yol! Yol! Yol! Yolyolyol Yolyolyol Ah, I feel so good, Yolyolyol. Yes, it's Yol! From now on, my name is Yol! Yolyolyol~ Hmm~~~ Sniff, sniff, where is that smell coming from? Sniff, sniff! Sniff, sniff! It smells so sweet! Sniff, sniff! Sniff, sniff! Oh, the smell is lovely! Sniff, sniff, sniff, it's this way!

Yol out.

Narrator	With the soft breeze, like a mother's breath, Yol followed the scent of flowers, his nostrils flaring as he sniffed.

Music 3. Yol on the Hill

(As the set changes) The small house set rises, and little Yol crosses a field, climbing the hill.

Yol	It's you guys! You're so cute! (Looking at the audience) Flowers here, flowers there! I'm Yol! Yol~ Yolyolyol~
Guroom	Who are you? You look like a pig, but what's with that weird sound?
Yol	I'm Yol! Does mine sound weird to you?
Guroom	No! It's not that. It's just that you seem a little different from the other pigs. Yol? Yol! What a pretty name.
Yol	Thank you. What's your name?
Guroom	I'm Guroom. My parents gave me that name because my fur is as white as a cloud.
Yol	Guroom? Guroom? That's pretty! But you say it's as white as a cloud⋯ What's a cloud?
Guroom	What? You don't know what a cloud is? It's the white thing floating in the sky. Like snow!
Yol	Where? What do you mean, the sky?
Guroom	You need to look up more. Here, look up like me.
Yol	How?
Guroom	Like this!
Yol	How?
Guroom	Oh, I just realized your neck is stiff! You're a pig with a stiff neck! I'm a goat with a tied neck! Those clouds in the sky float around, changing shapes all day long, and you can watch them

70

forever without getting bored. When I look at the clouds, I forget I'm tied up. That's why I like clouds! It's too bad you don't know what clouds are! I'd better go eat some grass now.

Guroom out.

Narrator   Yol had never heard of the sky or clouds before. The sky and clouds, which he had never seen, were right above him! But he couldn't see them⋯ Yol became a little sad.

Yol out.
Yol's house set is revealed.

Narrator   The morning after meeting Guroom, Yol is having breakfast with his brothers.

Rabbit   Where are you going, mountain rabbit? I'm hopping off to a picnic.

How's the weather? I'm so fast! Really fast! Super fast? Ultra fast? (With rhythm and at a fast pace, to the audience) Ah, it's a beautiful day! Let's go for a picnic!

Duck   Duck says Quack, quack, sparrow says chirp, chirp, pigeon says coo, coo!

We're going swimming today, but it's not going to rain, is it?

Oh, the sky is so blue! Let's go swimming! Duck says

quack, quack, sparrow says chirp, chirp!

Narrator   Now, Yol realized all the animals around him could see the sky. Yol stopped eating and hurriedly ran up the hill.

Pig Brothers   I'm full now. Since we've eaten, should we play a word chain? Yeah, yeah... Mandu, dubu, buchimgae, gaedduck, tteokbokki, wow! That sounds delicious! Let's sing now! What word ends in 'gi'? Baeksulgi, beondegi, bbungtuigi, jjondegi, mmm··· yummy Ddalgi (*Strawberry)! So tasty!

The house set closes, and the hilltop cardboard set is revealed, as Yol enters.

Yol   (Towards the audience) Hey, everyone! We pigs can't hold food with our hands, so when we eat, we have

72

to lower our heads. I think that's why our necks became stiff.

That's the reason we couldn't see the sky or the clouds. But if we start exercising our necks, maybe we can see them! Let's begin neck exercises. One, two, three, lift, turn, raise, lift, turn, raise⋯

Guroom (Clearing her throat) So, you're doing neck exercises now? I don't think that's going to work! Should I help you? Look closely at this leaf! (Guroom picks up a leaf and holds it in her hand.)

Don't take your eyes off it! Got it? (Guroom places the leaf in her mouth and slowly raises it, trying to catch Yol's attention.)

Yol Oh, I see it, I see it! (When Guroom lifts her head and disappears from Yol's sight) Ah! It's gone!

Guroom Really? Let's try again. I'll do it slowly this time. (Guroom raises the leaf again slowly.)

Yol Where did it go? (Looking around frantically)

Guroom Phew, this isn't working. You need to build up basic strength first. Let's do ten neck lifts!

Yol One, two, three⋯ ten⋯(after a big sigh) Guroom, but what shape do the clouds in the sky have right now?

Guroom Well, the clouds right now look like⋯

Music 4. Looking for Yol

Guroom Right now.

There are clouds shaped like cars, fish, airplanes⋯ they appear anddisappear.

Yol	Wow, that's so beautiful!

Narrator	After hearing Guroom's explanation, Yol became even more eager to see the clouds in the sky. How wonderful it must be for the clouds to transform into cars, fish, and airplanes!

Guroom	Yol, it's time to go back now. It's sunset.

Yol	Sunset? What's that?
Guroom	It's when the sun and the clouds say their beautiful goodbyes to each other. In the evening, the sky is filled with gorgeous colors, like those of balsam flowers, lilies, and bellflowers.
Yol	Really? That sounds so beautiful! Guroom, I will come every day, tomorrow, the day after tomorrow, and the day after that, to do my neck exercises. So, I will definitely watch the sunset with you.

After Yol exits, Guroom also exits.

Music 5. Spring in my Hometown

Narrator	From the next day, Yol began to climb the hill every day and exercise with Guroom. He gradually

74

increased his repetitions, from one hundred to two hundred, diligently continuing his exercises.

After a tiring workout of lifting his head, Yol's mother gently embraced him. Then, Yol would share the stories he had heard from Guroom with his family, one by one. The beautiful rainbow, the whoosh~~~shooting star, the flash-flash lightning, and sunset like a colorful flower field… The more he heard, the more amazing and fascinating the stories about the sky became! He also shared stories about the beautiful flowers and trees. Even though Yol's family was getting ready for bed, Yol couldn't fall asleep.

Yol   I wonder if Guroom is sleeping well? Won't Guroom be scared alone?

Music 6. Yol's Dream

Narrator   (Sound effect) Knock knock! Knock knock!

Yol   Who is it? (Yol appears as a balloon.)

Guroom   (Appears as balloon Guroom) Yol, come out! Let's go see the rainbow!

Yol   Oh, Guroom! How did you get here?

Guroom   Hurry, come out! We don't have much time!

Yol   Okay! (The window set is moved aside.)

Yol and Guroom, both as balloons, leave the house and fly

through the sky in rhythm with the music.

Music 7. Sound of Rain

Narrator   Despite the rain, they didn't stop exercising.

Pig Brothers   Ah! It's hot! So hot! I almost burned my nose! What's going on? Why are you so hot?

Aunt   (Wearing a hat, wiping sweat with a towel while trying to feed the pigs) Here! Eat up, little piggies! Eat well and grow big! Huh? How come is the youngest pig at home? Eat up! Huh? Why are you so limp? What's wrong? Hmm, you have a fever, and you haven't eaten properly! You've been out every day! Tsk, tsk! This is a problem! I'll have to sell the youngest pig when the market opens.

Pig Brothers   This is bad! She's going to sell the youngest! She's going to sell him! Yol! Wake up! Come on, Yol! We can't have fun when you're lying down. We want to hear the stories you tell about the outside world! Wake up and tell us! Little one, I didn't know before, but it's sad not being able to hear the stories you tell. Wake up, please!

Narrator   Soon enough, Yol's family had become eager listeners to the stories Yol told about the outside world. Until now, they had only waited for food, but now they were waiting for the stories Yol had to share. Yol's desire to lift his head and look at the sky became the wish of the whole family.

Pig Brothers We should help Yol feel better by getting some tomatoes!

Narrator For the first time, Yol's brothers stepped outside the fence. They remember hearing from their father that beyond the thorns, there is a tomato field, the same one the youngest pig had eaten from recently. Although they were scared, they gather the courage to go, for the sake of their younger brother.

Music 8. Let's Get the Tomatoes

The pig brothers bring the tomatoes and move them into the house.

Pig Brothers Tomatoes!

Narrator A week later, Yol has eaten a hearty meal and climbs up the hill.

Music 9. Yol Goes to the Hill

The hill set rises, and after Yol (Middle size) passes by, the hill set comes down.

Narrator	Guroom has been waiting for Yol to arrive.
Guroom	Yol!!! Come here! Over here~! It rained a lot recently, and this puddle is now full of water. Look! The sky and clouds are reflected in the puddle!
Yol	(Appearing with a face full of excitement) What's that sound? Wow~~~~ Oh my gosh, is that a cloud? Is that really the sky? It's so amazing! Even the sky reflected in the puddle looks so beautiful! How wonderful the real sky and clouds would be? I need to start my neck exercises right away.
Guroom	Yes, I'll help you.
Narrator	Yol had been resting for a long time, so his neck had become stiff, but he slowly began his neck exercises. As always, Guroom helped by keeping count.
Guroom	Yol, neck exercises, one thousand times!
Yol	Okay, One, Two, Three, Four··· Ten! One hundred, Two hundred, Three hundred, Four hundred,,,, One thousand!
Guroom	Now, neck turning exercises, one thousand times!
Yol	Okay, One, Two, Three, Four··· Ten! One hundred, Two hundred, Three hundred, Four hundred··· One thousand!
Guroom	Jumping in place, one thousand times!
Yol	One, two, three··· one thousand!

Narrator	Yol was out of breath, and it felt like his chest was about to burst. His legs were weak, and standing still seemed to be difficult.
Guroom	Yol, let's stop now.
Yol	No, I want to do a little more. I really want to see the sky! I will try jumping over the thorns this time.
Narrator	Yol's determination is incredible. But what about Guroom? Guroom is tied up and can't go far. What should we do? Can you guys help? Let's make the thorny bush with our fingers. Oh! This is tricky, but we need to count too! Can we do both? Alright! Let's start! Jumping over the thorny bush, one thousand times! Ready, set, go!

Music 10. Fox, Fox

Narrator	One, Two, Three, Four······ Ten! One hundred, Two hundred, Three hundred, Four hundred······ Nine hundred, Nine hundred ninety, Nine hundred ninety nine!
	When he tried to jump over the thousandth thorn bush, suddenly everything in front of Yol went blurry, and his legs gave way.
Yol	Ah! (Rolls and falls to the floor under the table)
Guroom	Yol! No!
Narrator	Yol rolls down the hill uncontrollably. Guroom,

worried and with no clear thoughts runs towards Yol, hoping he's okay. (A stake pops out) Yol loses consciousness, then opens his eyes. For a moment, he thinks he can't breathe.

Ah! The dazzling blue sky! Yol, blinking from the brightness, tries to adjust his eyes. The sky he had long dreamt of is now spread endlessly before him. This isn't a dream, is it? Tears start to fall.

Guroom	Yol! Are you alright? Are you hurt?
Yol	I'm fine, Guroom. I can see the sky! It's as white as your fur! I can't believe I'm seeing it. How did I not know this before? If I lie here, I can see the sky. If I hadn't jumped a thousand times, I would have never known this.
Narrator	Just when Yol thought everything was over after falling, miraculously, a new path appeared. A completely different path that he had never noticed before.
Yol	(Standing up) Guroom! Guroom! What happened? You're bleeding from your neck!
Guroom	I must have gotten hurt by the rope tied to the stake. I didn't know it could break so easily. But really, I'm okay!
Yol	Thank you, Guroom! If it weren't for you, I would have never seen the sky. But I'm even happier to be

your friend.

Guroom   I feel the same, Yol. You're no longer a sad little pig with a stiff neck. You can see the clouds anytime you want! And I'm no longer a sad little stuck goat tied by the neck. Now I can go anywhere!

Yol   This is great! Let's go to the dandelion field down there together!

Music 11. The Journey

Narrator   Though Yol couldn't lift his head to see the sky before, he now knows that whenever he wishes, he can gaze at the clouds. because he realised that if he lies flat, he can see the sky. But Yol won't stop exercising. One day, not by lying down, but by standing tall, he hopes to look up and see the sky for himself.

Yol runs energetically with Guroom, and when they grow tired, they lie down together to watch the clouds. They'll even enjoy the sunset, something Yol has longed for.

We thank all the friends who supported Yol through his challenge.

We'll be cheering for your dreams, too!

Guroom and Yol are rooting for you!

Thank you!

⟨Curtain Call⟩

창작자의 글

역할 : 연출, 배우
이름 : 문재현

저는 1993년 서울인형극회에서 인형극 배우로 인형극을 처음 시작한 이후 여러 인형극단에서 배우로 또는 제작 스태프로 참여해 오다 2006년 출산 이후 관객으로만 10여 년을 지내왔습니다. 그러던 어느 날 나는 동네 도서관에서 아이에게 읽힐 동화를 찾다가 〈꿈꾸는 꼬마 돼지 욜〉을 집어 들었습니다.

꿀꿀꿀!이 마음에 들지 않아 다른 소리를 찾는 엉뚱한 캐릭터인 꼬마 돼지가 주인공입니다. 자신을 욜이라고 불러달라 말하며 욜욜욜하고 울기 시작하자, 꿀꿀꿀하며 옆에서 핀잔주는 형제들이 있고요. 그리고 울타리 밖에서 만나게 되는 구름이라는 이름의 아기 염소가 있습니다. 이 구름이로 인해 하늘의 존재를 그제야 알게 되고, 목이 굳어 있어 위를 올려다볼 수 없었던 꼬마 돼지는 하늘을 보겠다는 꿈을 품게 됩니다.

몸이 아파도 비가 오는 날에도 고개 드는 운동을 멈추지 않았던 욜을 핀잔주던 형제들도 욜의 꿈을 응원하게 됩니다.

어느 날 고개 운동을 하던 욜은 언덕 아래로 굴러떨어져 정신을 잃게 됩니다. 그런데 잠시 후 눈을 뜬 욜의 눈앞에 그렇게나 꿈꾸던 파란 하늘이 펼쳐져 보입니다. 이 대목에서 작가는 이렇게 욜의 마음을 표현합니다.

"쓰러져 모든 게 끝났다고 생각했을 때 신기하게도 다른 길이 보였습니다. 지금까지와는 다른 전혀 새로운 길!"

욜은 혼비백산해서 달려온 구름이에게 이렇게 말합니다.

"이렇게 벌렁 누우면 하늘이 보인다는 걸 왜 몰랐을까! 천 번을 뛰지 않았더라면 영영 몰랐을 거야!"

도서관 구석에서 책을 읽던 내 눈에 눈물이 마구 흘렀습니다. 한 번 쓰러졌다고 그것이 끝이 아니라고, 내가 바라보는 그곳만이 길이 아니라고 말해주는 욜에게서 커다란 위로를 받았습니다. 더불어 그늘진 곳에서, 남이 알아주지 않는 곳에서, 저마다의 꿈을 품고, 그것을 이루기 위해 한 걸음씩 나아가는 모든 이들을 응원하는 작가의 마음에 큰 감동을 받았습니다. 바로 그날, 아름다운 이 동화를 인형의 움직임으로 표현하고 싶어졌습니다.

바로 그날, 이 작품을 테이블 인형극 형태의 1인극을 만들기고 마음먹게 되었지요.

인형과 소품 제작은 아기 동물들의 무해한 이미지를 표현하기 위해 자연과 가까운 재료인 나무와 종이로 정하고 폐가구의 목재와 버려진 택배 상자를 사용했습니다. 전체적인 색감도 밝고 귀여운

노랑, 연두, 초록 계열의 색감을 사용했습니다. 인형극으로 인물들이 만들어지면서 형제 돼지들의 성격을 재미나게 표현하기 위해 끝말잇기, 노래 부르기 그리고 꼬마 돼지 욜의 반복적으로 되묻는 대사를 넣었습니다. 형제들과 함께 있는 집과 구름이를 만나는 언덕 공간을 잘 표현하기 위해 네 개의 크기가 다른 욜 인형을 제작했고, 꿈속에서 구름이와 욜이 하늘을 나는 장면에서는 풍선으로 만든 구름이와 욜을 등장시켰습니다.

2018년 춘천인형극제에서 초연된 이 작품은 이후 여러 장소에서 많은 관객을 만났습니다. 공연 후 다가와 정말 아름다운 이야기였다고 인사해 주는 다양한 연령대의 관객을 종종 만나게 됩니다. 꿀꿀꿀이 싫은 목이 굳어버린 엉뚱한 꼬마 돼지 욜은 나뿐만이 아니라 많은 관객에게도 큰 위로와 응원이 돼주길 바랍니다.

The Creator's Story

Role : Director, Actor

Name : Moon Jae-Hyun

I started puppet theater as a puppet actor in 1993 with the Seoul Puppet Theater, and since then, I have participated as an actor or production staff in various puppet troupes. After giving birth in 2006, I spent about ten years one of the audience members. One day, while looking for a fairy tale to read to my child at the local library, I picked up ⟨The Dreaming Little Pig, Yol⟩.

The main character is a little pig who doesn't like the sound of 'oink, oink, oink!' and is looking for another sound. He asks to be called 'Yol,' and when he starts crying 'Yol, yol, yol,' his brothers, who are nearby, scold him with 'oink, oink, oink.' Then, outside the fence, he meets a baby goat named 'Guroom'(meaning 'Cloud' in Korean). It is because of Guroom that Yol finally learns about the existence of the sky, and the little pig, who had a stiff neck and couldn't look up, starts dreaming of seeing the sky. Even his brothers, who once mocked him for doing neck exercises despite being sick or on rainy days, begin to support Yol's dream.

One day, while doing neck exercises, Yol rolled down the hill and lost consciousness. But after a while, when Yol opened his eyes, the blue sky he had dreamt of so much unfolded before him. At this point, the writer expresses Yol's feelings:

"Just when Yol thought everything was over after falling, miraculously, a new path appeared. A completely different path that he had never noticed before."

Yol, in a panic, says to Guroom, who had rushed over:

"If I lie here, I can see the sky. If I hadn't jumped a thousand times, I would have never known this."

Tears flowed freely from my eyes as I read in the corner of the library. I received great comfort from Yol, who told me that just because I fell once, it's not the end, and that the place I see is not the only path. Along with that, I felt a strong desire to support all those who, in the shaded places, in the spots where no one notices, are carrying their dreams and taking steps towards achieving them.

I've been inspired to bring this beautiful fairy tale to life through puppet movements. For the puppet and prop production, I decided to use natural materials like wood and paper to express the innocent image of baby animals, and

I utilized wood from discarded furniture and abandoned cardboard boxes. The overall color scheme also used bright and cute colors like yellow, light green, and green. As the characters came to life through puppetry, I incorporated word chain games, singing, and the little pig Yol's repetitive questioning to playfully express the personalities of the brother pigs. To properly represent the house where the brothers live and the hill where they meet Guroom, I created four different sizes of Yol puppets. In the dream scene where Yol and Guroom fly through the sky, I introduced balloon-made Guroom and Yol.

This work, which was first performed at the 2018 Chuncheon Puppet Festival, has since met many audiences at various locations. After the performance, I often meet audiences of various ages who come up to me and say that it was such a beautiful story. I hope that Yol, the quirky little pig with a stiff neck who dislikes "oink oink," will bring great comfort and encouragement not only to me but also to many audience members.

[구름이와 욜] 초연기록

· 단체명 : 인형극단 아토
· 일시/장소 : 2018년 10월 1일 춘천인형극장 내 인형박물관
· 작가/연출 : 오미경 / 문재현
· 출연 : 문재현
· 창작 스태프 : 인형디자인·제작_옥종근
· 저작물 이용 문의 : fish287@naver.com

주요 공연 기록

2018.10.01   인형박물관 / 제30회 춘천인형극제
2019.08.02   한강 뚝섬 일대 / 한강몽땅축제
2019.08 10~11   명주예술마당 / 제6회 명주인형극제
2021.08.25   온라인영상송출 / 제1회 서울환경연극제
2022.010.07   포항리라유치원 / 포항바다국제연극제(찾아가는공연)
2024.12   충남어린이인성학습원

소금인형

극작 배근영

극단 로.기.나래

등장인물

소금인형
물
먹구름
고목나무
들꽃
숫자
소녀인형
얼음
태양
바다
소리

1. 탄생

모든 움직임이 정지된 세상, 몇 개의 반짝임이 보이기 시작한다.

이어 바람에 자연스럽게 날린다.

공간은 마치 바다처럼 그리고 하늘처럼도 보인다.

바람이 느껴지기 시작했을 때 반짝이는 것들의 움직임이 커진다.

그것은 서로 다른 빛으로 반짝임은 크기도 움직임도 불규칙하여 여러 개의 생명처럼 보이며 각자 살아 숨 쉬는 듯하다.

그중 하나의 반짝임이 강하게 움직이다가 날아오르듯 무대를 가로질러 가 무대의 한곳에 있는 하얀 무더기(탄생의 자리) 위에서 내려앉듯 멈춘다.

심장 소리가 들리기 시작하면 무대 서서히 밝아진다.

심장 소리에 이끌려 온 배우가 무엇인가 찾고 있다.

무대를 서성이다 드디어 무엇인가 발견한다.

하얀 무더기에 천천히 다가가 아주 조심스럽게 바라본다. 작고 하얀 소금인형이 누워 있다. 작은 숨을 쉬고 있다.

배우는 어머니처럼 소금인형을 소중하게 안고 어른다.

편안히 안겨있던 소금인형은 서서히 자신의 몸을 의식한다.

자신의 움직임을 발견하며 스스로 일어나고, 시선을 갖는다.

살아난 시선으로 모태의 숨(배우)과 눈을 마주치며 독립된 개체의 자신을 느끼기 시작한다.

소금인형은 분리되고자 하는 의지를 갖고 제 다리로 선다.

그리고 처음 만나는 모든 것이 신기한 듯 잠시 주위를 살핀다.

주변의 뭔가를 발견하고 따라 하는 몸짓을 한다.

세상의 여러 감정을 만나는 소금인형은 경쾌하거나 무겁거나 즐겁거나 호기심 강한 모습을 보여준다.

각각 다른 몸짓으로 몇 번 되풀이하고 음악에 맞추어 걷고 뛰고 춤을 춘다.

소금인형의 시선과 만나는 세상의 장면들이 그림자막을 통해 이미지로 보인다.

소금인형은 놀이를 멈추고 보다 차분한 호흡으로 주위를 둘러본다.
잠시 침묵.
아무런 소리도 들리지 않는다.
소금인형 뭔가를 찾듯 두리번거리다가 웅크리고 앉는다.
그리고 바닥에 낙서를 하듯 그림을 그린다.

산. 꽃. 사람. 나. 물음표.

소금인형의 낙서가 그림자막을 통해 이미지로 보인다. 낙서의 끝에 그려진 물음표가 파도 소리를 만난다.
이어지는 심장박동 소리.
소금인형은 자신을 움직이고 있는 배우들과 눈빛을 교환하고 다시 시선을 멀리 둔다. 그리고 말한다.

소금인형 무엇일까?

다시 파도 소리가 들린다.

소   리 난 누구지?
소금인형 (나지막이 따라한다) 누구지?
소   리 무엇으로부터 왔으며.
소금인형 무엇으로부터.
소   리 어느 곳을 향해 가고 있지?

소금인형 어느 곳으로…… (주위를 둘러보며) 알고 싶어.

소　리 바다.

소금인형 바다?

소　리 바다를 찾는다면… 바다를 찾는다면…… 소금인형!
　　　　바다를 찾는다면…

소금인형 (서서히 고개를 들며) 알 수 있어.

소　리 바다를 찾는다면…… 바다를 찾는다면… 소금인형…
　　　　바다를 찾는다면…….

소금인형 (소리를 따라 움직이다 멈추어서) 바다…? 바다… 찾고 싶어.
　　　　바다를 찾고 싶어.

　　　　서서히 일어나는 소금인형. 걷기 시작한다.
　　　　암전.
　　　　동그라미를 그리며 걷는 소금인형의 모습이 그림자막을 통해 보인다.
　　　　_밝은 모습으로 길을 걷기 시작하는 소금인형.

　　　　소금인형 노래
　　　　무엇일까? 나의 그리움
　　　　나를 떠나게 하는 그리움
　　　　나는 찾으리 나는 찾으리
　　　　나의 바다 나의 바다
　　　　어디에 있을까? 나의 바다는

2. 물을 만나다 – 내안의 긍정, 낙관, 순종

그림자극 장면이 끝나면 물 흐르는 소리 들리고 밝아진다.
무대 위에 물 등장, 물은 흐름을 표현하며 지속적인 움직임을 갖는다.

물	(낮은 흥얼거림이 여러 목소리가 겹쳐 들린다) 우리가 흐르는 것은 물이기 때문이라네… 우린 그곳으로 가네… 그곳으로 간다네…
소금인형	(등장해서 지켜보다가 방긋 웃으며) 당신들은 누구세요?
물	우리는 물이에요.
소금인형	당신들의 노래는 행복하게 들려요.
물	우리는 언제나 행복하지요.
소금인형	어떻게 그럴 수 있어요?
물	우리는 우리가 가야 할 그곳으로 가고 있기 때문이지요.
소금인형	나도 가야 할 그곳이 있는데…
물	어디?
소금인형	바다.
물	바다? 어쩌면 우리가 가는 그곳이 바다라는 느낌이 드는걸요. 우리와 함께 그곳으로 가요.
소금인형	고마워요 물님. (가까이 다가간다. 움찔 놀라며) 어? 이상해요. 물님에게 다가가면 아픔이 느껴져요.
물	그럴 줄은 몰랐는데. 우린 늘 함께이지만 아프지 않으니까… 우린 서로가 각자이고 또 하나이거든요. 그럼, 조금만

94

떨어져서 그곳으로 함께 가요.

소금인형 (망설이다가) 네, 물님! 그렇게 할게요.

음악과 함께 물소리 흐르고 물과 함께 걷는다 – 유쾌한 물의 춤

소금인형 (지쳐서) 그곳에는 언제쯤 도착할 수 있나요?

물　　　그건 알 수 없어요.

소금인형 알 수 없어요?

물　　　하지만 언젠가는 꼭 그곳에 가게 될 거예요. 인내를 가지세요!

소금인형 (풀이 죽어) 어쩌면 물님이 가는 그곳이 내가 찾는 바다가 아닐 수도 있어요. 그렇죠?

물　　　(대수롭지 않게) 그야 뭐……

소금인형 그렇다면 난 다른 길을 찾아보고 싶어요.

물　　　(빠져나가며) 길을 찾지 못하면 우리에게로 돌아오세요. 우리는 꾸준히 그곳을 향해 갈 테니까… 그럼 안녕~

물은 빠르게 자취를 감춘다.
서서히 멀어지는 물소리. 소금인형만 남는다.

소금인형 어느 쪽일까? (주위를 둘러본다) 길은 어디에도 있지만 나의 길은… 선택해야 해.

동그라미를 그리며 걷는 소금인형의 모습이 그림자막을 통해 보인다.
_혼란스럽지만 길을 이어가는 소금인형.

소금인형 노래
무엇일까? 나의 이 마음

나를 떠나게 하는 이 마음
나는 찾으리 나는 찾으리
나의 바다 나의 바다
어디에 있을까? 나의 바다는

3. 태양 – 신념

강렬한 햇빛이 쏟아 내는듯한 음악이 흐른다. 붉은빛의 태양이 이글
거리고 있다.
태양과 반대편에 소금인형. 소금인형에게 빛이 강렬하게 닿는다.

소금인형 어디로 가는 길일까?
태　　양 단지 나의 길.
소금인형 왠지 뛰어도 좋을 것 같은 느낌.
태　　양 앞으로만 향한 길.

태양은 점점 붉은 빛을 낸다.

소금인형 강한 이 빛. 주위가 보이지 않아.
태　　양 다른 건 볼 필요도 없지.
소금인형 세상에는 나와 저 빛만이 있는 것만 같아.
태　　양 나를 향해서만.
소금인형 너무 뜨거워. 강한 이 빛 눈이 부셔.
태　　양 숨고 싶은 거야?
소금인형 좀 쉬어야겠어.
태　　양 숨고 싶은 거야.
소금인형 쉬어야겠어.

태양의 강렬한 붉은 빛은 점점 약해지고 소금인형은 배우에게 안 긴다.

4. 고목나무를 만나다 – 고정관념, 안일

고목나무가 있고, 소금인형은 그 아래서 잠들어 있다. 따뜻하고 평화 로운 풍경이다.

소금인형 (잠에서 깨어나며) 아, 잘 쉬었다. 여기는 따뜻하고 참 아늑하다. (나무에 기대며) 기대기도 좋고 편안한 곳이야.

고목나무 그럼.

소금인형 (놀라서 올려다본다) 어?

고목나무 (다정하게) 너를 포근하게 안아줄 만큼 크고 또 오래 살았거 든. 잘 잤니?

소금인형 네, 안녕하세요. 나는 소금인형이에요.

고목나무 네가 누군가는 중요하지 않아. 네가 나의 그늘에서 보호받 고 있다는 것만 잊지 않는다면 말이다.

소금인형 당신은 누구세요?

고목나무 나는 고목나무란다.

소금인형 고목나무님.

음악이 흐르고 소금인형은 탐색하듯 고목나무 가지를 타고 위로 오 른다.

고목나무 잘하는구나? 재밌니?

소금인형 (신이 나서) 네! 재밌어요.

고목나무 자 이리 와 보렴. (그네를 태워준다)

소금인형 와!

고목나무 이것도 아주 재미있지?

소금인형 네, 아주 재밌어요.

나비가 등장한다. 소금인형은 나비를 바라본다.

소금인형 어? 나비예요.

고목나무 그래 나비구나.

소금인형 나비야 안녕?

고목나무 (흐뭇하게 웃는다)

소금인형 아주 예쁜 나비예요.

고목나무 그렇구나.

소금인형 나비가 저 위에까지 올라갔어요.

고목나무 그럼, 너도 나비처럼 올라가 보겠니?

소금인형 네.

고목나무 (소금인형이 올라갈 수 있도록 돕는다) 조심해야 한다. 다치지 않게.

소금인형 네.

고목나무 조심조심.

소금인형 이것 봐요, 여기까지 올라왔어요!

고목나무 어떠냐? 아주 시원하지?

소금인형 네, 시원해요.

고목나무 이 시원한 바람을 느껴봐라.

소금인형 음~ 아주 좋아요.

소금인형, 여기저기 살피다가 문득 멈추어서 먼 하늘을 바라보며

소금인형 바다에 가면 이런 기분일까?

고목나무님! 혹시 바다를 아세요?

고목나무 바다?

소금인형 네. 전 바다를 찾아가고 있거든요.

고목나무 바다는 누군가 상상으로 지어낸 이야기일 뿐이야.

소금인형 그렇지 않아요. 바다는 분명히 있어요. 느낄 수 있는걸요.

고목나무 어험 내 말을 믿지 않는군.

(달래듯이) 얘야! 흔히들 뭐가 잘 안되면 상상으로 어떤 걸 만들어 내서 그걸 행복이라고 여기고는 한단다. 너도 그런 거야.

소금인형 그럴 리 없어요.

고목나무 (타이르듯이 안고) 얘야! 넌 이렇게 내 품 안에 쉬면서 따뜻함과 위로를 느끼지 않니?

소금인형 (잠시 생각한 후에) 네, 여기 있으면 따뜻해요.

고목나무 편안하지?

소금인형 네.

고목나무 바로 이런 게 행복이란다. 네가 마음을 바꾼다면 넌 내 품 안에서 언제까지나 이렇게 쉴 수 있단다.

소금인형 그렇지만…

저만치 들꽃이 고개를 든다. 들꽃의 말에는 맑은 방울 소리가 들어 있다.

들 꽃 당신은 바다에 가야 행복해지겠군요.

고목나무 그런 소리 마라. 소금인형은 여기서도 충분히 행복해질 수 있어.

들 꽃 소금인형은 마음속에 있는 그리움을 떨쳐버릴 수는 없을 거예요. 내가 늘 바람을 기다리듯이…

소금인형 꽃님은 나를 이해하는군요. 그래요, 전 꼭 바다를 찾아야겠어요.

고목나무 (소금인형을 내려놓으며) 그렇다면 할 수 없지. 요즘 애들은 경험 많은 우리의 얘기를 듣지 않는단 말이야. 가려면 가거라. 어험…

고목나무는 사라지고 소금인형과 들꽃만 남는다.

소금인형 (들꽃을 보며) 고목나무님 곁에 남아야 했을까요?
들　꽃 당신은 당신의 마음을 따라가세요. 그게 당신의 길이니까.
소금인형 나의 길. 그래 나의 길… (결심한 듯) 고목나무님, 꽃님 안녕.

들꽃만 남는다.

들　꽃 난 바람을 기다려. 바람과 하나가 되어 흔들릴 수 있다면 정말 행복할 거야. 하늘의 별이 뜨고 또 지는 것처럼 나의 기다림은 끝없는 반복이지…

암전.
동그라미를 그리며 걷는 소금인형의 모습이 그림자막을 통해 보인다.

소금인형 노래
무엇일까? 나의 그리움
나를 떠나게 하는 그리움
나는 찾으리 나는 찾으리
나의 바다 나의 바다
어디에 있을까? 나의 바다는

5. 숫자를 만나다 – 이성과 냉정의 시간

숫자와 공식들이 있는 무대, 음악은 냉정하고 체계적인 느낌이 강조된다.

숫　자 (컴퓨터 자판 두드리는 소리) 정확한 계산도 없이 그냥 뭐든 한다는 건 참 위험한 일이지. 물론 어떤 믿음도 가지 않고. 뭐든 계산을 해야지. 이성적인 사고. 그것만이 진실이야. 명료하고 정확한 통계만이 의미 있는 삶을 살게 해 줄 뿐이야.

소금인형 (둘러보며) 여긴…

숫　자 빨간색은 맨 아래 줄, 보라색은 그 위로, 절대로 흔들리지 않게. 어? 이것 보라구 흔들리는 순서, 이렇게 엉망인 공식은 처음이야.

소금인형 순서가 바뀌면 왜 안 돼요?

숫　자 계산된 규칙이니까.

소금인형 하지만~

숫　자 의심하지 마. 규칙을 지키는 게 안전하지.

소금인형 규칙.

숫　자 언제나 정해진 모든 규칙을 지키며 냉정하게 생각해야만 해. 계산에 어긋나지 않도록 말이야.

소금인형 하지만 내 마음은…

숫　자 마음이라니? 그런 건 아무 의미가 없어. 모든 것을 흐트러뜨릴 뿐이라고.

소금인형 하지만. (숫자에 다가서려고 한다)

숫　자 너는 세 걸음 이상 다가오지 마.

소금인형 그건 왜요?

숫　자 규칙이니까.

소금인형 역시 규칙.

숫　자 너도 여기에 있으려면 정확한 계산에 의한 정확한 규칙을 정해야만 해.

소금인형 난 바다를 찾아야 해요. 내가 어떻게 바다를 찾을 수 있을까요?

숫　자 (당황한다) 그게 도대체 뭐지? 바다? (여기저기 뒤적이며 뭔가를 찾는다) 정보가 필요해. 넌 어떤 규칙으로 여기까지 온 거지?

소금인형 나는 그냥…

숫　자 그냥이라니? 너는 공연한 낭비를 하고 있어. 책을 찾아보고 찾을 수 없다면 우리가 바다를 찾는 법에 대한 새로운 규칙을 정해보자. 많은 시간이 필요할거야. 내가 그곳을 가는 방법을 찾기 위해 파란색을 위로 올릴 거야. 그러면 너는 '아!' 라고 말을 해줘.

소금인형 그건 왜요?

숫　자 규칙을 약속하는 거야.

소금인형 역시 규칙.

숫　자 계산에 의한 거리를 정하고, 알맞은 규칙을 정하고, 속도랑 방향도 정해야 넌 그 바다에 안전하게 갈 수 있어. 자, 시작해 볼까?

숫자의 노래

하나가 가면 하나가 오고 (규칙!)

파란색을 들면 아! 하고 말해, 아!

앞으로 갈 땐 왼발을 내밀어 (규칙!)

파란색을 들면 아! 하고 말해, 아!

초록색이 움직일 땐 고개를 들어 (규칙!)

파란색을 들면 아! 하고 말해, 아!

흰색이 가면 네모가 오고 (규칙!)

왼쪽으로 갈 땐 콩나무가 자라지 (규칙!)

파란색을 들면 아! 하고 말해, 아!
파란색을 들면 아!

소금인형 이렇게 하면 정말 바다에 갈 수 있어요?

숫   자 1과 1이 만나 2가 되는 이 세상엔 무엇이든 분명한 답이
있어.

소금인형 분명한 답.

숫   자 난 규칙을 믿어, 철저한 분석, 너를 바다로 데려가 줄 거야.

숫자의 계산이 계속되며 어떤 틀에 갇히기 시작하는 소금인형.

소금인형 내가 안전해진 느낌.

숫   자 바로 그거야. 안전하지.

소금인형 하지만.

숫   자 숫자를 믿어, 철저한 분석 너를 바다로 데려가 줄 거야.
이게 바로 바다로 가는 길…

소금인형 정말 바다에 갈 수 있을까요?

숫   자 안전하게.

소금인형 하지만 나는

숫   자 숫자를 믿어, 규칙을 믿어, 철저한 분석 너를 바다로 데려가
줄 거야.
이게 바로 바다로 가는 길, 바다로 가는 길, 숫자를 믿어…

소금인형 (강한 의지를 담아) 난 너무 답답해. (틀을 깨고 나온다) 나는… 내
마음을 따라가 볼래.

소금인형 노래
무엇일까? 나의 그리움
나를 떠나게 하는 그리움

나는 찾으리 나는 찾으리
나의 바다 나의 바다
어디에 있을까? 나의 바다는

6. 무지개 너머의 소녀를 만나다
– 안락, 안주, 타협, 쾌락

무대는 평화롭게 유영하는 배. 바람이 든 돛.
소금인형은 돛 위에 경쾌한 바람을 맞으며 앉아 있다.
귀여운 음악 흐르고 수줍은 듯 먼발치서 나타났다가 다시 숨는 소녀
인형.
소금인형은 주변을 장난스러운 모습으로 오가다 소녀인형을 발견
한다.

소금인형 안녕!
소녀인형 (수줍게) 안녕!
소금인형 안녕!
소녀인형 안녕!
소금인형 넌 누구니?
소녀인형 나? 난 그냥 나야.
소금인형 너랑 있으니까 기분이 좋아.
소금인형 나도 그래 너를 만나서 좋아.
소금인형 넌 마치 무지개 같구나. 아니 향긋한 꽃 같구나. 아니, 시원
한 산들바람.
소녀인형 홋, 그만해.
소금인형 너 언젠가 나를 본 적 있니?
소녀인형 글쎄… 그런 것 같기도 하고…

소금인형 너랑 있고 싶어. 너랑 있으면 행복할 것 같아.

소녀인형 너는 어떻게 여기에 왔니?

소금인형 난 바다를 찾아가는 중이야.

소녀인형 (갸우뚱거리며) 바다?

소금인형 넌 어디로 가니?

소녀인형 난 그냥 여기 살아.

소금인형 바다를 본 적 있니?

소녀인형 본적은 없지만 나도 바다에 대해서 들었어. 그런데 왜 그곳에 가려고 하지?

소금인형 그건… 음…. 그곳에 가야만 행복할 것 같아서.

소녀인형 꼭 바다에 안 가도 여기서 그런대로 행복할 수 있어.

소금인형 (활짝 웃으며) 그래, 지금은…

소녀인형 노래

누가 널 불렀을까? 나의 친구야

이렇게 널 만났으니 즐겁게 놀아보자

바다는 더 이상 필요치 않아 여행도 필요 없어

이렇게 춤을 춰봐 즐겁지 않니?

내가 너의 바다가 되어줄게

작은 나의 친구여 어여쁜 나의 친구여

춤을 추는 소녀인형을 넋을 잃고 바라보던 소금인형은 어느새 소녀인형과 함께 즐겁게 춤을춘다.

소녀인형 어때? 기분이 좋지 않아?

소금인형 그래. 네 덕분에 즐거웠어.

소녀인형 그럼, 너도 여기에 머무르면서 나와 함께 지내자.
　　　　　네가 마음만 정한다면 여기가 네가 찾는 바다가 될지도 몰라.

소금인형 그래.

소녀인형 자, 그 끝에 가서 서봐. 더 재미있게 해 줄게. (음악)
         저 하늘까지 뛰어오른다. 준비됐지? (뛰어오른다)

소금인형 응.

         둘은 시소를 타듯 돛의 양 끝에 서서 한껏 뛰어오른다.

소녀인형 (뛰면서) 이렇게 높이 뛰어오르면 머릿속 생각들이 모두 빠져
         나가는 것 같아.

소금인형 정말 머릿속의 생각들이 다 빠져나갈까?

소녀인형 정말 가벼워진다구. 어때?

소금인형 정말 시원해졌어.

소녀인형 저기. 저기 있는 큰 나무 좀 봐. 저 나무가 보이니?

소금인형 응, 보여.

소녀인형 저 나무에게도 바람은 있지만 우린 그 바람을 알 수 없어.

소금인형 그래.

소녀인형 바람은 어디에나 있지만 우린 우리에게 다가오는 바람만
         느낄 뿐이야.

소금인형 으응.

소녀인형 그런 거야! 보이지 않는 것에 대해서 애써 생각할 필요 없
         다니까.

소금인형 그럴까?

소녀인형 그럼.

소금인형 볼 수는 없지만 느껴지는걸. 바다처럼…

         하얀 나비 한 마리가 날아들자, 소금인형은 나비를 바라보다가 먼 곳
         을 응시하며 잠깐 동작을 멈춘다. 바닷소리가 들린다.

소녀인형 뭐 하는 거야. 그렇게 심각할 필요 없다니까.

소금인형 넌 여기서 진짜로 행복을 느끼니?

소녀인형 넌 참 이상한 말만 하는구나. 진짜든 가짜든 행복하다고 느끼면 되는 거지 뭐.

소금인형 난 바다를 찾지 못한다면 완전히 행복하지 못할 것 같아.

소녀인형 골치 아프게 따지지 말고 나랑 같이 놀자.

파도 소리가 들려온다.

소금인형 이제 알겠어. 여기가 너에게는 진짜 행복을 주는 곳이야. 하지만 이상해… 난 마음이 텅 빈 것 같이…

소녀인형 넌 참 골치 아픈 애구나. 행복한 게 뭔지 모르는 바보야.

소금인형 네 말이 맞는지도 모르지. 그렇지만 난 역시 바다를 찾아야 해. 그 전엔 무엇으로도 나를 채울 수 없을 것 같아.

소녀인형 넌 괴상한 망상가야. 바다만 찾고 있는…

암전.
동그라미를 그리며 걷는 소금인형의 모습이 그림자막을 통해 보인다.
몸은 지치고 마음은 혼란스럽지만 계속 길을 간다.

소금인형 노래

무엇일까? 나의 그리움
나를 떠나게 하는 그리움
나는 찾으리 나는 찾으리
나의 바다 나의 바다
어디에 있을까? 나의 바다는

7. 태양 – 신념

강렬한 빛으로 이글거리는 태양과 소금인형이 대치를 이루고 있다.

소금인형 너무 뜨거워. 강한 이 빛 눈이 부셔.

태　　양 너무 뜨거워. 강한 이 빛 눈이 부셔.

소금인형 너무 뜨거워. 강한 이 빛 눈이 부셔.

태　　양 너무 뜨거워. 강한 이 빛 눈이 부셔.

소금인형 쉴 곳이 필요해. 더 걷지 못하겠어.

태　　양 숨고 싶은 거야?

소금인형 어디로 가야 하지?

태　　양 나를 피해. 난 타협하지 않으니까.

소금인형 어디로 가야 하지?

태　　양 나를 피해. 난 타협하지 않으니까.

소금인형 잠이 들것 같아.

태　　양 단지 숨고 싶은 거야. 난 타협하지 않아 내 빛은 옳으니까.

소금인형 어디로 가야 하지?

태　　양 나의 세상을 이룰 수 있어. 난 결코 타협하지 않아.

소금인형 나의 세상?

먹구름이 몰려오기 시작하면 태양은 사라져 간다.

태　　양 나는 사라지는 게 아니야. 잠시 가려져 있을 뿐.

소금인형 타협하지 않는 나의 세상이 가려져…?

8. 먹구름을 만나다 – 권위, 자아도취, 독선

북소리가 섞인 큰바람 소리, 먹구름이 여러 갈래로 요동을 치며 노래를 부른다.
소금인형은 몸을 숨기고 먹구름을 지켜본다.

먹구름의 노래
오호 오호 나의 세상~ 오호 오호 나의 세상~
언제나 어둡고 축축하지
오호 오호 나의 세상~ 오호 오호 나의 세상
어둡고 축축한 나만의 세상~ 하하하하 (천둥소리)

먹 구 름 (소금인형을 보고) 자 이리로. 내가 잘 볼 수 있는 곳으로 오너라.
소금인형 (빼꼼히 나오며) 당신은 참 멋져 보여요.

먹구름이 대사를 할 때마다 낮은 바람 소리가 들린다.

먹 구 름 당연하지. 세상이 내 마음대로 움직이거든.
소금인형 정말 그래요? 어떻게 그럴 수가 있어요?
먹 구 름 간단해. 나를 중심으로 세상에 대해 생각하는 법을 알면 돼.
소금인형 아… 조금 어렵지만 그럴듯해요. 저는 소금인형이에요. 바다를 찾아가는 중이에요.
먹 구 름 바다라구?
소금인형 바다를 본 적이 있나요?
먹 구 름 물론 나야 바다를 본 적이 있지.
소금인형 정말이요? 기분이 어땠어요? 분명 굉장했겠죠? (들떠있다)
먹 구 름 음…
소금인형 (여전히 들떠서) 바다는 어떻게 생겼어요? 어디로 가야 찾아갈

수가 있죠? 제가 찾아갈 수 있을까요? 너무 멀지는 않겠죠?

먹 구 름 (단호하게) 너무 멀어. 그리고 거기까지 가야 할 필요는 없다.

소금인형 (당황해서) 왜요?

먹 구 름 내가 봤으니까. 바다는 내게 아무 의미도 주지 못했어. 바다
는 그저 바다일 뿐이야. 거기는 어디나 그런 것처럼 어둡고
축축했어. 그러니 너에게도 마찬가지일 거야.

소금인형 그 말은 이상해요.

먹 구 름 (화를 내며) 뭐가 이상하다는 거야? 내 말을 믿지 못하겠다는
거냐?

소금인형 그게 아니라.

먹 구 름 내 말을 들어. 너는 바다에 가기 전에 쓰러지고 말 거야. 그
러니 포기하는 게 좋아.

소금인형 (강하게) 안 돼요. 난 바다에 꼭 가야 돼요.

먹 구 름 흠! 고집도 세군. 다 너를 위해 하는 소리야. 내 얘기를 들으
라니까…

소금인형 난 바다에 꼭 갈 거예요.

먹 구 름 건방진 녀석! 내 말을 의심하고 있어. (비를 내린다)

소금인형 그만 해요. 당신의 빗줄기가 나를 아프게 해요.

먹 구 름 너의 상처 따위 내게는 아무 의미가 없어.

천둥소리 빗소리 더 크게 들리고, 먹구름의 움직임은 더 거칠어진다.
비를 맞은 소금인형은 고통을 느끼고 놀라 이리저리 뛰어다니며 어쩔 줄 모른다.

소금인형 아아… 아파. 사라져 버릴 것 같아. 날 내버려둬. 너무 아파.
너무 아파요.

비를 피해 겨우 몸을 숨기는 소금인형, 먹구름의 분노는 서서히 사그라든다.
먹구름이 사라지고 혼자 남은 소금인형은 고통에 흐느끼며 창백한 모습으로 쓰러져있다.
어디선가 들리는 소리, 소금인형이 말하는 듯 다른 누군가 말하는 듯하다.

소   리 난 누구지?

소금인형 (나지막이 따라한다) 누구지?

소   리 무엇으로부터 왔으며.

소금인형 무엇으로부터.

소   리 어느 곳을 향해 가고 있지?

소금인형 어느 곳으로…. (주위를 둘러본다)

소   리 바다.

소금인형 바다?

소   리 바다를 찾는다면.. 바다를 찾는다면…. 소금인형! 바다를 찾는다면.

소금인형 바다에는 무엇이 있을까? (사이) 어쩌면… 바다는 없을지도
          몰라…

소   리 바다를 찾는다면.. 바다를 찾는다면…. 소금인형!

소금인형 그만둬. 듣고 싶지 않아. 가버려! 난 너무 피곤해.

          가지 마. 아니 가버려. 가지 마. 모든 것이 다가왔다가는 사
          라져 버려.

          다가온다는 것은 떠난다는 뜻이야. 이젠 만난다는 게 두려워.

9. 얼음을 만나다 – 상처, 고독, 단절, 두려움

얼음의 노래와 함께 무대는 차가운 겨울 느낌으로 서서히 변화.
음악 또한 환상적이면서도 차가운 느낌을 돕는다.

얼음의 노래

모든 것들은 발을 멈추어라
내 안에 가두어 보내지 않으리
모든 것들은 바람조차도
내 안의 흐름으로 남으라

소금인형 추워.

얼   음 내게 들어와 심장 소리를 내며 움직이는 넌 누구지?

소금인형 (멈칫 놀라면서) 난…

얼   음 움직이지 마.

소금인형 당신은 창백해요. 쓸쓸해 보여요.

얼   음 나에게 어울리지 않는 표현이군. 난 많은 것을 가졌어. 자
          이것들을 봐.

차가운 바람 소리와 함께 얼음 속에 갇힌 듯한 수많은 형상들이 드러난다.

소금인형 그것들은…

얼 음 내게 온 것들이야.

소금인형 모두 갇혔네. 당신 안에 모두 가두어 버렸군요.

얼 음 떠나려 할 테니까. (차갑게 웃는다)

소금인형 모두 마음이 없는 것들이야.

얼얼음음 하지만 내 것이 됐지.

소금인형 또 다른 당신을 만들어 버린 거죠? 아.. 여긴 너무 추워.

얼 음 뭐든 나를 떠나는 건 참을 수가 없어. 떠나려면 오지 말았어야지.
  내게 오는 모든 것은 내 것이야.

소금인형 하지만 보세요. 당신에게 당신조차 묶여 있어요. 더 많은 걸 가둘수록 더 차가워질 거예요. 더 꽁꽁 묶이게 될 거 같은데…

얼 음 점점 안전해지는 거지. (냉소적인 웃음)

소금인형 혼자 있는 것을 두려워하는군요.

얼음 바람을 일으킨다.

소금인형 아, 추워. 뭐 하는 거예요?

얼 음 널 붙잡아 두려는 거야.

소금인형 안 돼요. 난 여기에서 멈출 수는 없어요.

얼 음 그런 건 관심 없어.

소금인형 그렇군요. 당신이 이렇게 창백한 이유를 이제야 알겠어요.

얼 음 뭐?

소금인형 당신은 마음을 허락하지 않아요. 그렇게 모든 걸 가두어 놓는다고 해도… 보세요. 당신은 혼자예요.

얼음 주변의 많은 형상들이 사라진다.

소금인형 그리고 두려움은 더 커질 거예요. 이리 나와요. 여기서 자유
　　　　　로워질 수 있어요.
얼　　음 그럼 난 없지. 나는 사라지지.
소금인형 함께 있는 거예요.
얼　　음 하하하하. (차갑게 웃으면 얼음 부딪히는 소리가 함께 들린다)
소금인형 추워…

얼음의 대사가 서서히 노래로 이어지고, 소금인형의 노래와 만난다.
유리 벽이 있는 것처럼 보이지 않지만 더 이상 어느 선을 벗어나지
못하는 얼음.
그 안의 것들 역시 괴로워 하지만 벗어날 수는 없다.
소금인형과 점점 멀어지면서 얼음은 사라진다.
소금인형의 노래가 이어진다.

얼음과 소금인형의 노래
모든 것들은 발을 멈추어라
내 안에 가두어 보내지 않으리 (당신을 묶고 있어요)
내게 오는 모든 빛을 가두고
흐르는 물소리를 조각하자 (자유로워져야 해요)
시간을 가두어 밟고 선 내 앞에 (당신을 놓아주세요)
모든 것들은 바람조차도 내 안의 흐름으로 남으라
(두려움을 이겨요) 흐름으로 남으라

얼음의 노래와 소금인형의 노래가 오버랩 된다.

무엇일까? 나의 그리움
나를 떠나게 하는 그리움
나는 찾으리 나는 찾으리
나의 바다 나의 바다
어디에 있을까? 나의 바다는

소금인형　내가 무엇을 찾고 있었지.
　　　　　나는 왜 바다를 그리워하는 걸까?

　　　　　소금인형이 경험한 여러 가지 장면들이 그림자막을 통해 희미하게
　　　　　보인다.
　　　　　여러 가지 희미한 이미지들이 뚜렷한 하나의 이미지로 모아졌다가
　　　　　모두 사라진다.
　　　　　이어 처음의 자장가 소리 들리고 파도 소리가 이어진다.

10. 바다를 만나다 – 나, 꿈, 사랑, 절대자

소금인형　이 소리…. (천천히 일어난다) 어? (앞을 응시한다) 아!! 아름답다.
　　　　　빛이 나는 저 거대한 것은 뭘까? 뭘까? 아… 숨이 멎을 것
　　　　　만 같아.
　　　　　알 수 없는 이 느낌은 무엇일까?
　　　　　(천천히 다가가 크게 묻는다) 이봐요! 당신은 누구시죠?

　　　　　순간 무대는 바다로 가득 채워진다. 작은 바위 위에 소금인형이 서서
　　　　　바다를 바라보고 있다.

바　　다　난 바다야.

심장박동 소리 점점 커진다.

소금인형 바다라구요? 바다…?

바　다 드디어 나를 찾았구나.

소금인형 바다. 바다… 나의 바다.

바　다 그래.

소금인형 당신을 찾아 먼 여행을 했어요. 언제부터 여기 있었나요?

바　다 네가 나를 찾으려고 했을 때부터.

소금인형 내가 찾으려고 했을 때부터? 당신을 알고 싶어요.
　　　　　당신의 신비스러운 푸른빛 속엔 무엇이 있지요?

바　다 내가 궁금하니? 나에게 발을 담가 보렴. 그럼 내가 누군지
　　　　　알 수 있어.

소금인형 (한발을 내밀어 바다에 담가본다) 어, (놀라 발을 다시 빼며) 이상해
　　　　　요. 내가 조금 사라졌어요.

바　다 이제 알겠니?

소금인형 아직은…

바　다 곧 알게 될 거야.

소금인형 내가 모두 사라지고 나면 당신을 알게 되나요?

바　다 사라지는 것은 없어.

소금인형 내가 당신이 되나요?

바　다 우린 처음부터 하나란다.

소금인형과 같은 실루엣의 바다 모습이 드러나기 시작한다.

소금인형 난 바다고.. 바다님은 나.

바　다 네가 걸어온 모든 길 또한 너야.

소금인형의 손과 바다의 손이 일렁이며 서로를 향해 다가간다.

소금인형 내가 당신에게 닿았습니다. 그러므로 내가 내게 닿았습니다.

파도 소리와 함께 바다와 소금인형의 목소리가 동시에 들린다.

함   께 내가 당신에게 닿았습니다. 그러므로 내가 내게 닿았습니다.

암전.

소금인형 (어둠 속에서 대사) 나는 나를 찾아 나를 걸어서 왔다. 끝없는 나…

다시 심장박동 소리가 시작된다. 푸르고 어두운 무대, 탄생의 자리에 작고 하얀 소금인형이 누워 있다.
조금씩 조금씩 숨을 쉬듯 움직이며 음악과 심장박동 소리 고조된다.
무대는 어두워진다. 심장박동 소리만 남는다.

〈끝〉

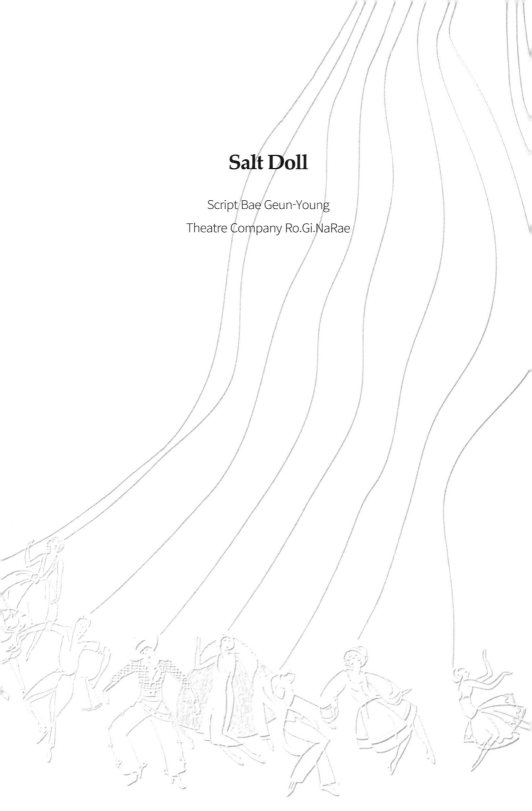

Salt Doll

Script Bae Geun-Young

Theatre Company Ro.Gi.NaRae

Characters

Salt Doll
Water
Rain cloud
Old tree
Wildflowers
Girl
Ice
Sun
Sea
Voice

1. Birth

In a world where all movement has ceased, a few glimmers begin to appear.

Then, they are naturally carried by the wind.

The space appears to be like the sea and the sky.

As the wind becomes stronger, the movement of the glimmers becomes stronger.

They shine in different colors, and their movements are irregular, making them appear like several living beings, each seemingly breathing life.

One of the glimmers moves strongly, flying across the stage, and lands softly on a white mound(the place of birth) in one corner of the stage.

As the sound of a heartbeat is heard, the stage slowly brightens.

Drawn by the heartbeat, the actor enters, searching for something.

The actor wanders on stage and finally discovers something.

The actor carefully approaches the white mound and gazes gently. A small, white Salt Doll lies there, breathing lightly.

The actor gently holds the Salt Doll as a mother would, soothing it with care.

The Salt Doll, comfortably nestled, slowly becomes aware of its own body.

It discovers its own movement, stands up on its own, and gains focus.

With a revived gaze, it locks eyes with the breath of the womb(actor), beginning to feel that it is an independent being.

The Salt Doll now gets the will to separate and stands on its own legs.

It pauses for a moment as if everything it encounters is new, curiously observing its surroundings.

The Salt Doll mimics movements it discovers in its environment.

Experiencing various emotions of the world, the Salt Doll shows a range of expressions - playfulness, gloom, joy, and full of curiosity.

It repeats different movements several times, walking, running, and dancing to the rhythm of the music.

Images of the world, as seen through the Salt Doll's eyes, appear on the shadow screen.

The Salt Doll stops playing, takes a more measured breath, and looks around.

A moment of silence.

No sound is heard.

The Salt Doll, searching for something, glances around and sits down.

It begins to draw on the floor as if doodling.

Mountain. Flower. Person. Myself. Question mark.

The doodles of the Salt Doll appear as images through the shadow screen. The question mark drawn at the end of the doodle meets the sound of waves.

The sound of a heartbeat follows.

The Salt Doll exchanges glances with the actors who are moving it, then looks off into the distance again.

And then it speaks.

Salt Doll   What could it be?

The sound of the waves is heard again.

Voice   Who am I?
Salt Doll   (softly repeats) Who am I?
Voice   From where did I come?
Salt Doll   From where?
Voice   Where am I going?
Salt Doll   Where··· (looks around) I want to know.
Voice   The sea.
Salt Doll   The sea?
Voice   If you find the sea··· If you find the sea··· Salt Doll! If you find the salty sea···
Salt Doll   (slowly raises its head) I will know.
Voice   If you find the sea··· If you find the sea··· Salt Doll··· If you find the sea···
Salt Doll   (moves as the voice moves, then stops) The sea···? The sea···
            I want to find it. I want to find the sea.

Slowly, the Salt Doll rises. The Salt Doll begins to walk. The stage goes dark.

The image of the Salt Doll walking in circles is shown through the shadow screen.

_ The Salt Doll sets off on the path, delighted.

Salt Doll's Song:

What could it be? My longing

The longing that makes me want to leave

I will find it I will find it

My sea my sea,

Where could it be? My sea

2. A Chance Encounter with Water – My Inner Positivity, Optimism, and Compliance

As the scene of the shadow play ends, the sound of flowing water is heard and the stage brightens. Water appears on stage, expressing its flow with continuous movement.

Water   (Low humming of multiple voices overlapping) We flow because we are water⋯ We go to that place⋯ We go there⋯

Salt Doll   (Appears, watching, then smiles) Who are you?

Water   We are water.

Salt Doll	Your song sounds happy.
Water	We are always happy.
Salt Doll	How can that be?
Water	Because we are going to the place we must go.
Salt Doll	I also have a place I need to go…
Water	Where?
Salt Doll	The sea.
Water	The sea? Perhaps the place we are going is the sea. Come with us to that place.
Salt Doll	Thank you, Water. (Approaches, then suddenly pulls back in surprise) Huh? That feels weird. I felt pain as I got closer to you.
Water	We didn't know that. We are always together, but we never/don't feel pain…. We are separate, yet we are one. Let's make some space and go together to that place.
Salt Doll	(Hesitates) Yes, Water! Let's do that.
	With music playing, the sound of water flows, and the Salt Doll walks with the water - a joyful dance of
Salt Doll	(Exhausted) When will we reach that place?
Water	I don't know.
Salt Doll	You don't know?

Water	But one day, we will surely get there. Be patient!
Salt Doll	(Disheartened) Perhaps the place you are going isn't the sea I'm looking for.
Water	(Unconcerned) Well···
Salt Doll	In that case, I want to find another way.
Water	(Leaving quickly) If you don't find a way, come back to us. We will continue to head to that place··· Then, goodbye~

Water quickly disappears. The sound of water slowly **fades away. The Salt Doll is left alone.**

Salt Doll	Which way should I go? (Looks around) The path is everywhere, but my path··· I must choose···

The Salt Doll's figure walking in circles is seen **through the shadow screen.**
_Salt Doll is confused but continues walking.

Salt Doll's Song:

What could it be? My longing
The longing that makes me want to leave
I will find it I will find it
My sea my sea,
Where could it be? My sea

3. The Sun – Belief

Intense music flows as if it were intense sunlight pouring down. The red sun is blazing. On the opposite side of the sun is the Salt Doll. The light from the sun strikes the Salt Doll intensely.

Salt Doll	Where is the path going?
Sun	It's simply my path.
Salt Doll	It feels like I could run on it.
Sun	The path that leads only forward.

The circle of light gradually turns red.

Salt Doll	This light is so intense, I can't see anything around me.
Sun	You don't need to see anything else.
Salt Doll	It feels like only I and this light exist in the world.
Sun	Only towards me.
Salt Doll	It's scorching. The light is blinding.
Sun	Do you want to hide?
Salt Doll	I need to rest.
Sun	You want to hide.
Salt Doll	I need to rest.

The intense red light of the sun gradually weakens and the Salt Doll is embraced by the actor.

4. A Chance Encounter with an Old Tree – Stereotypes, Complacency

There is an old tree, and the Salt Doll is sleeping under it. It is a warm and peaceful scene.

Salt Doll   (Waking up) Ah, I've had a good rest. It's warm here, and really cozy.
(Leaning against the tree) It's a great place to lean, very comfortable.

Old Tree   Of course.

Salt Doll   (Surprised, looking up) Huh?

Old Tree   (Affectionately) I'm big and have lived for a long time, enough to embrace you warmly. Did you sleep well?

Salt Doll   Yes, hello. I'm without the Salt Doll.

Old Tree   It doesn't matter who you are. As long as you don't forget that you are protected in my shade.

Salt Doll   Who are you?

Old Tree   I am an old tree.

Salt Doll   Old Tree.

Music plays, and the Salt Doll climbs the branches of **the old tree as if exploring.**

Old Tree   You're doing well, aren't you? Isn't it fun?

Salt Doll   (Excited) Yes! It's fun.

Old Tree   Here. (Gives the puppet a swing.)

Salt Doll	Wow!
Old Tree	This is fun, too, right?
Salt Doll	Yes, it's very fun.

A butterfly appears. The Salt Doll watches it.

Salt Doll	Oh! It's a butterfly.
Old Tree	Yes, it's a butterfly.
Salt Doll	Hello, butterfly.
Old Tree	(Smiling gently)
Salt Doll	It's a very pretty butterfly.
Old Tree	It is.
Salt Doll	The butterfly has gone up the tree!
Old Tree	Then, would you like to go up like the butterfly?
Salt Doll	Yes.
Old Tree	(Helping the Salt Doll climb) You have to be careful. Don't get hurt.
Salt Doll	Yes.
Old Tree	Careful, careful.
Salt Doll	Look! I made it up here!
Old Tree	How is it? Isn't it refreshing?
Salt Doll	Yes, it's refreshing.
Old Tree	Feel the cool breeze.
Salt Doll	Mmm, it's really nice.

The Salt Doll looks around for a while, then suddenly stops and gazes at the distant sky.

Salt Doll	(To itself) Is this the feeling I would have if I reached the sea?
	Old Tree! Do you know the sea?
Old Tree	The sea?
Salt Doll	Yes, I'm on my way to find the sea.
Old Tree	The sea is just a story made up by someone with a big imagination.
Salt Doll	That's not true. The sea definitely exists. I can feel it.
Old Tree	(Annoyed) Hmph, you don't believe me, do you?
	(Soothingly) Hey, little one, when things don't go well, people often create something with their imagination and think of it as happiness. You are doing the same.
Salt Doll	That's not true.
Old Tree	(Hugging and comforting the Salt Doll) Little one! Don't you feel warm and comforted while resting in my arms like this?
Salt Doll	(Thinking for a moment) Yes, it's warm here.
Old Tree	Isn't it comforting?
Salt Doll	Yes.
Old Tree	This is what happiness is. If you change your mind, you can rest here in my arms forever.
Salt Doll	But⋯

In the distance, wildflowers begin to bloom. Their words carry a clear bell-like sound.

Wildflowers	You must go to the sea to be happy.

Old Tree	Don't say that. The Salt Doll can be happy right here.
Wildflowers	The Salt Doll will never be able to shake off the longing inside. Just like I am always waiting for the wind···
Salt Doll	Flower, you understand me. Yes, I must find the sea.
Old Tree	(Putting the Salt Doll down) Then I can't stop you. These days, the kids don't listen to our experienced words. If you want to go, then go. Hmph···

The Old Tree disappears, leaving only the Salt Doll and the wildflowers.

Salt Doll	(Looking at the wildflowers) Should I stayed with the Old Tree?
Wildflowers	Follow your heart. That's your path.
Salt Doll	My path. Yes, my path··· (Decisively) Old Tree, Wildflowers, goodbye.

Only the wildflowers remain.

Wildflowers	We wait for the wind. If we can sway with the wind, we'll truly be happy. Just like the stars rise and set, our waiting is an endless repetition···

Blackout.

The Salt Doll's figure walking in circles is seen **through the** shadow screen.

Salt Doll's Song:

What could it be? My longing

The longing that makes me want to leave

I will find it. I will find it

My sea my sea,

Where could it be? My sea

5. A Chance Encounter with a Number – Time of
Reason and Calm

A stage with numbers and formulas, the music emphasizes a cold and systematic feeling.

Number   (Sounds of typing on a computer keyboard) Doing anything without accurate calculations is a very dangerous thing.
Of course, having no credibilities. Everything must be calculated.
Logical thinking. That's the only truth. Only clear and precise statistics can give you a meaningful life.

Salt Doll   (Looking around) Where···?

Number   Red is on the bottom row, purple should be directly above it, never confuse the two. Oh? Look at this, the irregular order, this is the first time I've seen such a messy formula.

Salt Doll	Why can't the order be changed?
Number	Because it's a calculated rule.
Salt Doll	But···
Number	Don't doubt it. It's safer to follow the rules.
Salt Doll	Rules.
Number	You must always keep you cool while following all the established rules. So that it doesn't deviate from the calculations.
Salt Doll	But my heart···
Number	Heart? That means nothing. It only disrupts everything.
Salt Doll	But··· (Trying to approach the number)
Number	Don't come closer than three steps.
Salt Doll	Why not?
Number	Because it's a rule.
Salt Doll	Again, a rule.
Number	If you want to be here, you must set precise rules based on accurate calculations.
Salt Doll	I need to find the sea. How can I find the sea?
Number	(Becomes flustered) What on earth is that? The sea? (Looking around, searching for something) I need information. What rule did you follow to get here?
Salt Doll	I just···
Number	Just? You're wasting your time. Let's find a book, and if we can't find it in the book, let's set a new rule for how to find the sea.

	It will take a lot of time. I'll raise the blue card to find the way to the sea. Then, you must say 'Aye!'
Salt Doll	Why?
Number	It's to set the rules to follow.
Salt Doll	Again, a rule.
Number	By setting the distance through calculation, determining the right rules, adjusting speed and direction, you can safely reach the sea. Shall we start?

Song of the Numbers

"When one goes, another comes(rule!)

When I lift the blue card, say 'Ah!', Ah!

When going forward, lift your left foot(rule!)

When I lift the blue card, say 'Ah!', Ah!

When the green card moves, lift your head(rule!)

When I lift the blue card, say 'Ah!', Ah!

When white goes, a square comes(rule!)

When you turn left, the bean plant grows(rule!)

When I lift the blue card, say 'Ah!', Ah!

When I lift the blue card, say 'Ah!'"

Salt Doll	Can I really reach the sea by doing this?
Number	In this world where one and one make two, there's a clear answer to everything.
Salt Doll	A clear answer.
Number	I believe in the rules, thorough perfect analysis, it will take you to the sea.

As the calculations of number continue, the Salt Doll begins gettingl trapped in a frame.

Salt Doll	I feel safe now.
Number	Exactly. It's safe.
Salt Doll	But.
Number	Believe in numbers, trust the rules, thorough perfect analysis it will take you to the sea. This is the way to the sea⋯
Salt Doll	Can I really reach the sea?
Number	Safely.
Salt Doll	But I⋯⋯
Number	Believe in numbers, believe in rules, thorough perfect analysis it will take you to the sea. This is the way to the sea, the way to the sea, believe in numbers⋯
Salt Doll	(With strong determination) I'm feeling trapped. (Breaking out of the frame) I will follow my heart.

Salt Doll's Song:

What could it be? My longing

The longing that makes me want to leave

I will find it, I will find it

My sea my sea,

Where could it be? My sea

6. A Chance Encounter with a Girl Beyond the Rainbow – Comfort, Settling, Compromise, Pleasure

> The stage is a ship peacefully sailing, with wind in its sails. The Salt Doll sits on the sail, enjoying the lively breeze. Cute music plays as the shy Girl peeks from behind the sail and quickly hides again. The Salt Puppet playfully moves around, discovering a Girl Puppet.

Salt Doll	Hello!
Girl	(shyly) Hello!
Salt Doll	Hello!
Girl	Hello!
Salt Doll	Who are you?
Girl	Me? I'm just me···
Salt Doll	I feel good being with you.
Salt Doll	Me too. I'm happy to meet you.
Salt Doll	You're like a rainbow. No, you're like a fragrant flower. No, like a cool breeze.
Girl	Heh, stop it···!
Salt Doll	Have you ever seen me before?
Girl	Hmm··· Maybe I have···
Salt Doll	I want to be with you. I think I'll be happy if I'm with you.
Girl	How did you come here?
Salt Doll	I'm on a journey to find the sea.

Girl	(Tilting head) The sea?
Salt Doll	Where are you going?
Girl	I just live here.
Salt Doll	Have you ever seen the sea?
Girl	I haven't, but I've heard of it. But why do you want to go there?
Salt Doll	Well⋯ I think I'll be happy if I go there.
Girl	You don't have to go to the sea. You can be happy here, just fine.
Salt Doll	(Smiling brightly) Yeah, maybe for now⋯

Girl`s song

Who called you, my friend?
Now that I've met you, let's play and have fun.
The sea is no longer needed, no more journeys needed.
Come, dance with me, aren''t you happy?
I'll be your sea.
My little friend, my lovely friend.

The Girl dances, and the Salt Doll watches, mesmerized, then joins her in the dance.

Girl	How is it? Isn't it nice?
Salt Doll	Yeah. I really enjoyed it, thanks to you.
Girl	Then stay here with me. If you decide so, this place might be the sea you're looking for.
Salt Doll	Alright.
Girl	Come, stand at the end. I'll make it even more fun.

(Music) Let's jump all the way to the sky. Ready? (Jumps)

Salt Doll	Yeah.

They stand at both ends of the sail like on a seesaw and jump up high.

Girl	(Jumping) When I jump this high, it feels like all the thoughts in my head are flying away.
Salt Doll	Do you think all the thoughts in your head will really disappear?
Girl	It really feels lighter. How about you?
Salt Doll	I feel really refreshed.
Girl	Look over there. Do you see that big tree?
Salt Doll	Yeah, I see it.
Girl	That tree also feels the wind, but we can't feel that wind.
Salt Doll	Yeah.
Girl	The wind is everywhere, but we can only feel the wind that comes to us.
Salt Doll	Hmm.
Girl	That's it! There's no need to overthink about things we can't see.
Salt Doll	Really?
Girl	Really.
Salt Doll	I can't see it, but I can feel it. Like the sea…

A white butterfly flies in. The Salt Doll stares at the butterfly, then stops, gazing into the distance. The sound of the sea is heard.

Girl	What are you doing? There's no need to be so serious.
Salt Doll	Do you really feel happy here?
Girl	You always say weird things. Whether it's real or not, if you feel happy, that's what matters.
Salt Doll	I think I won't be truly happy if I don't find the sea.
Girl	Stop thinking too much and just play with me.

The sound of waves is heard.

Salt Doll	I understand now. This is the place where you find true happiness. But, it's strange⋯ I feel like my heart is empty...
Girl	You really are a troublesome one. You don't even know what happiness is.
Salt Doll	Maybe you're right. But still, I have to find the sea. Before that, I don't think I can fill myself with anything else.
Girl	You're a strange dreamer. Always searching for the sea⋯

Blackout.

The Salt Doll's figure walking in circles is seen through the shadow screen. It's body is exhausted, and it's mind is in turmoil, but it keeps walking.

Salt Doll's Song:

What could it be? My longing
The longing that makes me want to
leave
I will find it, I will find it
My sea my sea,
Where could it be? My sea

7. The Sun – Belief

The intense, blazing sun is in a standoff with the Salt Doll.

Salt Doll   It's too hot. This intense light is blinding.
Sun   It's too hot. This intense light is blinding.

Salt Doll	It's too hot. This intense light is blinding.
Sun	It's too hot. This intense light is blinding.
Salt Doll	I need a place to rest. I can't walk anymore.
Sun	Do you want to hide?
Salt Doll	Where should I go?
Sun	Avoid me. I don't compromise.
Salt Doll	I think I'm going to fall asleep.
Sun	You just want to hide. I don't compromise, my light is right.
Salt Doll	Where should I go?

140

| Sun | I can create my own world. I never compromise. |
| Salt Doll | My world? |

As Rain Clouds begin to gather, the sun begins to disappear.

| Sun | I'm not disappearing. I'm just temporarily hidden. |
| Salt Doll | The world that does not compromise is hidden···? |

8. A Chance Encounter with Rain Clouds – Authority, Narcissism, Dogmatism

A loud wind mixed with drum sounds, the Rain Clouds move restlessly and sing a song. The Salt Doll hides and watches the Rain Clouds.

Song of the Rain Clouds

Oh ho, oh ho, my world~ Oh ho, oh ho, my world~
Always dark and damp
Oh ho, oh ho, my world~ Oh ho, oh ho, my world
A dark and damp world of my own~ Ha ha ha ha (Thunder sound)

Rain Clouds	(Seeing the Salt Doll) Come here. Come to where I can see you clearly.
Salt Doll	(Poking out) You look really dashing.
	Every time the Rain Clouds speak, a low wind sound is heard.

Rain Clouds	Of course. The world moves as I wish.
Salt Doll	Really? How can that be?
Rain Clouds	It's simple. You just need to know how to see the way the world revolves around you.
Salt Doll	Ah⋯ it's a bit hard, but it sounds plausible. I'm the Salt Doll.
	I'm on my way to the sea.
Rain Clouds	The sea?
Salt Doll	Have you ever seen the sea?
Rain Clouds	Of course. I've seen the sea.
Salt Doll	Really? How did it feel? It must have been amazing! (Excited)
Rain Clouds	Hmm⋯
Salt Doll	(Still excited) What's the sea like? How can I find it? Can I go there? It can't be too far, right?
Rain Clouds	(Firmly) It's too far. And there's no need to go there.
Salt Doll	Why?
Rain Clouds	Because I've seen it. The sea didn't give me any meaning. The sea is just the sea. It was dark and damp like everywhere else.
	It will be the same for you.
Salt Doll	That's strange⋯
Rain Clouds	(Angrily) What's strange about it? Don't you believe me?
Salt Doll	That's not it⋯
Rain Clouds	Listen to me. Before you even reach the sea, you'll collapse. It's better to give up.
Salt Doll	(Strongly) No! I must go to the sea.

Rain Clouds	Hm! You're stubborn. I'm saying this for your own good.
	Listen to me…
Salt Doll	I must go to the sea.
Rain Clouds	You arrogant little thing! You're doubting my words.
	(Rain begins to pour)
Salt Doll	Stop it. Your rain hurts me.
Rain Clouds	Your wounds mean nothing to me.

Thunder and rain sounds grow louder, and the movement of the Rain Clouds becomes more violent. The Salt Doll, drenched in the rain, feels pain and runs around in panic, unsure of what to do.

Salt Doll	Ouch… It hurts. I feel like I'm going to disappear. Leave me alone.
	It hurts so much. It hurts so much for real.

The Salt Doll barely hides from the rain, and the fury of the Rain Clouds gradually subsides. When the Rain Clouds disappear, the Salt Doll is left alone, lying pale and weeping from the pain. A voice is heard from somewhere, almost as if someone else is speaking.

Voice	Who am I?
Salt Doll	(Repeats quietly) Who am I?
Voice	Where did I come from?
Salt Doll	Where did I come from?

Voice	Where am I going?
Salt Doll	Where am I······ (Looks around)
Voice	The sea.
Salt Doll	The sea?
Voice	If you find the sea··· if you find the sea··· Salt Doll! If you find the sea···
Salt Doll	What's in the sea? (Pauses) Maybe··· the sea doesn't even exist···
Voice	If you find the sea··· if you find the sea··· Salt Doll!
Salt Doll	Stop it. I don't want to hear it. Go away! I'm so tired. Don't Go. No, go away. Don't go. Everything that comes near just disappears. To come means to leave. Now, I'm afraid of getting to know someone.

9. A Chance Encounter with Ice – Wounds, Solitude, Isolation, Fear

With the song of ice, the stage slowly transforms into a cold winter scene. The music also adds a fantastic yet cold atmosphere.

Song of Ice

All things, stop your feet
I will not let you out of me
All things, even the wind
Remain as they move about inside me

Salt Doll	It's cold···
Ice	Come inside, who are you, moving with the sound of your heartbeat?
Salt Doll	(Startled) I······
Ice	Don't move.
Salt Doll	You're pale. You look lonely.

Ice	That's an expression that doesn't suit me. I have many things. Look at this.

Countless figures are frozen as if trapped inside the ice, accompanied by the sound of the cold wind.

Salt Doll	Those are···!
Ice	They came to me.
Salt Doll	They're all trapped. You've trapped them all inside you.
Ice	They tried to leave··· (cold laughter)
Salt Doll	They have no heart of their own.
Ice	But they're mine.
Salt Doll	You've made more of you, haven't you? Oh··· it's so cold here.
Ice	I cannot bear anything that leaves me. If you wanted to leave, you shouldn't have come. Everything that comes to me is mine.
Salt Doll	But look. You have even trapped yourself!. The more things you trap, the colder you'll become. You'll get more and more bound···

Ice	I am becoming more secure. (Cynical laughter)
Salt Doll	You're afraid of being alone.

Ice creates an icy wind

Salt Doll	Oh, it's cold. What are you doing?
Ice	I'm trying to keep you here.
Salt Doll	No, I can't stop here.
Ice	I don't care about that.
Salt Doll	I see. Now I understand why you're so pale.
Ice	What?
Salt Doll	You don't allow your heart to do its thing. Even if you trap everything······ look. You're alone.

The many figures around the ice begin to disappear.

Salt Doll	And the fear will only grow. Come out. You can be free here.
Ice	Then I don't exist. I disappear.
Salt Doll	We are together.
Ice	Hahahaha. (cold laughter, and the sound of ice clashing is heard)
Salt Doll	It's so cold···
	(In the following scene)

The dialogue of ice slowly transitions into a song, blending with the song of the Salt Doll. It appears as if there is no glass wall, but the ice cannot move beyond a certain line.

The things inside it also suffer but cannot escape.

The ice gradually disappears as it moves further away from the Salt Doll.

Only the Salt Doll remains, and the song of the Salt Doll continues.

Song of Ice and Salt Doll

All things, stop your feet

I will not let you out of me (I'm binding you)

I will trap all the light coming to me

Let's carve the sound of flowing water (You need to be free)

I will trap time and stand before me (Let me go)

All things, even the wind, remain as they move about

(Overcome the fear) Remain as they move

The song of Ice and the song of Salt Doll overlap.

What is it? My longing

The longing that makes me want to leave

I will find it, I will find it

My sea, my sea

Where could it be? My sea

Salt Doll   What was I looking for?

Why do I long for the sea?

The various scenes the Salt Doll has experienced appear

faintly through the shadow screen. Various faint images gather into a single clear image and then all disappear.

The sound of a lullaby begins, and the sound of waves follows.

10. A Chance Encounter with the Sea – Me, Dream, Love, Absolute Being

Salt Doll   This sound⋯ (slowly rises) Huh? (looks ahead) Ah!! It's so beautiful!

What is that enormous shining thing? What is it?

Ah⋯ I feel like I might stop breathing.

What is this feeling? (slowly approaches and asks loudly) Hey!

Who are you?

Suddenly, the stage is filled with the sea, and the Salt Doll stands on a small rock, gazing at the sea.

Sea   I am the sea.

The sound of a heartbeat grows louder.

Salt Doll   The sea? The sea⋯?

Sea   Finally, you found me.

Salt Doll   Sea⋯ sea⋯ my sea.

Sea   Yes.

Salt Doll   I've traveled far to find you. How long have you been here?

Sea	Since you started to look for me.
Salt Doll	Since I started to look for you? I want to know more about you.
	What's inside your mysterious blue light?
Sea	Would you like to know? Dip your feet in, and you'll know who I am.
Salt Doll	(Puts one foot in the sea) Oh, (pulls it back in surprise) This is weird… I've kind of disappeared.
Sea	Do you understand now?
Salt Doll	Not yet…
Sea	You'll understand soon enough.
Salt Doll	If I disappear completely, will I understand you?
Sea	There is no such thing as disappearing.
Salt Doll	Do I become you?
Sea	We've always been one from the very beginning.

The silhouette of the sea, resembling the Salt Doll, begins to emerge.

Salt Doll	I am the sea… Sea, you are me…
Sea	The road you've walked is you also.

The hands of the Salt Doll and the Sea wave and slowly approach each other.

Salt Doll	I reached you. And so, I reached myself.

With the sound of waves, the voices of the Sea and Salt Doll
are heard together.

Together   I reached you. And so, I reached myself.

Blackout.

Salt Doll   (In the darkness) I have walked on myself only to find.
I've been, I am⋯ I'll always be⋯

The whole stage shows a shining sea, and the sound of a
heartbeat can be heard faintly.
On the stage, a small white Salt Doll lies in the place of its
birth.
It moves slightly, as if breathing, and the music and
heartbeat grow louder.
The stage darkens. Only the sound of the heartbeat remains.

〈Curtain Call〉

창작자의 글

역할 : 연출, 극작, 제작
이름 : 배근영

• 극작 이야기

나만의 일기처럼, 모두의 시처럼.
혼자 그리고 함께 느끼는 이야기!

바다를 찾아가는 소금인형의 이야기는
모두가 읽는 시처럼 또 나만이 쓰는 일기처
럼 조용하게 다가가기를 바라는 마음으로
쓰여졌습니다.

소금인형이 바다를 찾아가는 과정은 자아
를 찾으며 완성해 가는 여정을 상징합니다.

어쩌면 이것은 진정한 사랑, 꿈, 신념, 종
교에 대한 이야기입니다.

이 이야기를 보는 관객들은 단순히 소금
인형의 여정을 따라가는 것이 아니라, 자신
만의 의식과 삶의 여정을 떠올리며 자신의
이야기와 만날 수 있기를 바랍니다.

소금인형이 바다를 만나는 순간은 끝이
아니라 변화와 발견의 시작입니다. 이는 우
리가 누군가를 만나고 세상을 경험하면서

151

변화하고 성장하는 과정의 은유이기도 합니다.

관객들에게 감정적이고 철학적인 울림을 줄 수 있는 상징적 서사를 전하고자 하였습니다.

소금인형의 여정을 통해 관객들이 자신의 삶과 의식에 대해 깊이 생각해 보는 기회가 되기를 바랍니다.

소금인형은 바다를 만나 자신이 처음부터 바다와 하나였음을 깨닫습니다. 그 만남 속에서 '사라지는 것'은 없다는 진실을 받아들이고, 의식의 흐름 속에서 다시 태어나는 여정을 겪습니다.

이 여정은 끊임없이 이어지는 의식의 흐름이자, 우리 삶 속에서 맞이하는 중요한 순간들, 내면의 변화와 성찰이 결국 하나의 진실을 향해 가고 있음을 상징합니다.

이 이야기를 통해 관객들도 자신의 삶을 되돌아보고, 일상의 한 장면, 문득 떠오른 기억, 조용한 마음의 움직임 속에서 자신만의 '의식의 지점'을 깊이 마주하게 되길 바랍니다.

• **연출 이야기**

'나는 누구지?'……

라고 질문을 던져보았습니다…

그리고

여행이 시작되었습니다…

- 언어가 되어 이야기하는 회화적인 음악
- 음악이 되어 흐르는 시적인 대사
- 우주와 생명을 상징하며 스케치한 푸른빛의 무대
- 하나의 존재가 되어 살아나는 인형과 배우의 호흡

세상은 하나의 큰 원이고 내 안의 나도 큰 원의 흐름을 가진다.

그것을 기반으로 모든 것이 이어져 있고 결국엔 하나의 원을 그
리며 흐르고 있다는 의미를 보여줄 수 있는 무대를 상상했습니다.
그리고 그 무대를 배우와 인형이 무대를 유기적으로 활용하며 함께
이동하거나 공간을 채우는 방식으로 하나의 생명체처럼 보이게 하
고 싶었습니다.

음악과 움직임이 결합되며 감각의 조화를 이루고 소리와 빛을 통
해 배우와 인형의 움직임을 강조하고, 감각적 몰입감을 높일 수 있
도록 고민했습니다.

소금인형이 긴 여정 속에서 이루어지는 모든 만남과 이야기를 지
나서 진심으로 원하는 바다에 닿는 순간을 함께하며 관객들도 자신
을 짙게 들여다 보게되고 내 안의 '나'에게 닿는 순간에 조금 더 가
까워지기를 바랍니다.

• 인형 제작 이야기 – 소금인형

이야기 속의 '소금인형'을 인형극 속의 '소금인형'으로 형상화하
기 위해서 소금인형이 가진 상징성과 극적 메시지를 효과적으로 전
달할 수 있는 인형의 모습을 찾아야 했습니다.

소금인형의 상징성을 담고 정서적인 표현을 해낼 수 있는 인형!
섬세하고 다양한 이야기를 하는 인형은 어떤 모습, 어떤 움직임
을 가져야 할까?

  1) 형태와 디자인: 외형이 단순한 모습의 인형으로 순수한 느낌
     을 주면서 소금인형의 상징성을 강화하면서 무엇보다 시선의
     움직임이 최대한 자연스럽고 섬세해야 한다.

2) 감정적 연결: 소금인형은 여정 중 여러 가지 감정을 만나며 표현해야 하므로 특정한 표정을 가진 마스크보다는 인형 자체가 모든 감정을 불러일으킬 수 있도록 하는 디자인과 연출이 필요하다.

이런 고민 끝에 드디어 소금인형이 태어났습니다.

소금인형의 흰색은 '소금'이라는 물리적 상징성과 순수함, 본연의 자아라는 정서적 상징성을 가집니다. 그리고 표정 없이 방향성만 가지고 있는 얼굴은 감정의 흐름에 따라 여러 가지의 표정을 상상하게 합니다.

소금인형은 구조적으로 자유로운 움직임이 가능하도록 만들어졌습니다. 그 섬세함 움직임은 내적 상태를 반영하는 중요한 요소로 작용합니다.

인형은
상상력에서 비롯되어.
손을 통해 형상화가 되고…
배우의 마음으로부터 생명을 얻어
비로소 무대 위에 섭니다.

The Creator's story

Role : Playwright, Director, Puppet Maker
Name : Bae Geun-Young

• **The story of the Playwright**

Like my own diary, like everyone's poem…
A story experienced both alone and together!

The story of the ⟨Salt Doll⟩ making its way to the sea was written with the hope that it would gently approach, like a poem read by all, yet written as if it were my own personal diary.

The journey of the Salt Doll finding the sea symbolises the process of discovering and completing one's true self. Perhaps, it is a story about true love, dreams, faith, and religion. The audience watching this story will not simply follow the Salt Doll's journey, but hopefully reflect on their own rituals and life paths, finding a connection with their own stories.

The moment the Salt Doll meets the sea is not the end, but the beginning of change and discovery. It is also a metaphor for the process of change and growth as we meet others and experience the world. Through this symbolic narrative, I aim to convey an emotional and philosophical resonance to the audience. I hope that through the Salt Doll's journey, the audience will have the opportunity to reflect deeply on their own lives and consciousness.

• The Story of the Director

"Who am I?"···
 I asked myself this question···
 And then,
 the journey began···

- Music that speaks in a conversational tone, as though it were a language
 - Poetic dialogue flowing like music
 - A stage sketched in blue light, symbolizing the universe and life
 - The breath of the puppet and the actor, coming to life as one existence

The world is one large circle, and "I" within me carries the flow of that great circle. Based on this, everything is interconnected, and I imagined a stage that shows the meaning of how everything flows, ultimately drawing a single circle. I wanted to create a stage where the actor and the puppet use the space smoothly, moving together or filling the space in a way that makes them appear as one living entity.

As music and movement merge, creating a harmony of the senses, I carefully considered how to emphasize the movements of the actor and the puppet through sound and light, increasing the sensory immersion.

As the Salt Doll goes through every encounter and story on its long journey, reaching the sea it truly desires, I hope that the audience will also deeply reflect on themselves and come a little closer to the moment of reaching "I" within.

• Creating the Puppet - The Salt Doll

In order to transform the 'Salt Doll' from the story into a puppet in the puppet theatre, I had to find a form of the puppet that would effectively communicate the symbolism and dramatic message held by the Salt Doll.

A puppet that embodies the symbolism of the Salt Doll and can express emotional depth.

What form and movement should a delicate puppet capable of telling a variety of stories have?

1) Form and Design: The puppet should have a simple appearance that conveys a sense of purity, while enhancing the symbolism of the Salt Doll. Above all, the movement of the eyes must be as natural and delicate as possible.

2) Emotional Connection: Since the Salt Doll encounters and expresses various emotions throughout its journey, a design

and direction are needed that allow the puppet itself to evoke all emotions, rather than relying on a mask with a specific expression.

The Salt Doll was finally created after much contemplation. The white colour of the Salt Doll conveys both the physical symbolism of "salt" and the emotional symbolism of purity and the true self. Its face, with no expression and only a sense of direction, allows the imagination to fill in various expressions depending on the flow of emotions.

The Salt Doll was designed to allow for free movement structurally. The delicate movements play an important element in reflecting its inner state.

The puppet originates from imagination.
It is brought to form through the hands.
Gaining life from the actor's heart,
it finally stands on the stage.

[소금 인형] 초연기록

· 단체명 : 극단 로.기.나래
· 일시/장소 : 2006년 8월 10일 춘천인형극장
· 작가/연출 : 배근영 / 배근영
· 출연 : 고은경, 이현주, 이다정, 홍용민, 이주희, 정수미
· 창작 스태프 : 인형 디자인_배근영/ 제작_극단 로.기.나래/ 무대 디자인_김교
　　　　　　　 은/ 조명_최진근/ 음향_이주환/ 음악_김영준
· 저작물 이용 문의 : ogi223@hanmail.net

주요 공연 기록

2006.08.10	춘천인형극장 / 제18회 춘천인형극제
2006.09	프랑스 샤르르빌세계인형극축제
	France Mondialdes Théâtresde Marionnettes
2010.10.15~17	성남아트센터 / 경기문화재단 우수작품 창작발표활동지원
	사업
2013.08.12	춘천인형극장/ 제25회 춘천인형극제공식초청
2013.08.03~04	이다시 공민관 / 일본 Iida Fasta 공식초청작
2021	제6회 예술인형축제 초청작

주요 수상 기록

2013	제25회 춘천인형극제 경연 우수상

이야기 쏙! 이야기야!

(원제 : 어느 날 거인의 뱃속에서)

극작 정승진

극단 별 비612

등장인물

＊우산장수 이야기
  우산장수 / 우산장수 친구 / 곰방대 도깨비 / 부채 도깨비 /
  고무신 도깨비 / 신부

＊짚신장수 이야기
  짚신장수 / 아버지 / 사회자

＊포수 이야기
  포수 / 어머니 / 호랑이 / 멧돼지 / 노루 / 거인

무대

장터
깊은 산 속
거인의 소굴
거인의 뱃속
재 너머

프롤로그

우산장수가 객석 사이를 돌아다니며 짚신을 팔고 있다.

우산장수 우산 사려. 우산 사세요. 곧 비가 옵니다. 우산 사려. 오늘 장에 사람이 참 많네요. 그런데 우산은 아무도 안 사주고, 뭘 사러 오셨나? 구경 왔어요? 그럼 구경해야지. 그런데 거 뭣이냐, 핸드폰? 그런 게 있어요? 꼭 *끄고* 보셔야 한대요. 왜 그러냐면 지금 시대가 아주 옛날이에요. 울리면 우리가 깜짝 놀라. 그러니까 꼭 끄고 봅시다.

1장. 만남

짚신장수가 등장한다.

짚신장수 짚신 사려. 발에 꼭 맞는 짚신. 한 번 신어보셔. 단돈 두 냥!
우산장수 (짚신장수를 밀어내고 자리를 잡으며) 여긴 내 자리! 우산 사세요. 튼튼하고 오래가는 멋진 우산이 단돈 두 냥!
짚신장수 (밀려나 약 오른 듯) 어린이용은 한 냥. 세상에서 제일 발이 편한 짚신이 왔어요. 엽전 두 냥, 한 짝에 한 냥!
우산장수 가볍고 예쁜 우산이 단돈 두… 아니 한 냥!

포수가 이를 쑤시며 등장한다.

포   수 아이고. 배부르다.
짚신장수 손님! 여기 짚신 하나 사세요. 물을 촥 먹여서 정성으로 만들어서 발에 꼭 맞는 짚신!

우산장수 기름을 촥 먹여서 빗물이 쪼르륵 미끄러지는 우산!
짚신장수 가시도 하나 안 박히는 보드라운 짚신!
우산장수 파리도 쪼르륵 미끄러지는 우산!
짚신장수 오늘 해가 반짝반짝해요!
우산장수 오늘 비가 옵니다!

노래. 짚신과 우산
짚신이요, 짚신. 세상에서 둘째가는 짚신!
(포수: 그럼 첫 번째는?)
짚신이요, 짚신. 이렇게 해가 쨍쨍한 날 짚신.
(우산장수: 비가 온다던데)
보들보들 짚신이요.
반들반들 짚신이요.
짚신이요, 짚신!
(포수: 이거 얼마에요?)
(짚신장수: 두 냥입니다.)
(우산장수: 두 냥 날리셨네.)
(짚신장수: 두 냥 날리셨네요. 엥?)
우산이요, 우산. 가볍고 예쁜 우산
(포수: 오, 예쁜데!)
우산이요, 우산. 먹구름이 몰려와요.
(짚신장수: 이렇게 해가 쨍쨍한데?)
빙글빙글 우산.
방글방글 우산.
우산이요 우산!
(포수: 이건 얼마에요?)
(짚신장수: 두 냥입니다.)
(우산장수: 두 냥 날리셨네.)

(짚신장수: 두 냥 날리셨네요. 엥?)

보들보들 짚신이요.

반들반들 짚신이요.

짚신이요. 짚신!

우산이요. 우산!

해가 쨍쨍! 우르르 쾅쾅! (우산장수, 짚신장수 동시에)

(포수: 대체 해가 뜬다는 거야, 비가 온다는 거야?)

(짚신장수: 해 뜬다!)

(우산장수: 비 온다!)

(짚신장수: 해 뜬다!)

(우산장수: 비 온다!)

해뜬다비온다해뜬다비온다해뜬다비온다해온다비뜬다해온다

비뜬다해온다비뜬다

해온다비뜬다해온다비뜬다.

짚신이요, 우산!

포 수 해 온다? 비 뜬다? 에이 사람 놀려요? 몰라요! 둘 다 안 사요!

포수 퇴장한다.

짚신장수 손님! 해가 온대요!

우산장수 비가 뜬대요!

짚신장수 (우산을 가리키며) 그 우산이라도 하나 팔 걸.

우산장수 (짚신을 가리키며) 그 짚신이라도 하나 팔 걸.

짚신장수 벌써 날이 저물어가네.

우산장수 짚신 하나만 주세요.

짚신장수 나 동정받는 건 싫어요.

우산장수 내 짚신이 잘 안 맞아서 그래요. 하나만 줘 봐요.

짚신장수 진짜지요? 여기 있어요.

우산장수 (짚신을 신어본다) 아이고, 발에 딱 맞네.

짚신장수 꼭 맞네. 저도 우산 하나만 주세요.

우산장수 나도 동정받는 건 싫어요.

짚신장수 비 온다면서요. 얼른 하나 줘 봐요.

우산장수 여기요.

짚신장수 고마워요.

우산을 써 본다.

짚신장수 우산이 아주 튼튼하고 좋네요.

우산장수 짚신도 튼튼하고 좋네요.

포 수 (지켜보고 있다가 슬그머니 끼어들며) 튼튼하다고?

짚신,우산 아주 튼튼하고 좋아요!

포 수 (펼쳐보고 신어보며) 재 너머 가는데 하나씩 사야겠소.

우산장수 재 너머요? 나도 재 너머 가는데?

짚신장수 어? 저도 그쪽으로 갑니다. 재 너머가 고향 집이거든요. 십 년 만에 고향 갑니다.

우산장수 나도 십 년 만이오.

포 수 이제 보니 다 같은 고향 사람들이네. 이왕 이렇게 된 거 우리 다 같이 갑시다!

짚신,우산 그럽시다!

짐을 챙겨서 출발한다.

포 수 저만 따라오세요.

2장. 고개 앞에서

밤이 되어 어두워진다.
우산장수, 짚신장수, 포수가 조족등(발밑을 비추는 등)을 들고 등장
한다.

포　　수　어! 나 갑자기 배가 너무 아프네요. 얼른 볼일 보고 올 테니
　　　　　까 잠깐만 계세요.
우산장수　(우산 바구니를 내려놓으며) 우리 여기서 잠깐 쉬었다 갑시다.
짚신장수　(지게를 내려놓으며) 그럽시다.

우산장수가 바위틈에 꽂혀있는 팻말을 발견한다.

우산장수　이게 뭐야? (팻말을 조족등으로 비추면서) 땡땡 조심.
　　　　　여기 뭘 조심하라고 씌어있어요.
짚신장수　여기에도 뭐가 쓰여 있어요. (팻말을 조족등으로 비추면서) 열
　　　　　명 이상 모아서
우산장수　여기 또 있네? (팻말을 비추면서) 지나가시오.
짚신장수　도대체 뭘 조심하라는 걸까요? 혹시 호랑이?
포　　수　(그림자로 호랑이를 만들며) 어흥!
우산장수　아니면, 산적?
포　　수　(그림자로 얼굴을 비추며) 가진 거 다 내놔!
우산장수　저는 가진 게 없어요!
짚신장수　저는 맛이 없어요!
포　　수　어흥! 가진 거 다 내놔! (짚신장수, 우산장수 쪽으로 총을 겨누며)
　　　　　아하하! 속았지요.
우산장수　아이고, 난 또 호랑인 줄 알았네요.
포　　수　그렇지, 내 존재감이 그 정도 되지요. 하하하.

짚신장수 간 떨어질 뻔했네요.

우산장수 여기 산속에서 무엇이 나타난대요.

포　수 뭐가 나타나요?

우산장수 열 명 이상 모아서 산을 넘으라는구먼요.

짚신장수 지금 여기는 우리 셋뿐이니까 오늘 넘어가긴 틀렸네요.

포　수 산에 사는 것이 아무리 무서워 봐야 호랑이만 할까요. 그러니 호랑이는 걱정 말고 저만 따라오세요!

짚신장수 예예. 따라갑니다.

우산장수 잠깐! 정말 괜찮겠어요?

포　수 두 분이 안 가신다면 저 혼자라도 갑니다.

짚신장수 저는 갑니다. 정 무서우면 여기 계시다가 내일 날 밝으면 그때 넘어오세요.

우산장수 누가 무섭대요? 갑시다, 가!

셋이 같이 출발한다.

3장. 거인을 만나다

비가 내린다.

짚신장수 비다! (우산을 쓰며) 우산 사길 잘했네.

포　수 (우산을 쓰며) 잘했네!

우산장수 (우산을 쓰며) 내가 비 온다고 그랬죠?

포　수 갑시다.

짚신장수 호랑이는커녕 개미 한 마리 없네요.

짚신장수가 조족등을 비추자, 포수 우산에 거인의 눈이 비친다.

짚신장수 어? 저기 뭐가 있어요!

우산장수가 조족등을 비추자, 짚신장수 우산에 거인의 눈이 비친다.

우산장수 으악!
포　　수 왜 그래요?
우산장수 시커멓고 얼룩덜룩한 게… 무서워서 나 못가!
포　　수 저기 뭐가 있다는 거야?

포수가 조족등을 비추자, 우산장수 우산에 거인의 입이 비친다.

포수, 짚신장수 (우산장수 우산에 비친 형상을 발견) 으악! 괴물이다!

모두가 비추는 공간마다 거인의 형상이 나타났다 사라졌다 한다.
가운데 모여서 떨며 조족등을 비추자, 거인의 얼굴이 비친다.
눈코입이 나타났다가 흩어진다.

모　　두 으악! 괴물이다.

모두가 놀라서 정신없이 우왕좌왕한다.

거　　인 으하하하, 지나가고 싶나?
우산/짚신 네.
거　　인 살고 싶나?
우산/짚신 네!
거　　인 그렇다면 대가를 치러야지!
모　　두 으악! 사람 살려!

거인 그림자가 어지럽게 왔다 갔다 한다.

우산, 짚신, 포수 여기저기 도망 다니다가 아수라장이 된다.

4장. 포수 이야기

거인의 감옥이다.

거   인 지금부터 살아서 집에 가야 하는 간절한 사연을 이야기해
라. 이야기를 다 듣고 너희 셋 중 딱 한 명만 살려주겠다.

포   수 (다른 사람들을 돌아보며) 딱 한 명만요?

거   인 (포수를 가리키며) 거기 맨 앞에 있는 잘생긴 놈! 너부터 이야
기해라.

우산장수 가보세요!

포   수 저, 저요? (쭈뼛쭈뼛 일어서서) 홀로 계신 어머니가 아프셨습니
다. 저는 산에 약초를 캐러 산에 갔지요.

포수가 숲을 돌아다니며 약초를 캔다.

포   수 오늘은 산에 뭐가 있을까? (산딸기를 발견하고) 맛 좋은 산딸기
네? 아이고 달다. (버섯을 발견하고) 몸에 좋은 버섯. 어머니 가
져다드리고. 쿵쿵. 이게 무슨 냄새지? (산삼을 뽑으며) 심 봤다!

호랑이가 나타난다.

호랑이 어흥!

포   수 아이쿠야, 호랑이잖아?

호랑이 어흥, 널 잡아먹겠다. 냠냠!

포   수   꼼짝없이 죽게 됐구나. 호랑이 굴에 들어가도 정신만 바짝
          차리면 된다고 했지? 에라이 모르겠다. 이판사판이다!

          포수가 호랑이에게 큰절한다.

포   수   아이고 호랑이 형님, 이제야 만나게 되었군요. 너무나 반갑
          고, 감사합니다.
호랑이   어쭈? 너는 사람인데 나보고 형님이라고? 어흥!

          호랑이가 잡아먹으려 한다.

포   수   (피하며) 저희 어머니께서 늘 말씀하시길,
어머니   아들아, 니 형이 어릴 때 산에 갔다가 돌아오지 못했단다.
          호랑이에게 물려가서 죽은 줄 알고 있었지. 어느 날 꿈을
          꾸었는데…
호랑이   어머니. 저는 길을 잃고 산을 헤매다 죽게 되었는데, 산신의
          가호로 호랑이가 되었습니다. 이 꼴을 하고는 집에 돌아갈
          수가 없어요. 보고 싶어요! 어머니!
어머니   아들아, 산속에서 혹시 널 닮은 호랑이를 만나거든 형님이
          라 부르거라!
포   수   딱 우리 형님 같아서 그럽니다. 형님!
호랑이   (절하려는 포수를 말린 후) 내가 어딜 봐서 니 형님 같으냐?
포   수   우리 집안이 예전부터 목소리가 천둥소리처럼 아주 큽니다.
호랑이   오, 내 목소리가 좀 우렁차지! 어흥!
포   수   (멋진 포즈) 그리고 이 날카로운 눈빛.
호랑이   부리부리하지!
포   수   그리고 발이 왕 발입니다.
호랑이   (발을 확인하며) 오, 내가 발이 좀 크다.

포 수	남의 말을 잘 믿고요.
호랑이	오, 내 귀가 얇아.
포 수	머리도 좀 나쁘고요.
호랑이	그래, 내 머리가 나빠. 뭐라구?
포 수	(얼른 절을 한다) 아이고 형님, 그동안 얼마나 고생이 많으셨습니까?
호랑이	(절을 받는다) 아이고, 아우야.

둘이 껴안고 운다.

포 수	형님을 만나면 어머니가 이 말을 꼭 전하라고 하셨습니다.
호랑이	그래, 아우야. 어머니께서 내게 뭐라고 하시더냐?
어머니	사랑한다. 아들아! 내 너를 한시도 잊지 않고 그리워하고 있다!
호랑이	(감격) 어머니! (호랑이, 어머니 계신 쪽으로 절한다) 당장 뛰어가서 어머니 품에 안겨 울고 싶지만, 이렇게 산짐승이 되었으니… (울며) 나는 못 간다. 내가 한 달에 두 번씩 사냥한 것을 갖다 줄 테니 어머니 맛나게 드시게 해드려라. 이게 내가 할 수 있는 전부다.
포 수	(호랑이를 안으며) 형님!
호랑이	(마주 안으며) 아우야!

호랑이가 사냥감을 갖다준다.

호랑이	으차!
어머니	이게 웬 멧돼지냐?
포 수	어머니! 이거 우리 호랑이 형님께서 가져다주셨나 봐요.
어머니	아이고! 그래!

호랑이	으차!
어머니	이게 웬 노루냐?
포 수	호랑이 형님! 감사합니다.
어머니	호랑이 아들이 아주 효자구나. 꿀까닥!

어머니가 죽는다.

포 수	어머니!
호랑이	어흥!
포 수	제가 우리 호랑이 형님께 그동안 감사했다고 사랑한다고 전해야 하는데… 제가 형님께 이 말을 전할 수 있게 저 좀 살려주세요!

5장. 짚신장수 이야기

포수를 밀쳐내고 짚신장수가 등장한다.

짚신장수 다음은 제 이야기를 하겠습니다. 저는 짚신장수입니다. 우리 아버지도 짚신장수. 저는 아버지께 새끼를 꼬아서 짚신 삼는 것을 배웠습니다. 어느 날 저는 아버지보다 짚신을 더 빨리 만들게 되었습니다. 아버지가 하나 만들 때 저는 두 개! 아빠가 두 개 만들 때 저는 네 개! 하지만 아버지는 배울 게 더 남았다며 제 짚신을 못 팔게 하셨습니다. 화가 난 저는 장에 나가서 누구 짚신이 더 많이 팔리는지 대결을 하자고 했지요.

사회자 지금부터 아빠와 아들의 짚신 대결을 시작하겠습니다! 홍 코너, 50년 경력을 자랑하는 짚신 장인이 만든 아빠 짚신!

아빠 짚신이 등장한다.

사회자 청 코너, 경력보다는 실력. 패기 넘치는 아들 짚신!

아들 짚신이 등장한다.

사회자 아들의 도전으로 시작된 이 대결, 과연 누가 승자가 될 것인가?

노래. 대결

아들짚신 : '나'는 짚신. 젊고 팔팔하지. 하루에 스무 개를 만든다네. 빠르고 정확하지 놀랍도록 튼튼하지.

아빠짚신 : 내 소개를 함세. 늙었지만 기본을 지킨다네. 하루에 다섯 개면 충분하지.

섬세하고 꼼꼼해. 고객을 생각하지.

아들짚신 : 내꺼 최고 내가 최고 내 짚신이 최고 최고야!

내꺼 최고 내가 최고
내짚신이 최고야! 내꺼 최고 내가 최고
내 짚신이 최고 최고야!
아빠짚신 : 내 짚~~~신이~~최고~~~~야~~!

사회자   그만! 제가 보기에는 똑같아 보이는데요?
아들짚신 똑같다고? 그럼 네 배나 빠른 내 승리!
아빠짚신 한번 신어나 보구려.
사회자   그럽시다.

사회자, 두 짚신을 신어본다.

사회자   똑같아 보이는데……
아들짚신 보나 마나 내 승리.
아빠짚신 지켜보자꾸나.

짚신 양쪽 발에 신어본다.

사회자   우승자를 발표하겠습니다. 짚신 대결의 우승자는 바로!
사회자   아빠 짚신!

아들 짚신 좌절한다.

아들짚신 어째서? 내가 네 배나 빠른데? 도대체 모르겠어. 어째서..
사회자   아빠 짚신과 아들 짚신의 차이를 구별 못 한다면 장인이 될
            자격이 없습니다!

우산장수가 짚신 두 짝을 들고 짚신장수 옆으로 다가온다.

짚신장수 무슨 차이일까.

우산장수가 열심히 본다.

우산장수 내가 알려 줄까요?
짚신장수 알려 주시오!
우산장수 비밀은 이 거스름에 있소. 당신 아버지 것은 이 거스름을
잘 다듬어서 보들보들한데 당신 것은 그대로 놔두어 까칠
까칠 따갑소. 이래서는 발이 따가워서 못 신지.
짚신장수 보들보들, 까칠까칠. 드디어 아버지의 깊은 뜻을 알게 됐
소! 아버지! 불효자를 용서하세요. 저는 집으로 돌아가야겠
어요! 아버지께 용서를 구하고 배울 것이 많이 남았습니다.
저 좀 집에 보내주세요!

우산장수가 짚신장수를 밀쳐낸다.

6장. 우산장수 이야기

우산장수 이제 제 이야기를 하겠습니다. 저는 어릴 때부터 이야기를
아주 좋아했습니다. 어디서 재미있는 이야기를 들으면 적
어 놓고.

이야기를 적은 종이가 쌓인다.

우산장수 들으면 또 적어 놓고.

주머니에 이야기를 집어넣는다.

우산장수　이야기를 적어서 주머니에 넣었어요.

주머니가 세 개가 된다.

우산장수　이야기를 모으는 데만 정신이 팔려서 적어 놓기만 했지,
　　　　　들려준 적은 없었죠.
　　　　　그러다가 장가를 가게 됐습니다.

친구가 등장한다.

친　　구　결혼 축하하네.
우산장수　고마워. 내일 잘 부탁하네.
친　　구　걱정 말고 푹 자둬. 재 너머 김부자 댁까지 가려면 먼 길이
　　　　　잖아. 그런데 이 주머니들은 뭔가?
우산장수　그동안 모은 이야기들이네.
친　　구　이걸 가져가려고?
우산장수　쓸데없는 걸 모았다고 뭐라 하려나? 일단 여기 두고 가야
　　　　　겠네.
친　　구　잘 생각했네.
우산장수　갈 길이 머니 이제 자자고.
친　　구　그러자고.

어두워지고 밤이 된다.
친구가 잠에서 깨어난다.

친　　구　저녁에 뭘 잘 못 먹었나? 왜 이렇게 배가 아프지?

밖으로 나온다. 그때 도깨비들이 주머니 속에서 하나씩 나온다.

친 구 저게 뭐지?

곰방대 저놈이 우릴 여기 가둬놓고 안 풀어준다.

부 채 낼 재 너머 장가를 가면 영영 못 볼 텐데.

고무신 억울해서 못 살겠다. 우리처럼 재밌는 이야기를 가둬놓다니.

곰방대 저놈이 우릴 영영 여기 가둬놓을 셈인가?

부 채 장가가서 재밌게 살다 보면 우리 생각이 나겠나?

고무신 우린 영영 세상에 나가지 못하고 사라지는 이야기가 될
        거야.

곰방대 늦기 전에 복수하자.

부 채 독을 먹이자.

고무신 복수하자!

부 채 복수는 나의 것!

도깨비들 복수는 우리의 것! 복수! 복수! 복수!

        도깨비들 사라진다.

친 구 이야기들이 오래 묵어서 도깨비가 되었구나. 이를 어쩐다?

아침이 된다.
결혼식장으로 출발하는 우산장수와 친구를 곰방대 도깨비가 기다리고 있다.

우산장수 자! 가세나.
곰방대 저기 온다. 먹음직스러운 독 사과로 변신!
우산장수 저기 좀 봐! 아주 먹음직스러운 사과가 있네. 우리 나눠 먹을까?
친　구 잠깐만 기다려보게.
　　　　이런 먹음직스러운 사과가 땅에 떨어져 있을 리가 없어.

사과를 밟아 뭉개 버린다.

우산장수 자네 왜 그러나?
친　구 결혼식 앞두고 땅에 떨어진 거 먹으면 못 써!
우산장수 맛있게 보였는데…
친　구 어서 가자고.

다시 출발하는 가마. 부채 도깨비가 기다리고 있다.

부　채 독 사과가 실패했구나. 그렇다면 독 꽃으로 변신!
우산장수 처음 보는 예쁜 꽃이 피었네. 새 신부에게 갖다줘야겠다.
친　구 잠깐! 기다려 보게.
　　　　이런 풀 한 포기 없는 곳에 예쁜 꽃이라니! 도깨비장난이 분명해! (꽃을 따서 던지며) 이런 건 그냥 버려!
우산장수 아니 왜 그래?
친　구 새 신부에게 빨간 꽃은 안 어울려.
우산장수 예쁜 꽃인데 왜 그러나?

친　　구　얼른 가세. 이러다 늦겠어.
우산장수　이제 다 왔네. 어서 가세.

　　　　　다시 출발한다.

소　　리　혼례를 시작하겠습니다.

　　　　　꼭두각시 음악과 함께 춤추는 신랑 신부.

고무신　　이건 못 피할걸. 독바늘로 변신!
소　　리　신랑 신부 맞절!

　　　　　도깨비가 독바늘로 변하고, 신랑 신부가 절하려고 엎드리는데 친구
　　　　　가 나타난다.

친　　구　잠깐!

　　　　　친구가 신랑을 밀치고 친구는 나가떨어진다.

우산장수　자네! 도대체 왜 이러는 거야? 세 번이나 나를 망신을 주다니!
친　　구　그게 아니야. 자네가 모아둔 이야기 주머니 안에 사는 도깨
　　　　　비들이 복수를 한다고 그러지 않는가?
우산장수　그 말을 나보고 믿으라고?
친　　구　내 말을 못 믿겠거든 자네 절하려고 엎드린 자리를 파보게나.
우산장수　그래, 파 보자구. 거짓말이면 각오해.

　　　　　신랑이 땅을 파자 바늘이 나온다.

우산장수 정말 독바늘이네. 자네 덕에 살았네. 내 이놈의 이야기 주머니들을 싹 불 싸질러버려야지!

바늘이 도깨비로 변신한다.

고무신 잠깐! 내 말 좀 들어봐라.
우산장수 너 잘 만났다. 니가 나랑 무슨 원수가 졌다고 이런 짓을 하느냐. 내가 이야기를 얼마나 좋아했는데.
고무신 이야기를 좋아했다고? 너는 욕심껏 이야기를 혼자 모으기만 하고 남들에게 들려주질 않았잖아! 이야기를 좋아한다면 다른 사람에게도 들려줘야지. 사람들 입에서 입으로 돌아다니는 게 얼마나 즐거운데. 귀를 간질간질하게 해주는 게 얼마나 행복한데!
우산장수 그날 저는 도깨비에 놀란 신부와 결혼도 못하고 온 세상을 돌아다니며 우산을 팔고 있습니다. 이렇게 떠돌다 보니 이제는 장가도 가고 싶고 고향이 그리워 돌아가는 길입니다. 제발 저 좀 살려주십시오!

7장. 거인의 결정

우산장수 자, 이제 이야기를 다 했으니 우리 중 한 명을 살려주십시오.
거 인 아하하하! 너희들은 이야기를 참 잘하는구나?
모 두 고맙습니다.
거 인 나도 이야기를 잘하고 싶지만 재주가 없다. 그래서 이야기를 잘하는 사람들을 보면 화가 난다.
우산장수 네? 왜 화가 나지? 이야기 잘하면 살려준다고 했잖아.
짚신장수 그랬잖아!

노래. 거인 랩소디

너희 사람들, 이야기를 잘하지.

(모두) 우리 사람들, 이야기를 좋아해.

이야기 잘하는 사람 싫어.

아무리 재미있는 이야기도 내가 하면 재미가 없어

(짚신장수) 그러면 저희 이야기 들으면 돼요.

나는 화가 났지. 생각했어.

이야기는 어디서 오는 걸까?

바로 너희들 같은 이야기꾼!

(우산장수) 맞아요! 이야기는 우리 사람들에게서 나오지.

결심했어! 없앨거야! 결심했어! 없앨거야! 이야기를

(모두) 이야기 살려! 결심했어! 없앨거야!

결심했어! 없앨거야! 사람들을!

(모두) 으악! 사람 살려!

사람들이 도망가고 거인이 잡으러 다닌다.

우산장수 이쪽이에요!

짚신장수 아니! 저쪽이에요!

모두가 도망 다닌다.

거 인 이놈들!! 잡았다!

모 두 으악! 사람 살려!

아수라장이 되며 거인에게 잡아먹힌다. 거인의 뱃속 위장이 나오면서 한 사람씩 위장에 빠져서 내려간다. 포수, 짚신장수, 우산장수 순서로 위장을 따라 아래로 미끄러진다.

포　　수 으악! 나 먼저 가요!

짚신장수 우리 아버지를 잘 부탁해요.

우산장수 이런다고 이야기가 없어질 것 같아? 이야기는 사라지지 않아!

뱃속으로 떨어지는 세 사람.

포　　수 어이쿠!

짚신장수 아이고!

우산장수 아고고! 소화되기 전에 죽을 뻔했네!

포　　수 이제 어쩌죠?

짚신장수 기다리면 돼요.

포　　수 뭘 기다려요?

짚신장수 죽기만 기다리면 돼요. 괜히 누구 말 듣고 한밤중에 산을
　　　　 넘다가 죽게 됐네요.

포　　수 아니, 왜 내 탓을 해요?

짚신장수 당신이 나만 따라오라고 했잖아.
포　수 당신? 당신이라고 했냐?
짚신장수 당신이라고 했다. 어쩔래?
우산장수 그만 싸우고 여기서 빠져나갈 방법을 찾아봅시다.
짚신장수 방법이 어디 있어요. 우린 다 죽었어요.
우산장수 그러지 말고 좋은 방법을 생각해 봅시다.
우산장수 가만… 저기 뭐가 보이는데요? 이리 와보세요!

　　　　셋은 무언가 보이는 쪽으로 가본다. 관객들 쪽이다. 사람들이 가득
　　　　있다.

우산장수 여기 사람들이 모여 있네요.
짚신장수 그동안 거인이 잡아먹은 사람들인가 봐요. 안녕하세요.
포　수 안녕할 리가 있겠소?
우산장수 아! 여기 먼저 잡혀 온 분들과 힘을 합쳐서 여기서 빠져나
　　　　갈 방법을 생각해 봅시다!
짚신장수 아! 여러분, 여기서 나갈 방법을 알고 계십니까?

　　　　관객에게 묻는다. 방법을 들어본다.

우산장수 우리가 가진 걸 다 꺼내 봅시다. 난 여기 대나무로 만든 우
　　　　산이 있소.
짚신장수 나야 가진 게 짚신뿐인데.
포　수 나는 화승총과 부싯돌. 이거밖에 없는데?
우산장수 무슨 좋은 방법이 없을까요, 여러분?

　　　　관객이 불을 붙이자고 제안한다.
　　　　관객의 제안이 없으면 짚신장수가 생각해낸다.

짚신장수 그래! 이 부싯돌로 짚신에 불을 붙이고,

우산장수 이 대나무 우산을 장작으로 같이 태우면 큰불을 만들어낼 수 있어요.

포　　수 그럼, 거인을 물리칠 수 있을 거예요.

우산장수 그거 좋은 생각이에요.

포　　수 당장 해 봅시다.

세 가지를 모아 불을 붙인다. 연기가 난다.

거인소리 에~~~춰!

에필로그. 탈출

거인의 기침으로 거인 뱃속에서 빠져나온 세 사람은 재 너머로 날아간다.

모두가 살아서 재 너머에 떨어진다.

우산장수 그 부싯돌이 아니었더라면!

포　　수 그 짚신 지푸라기가 아니었더라면!

짚신장수 그 우산 대나무가 아니었더라면!

모　　두 불이 붙지 않았을 것 아니오! 하하하하하하

짚신장수가 짐을 짊어진다.

짚신장수 이제 가야겠소. 그럼 안녕히들 가시오.

우산장수 아버지 만나러 가시오?

짚신장수 내 아버지는 20년 전에 돌아가셨소.

우산장수 아니 그럼, 아까 그 얘기는?

짚신장수 아이구~ 살려면 무슨 말을 못 해. 안녕히들 계시오.

짚신장수가 퇴장한다.

우산장수 그, 그렇긴 하지.

포수가 총을 어깨에 멘다.

포　　수 나도 이제 가야겠어요. 너무 늦으면 어머니가 걱정하실 거예요.

우산장수 아니, 어머니 돌아가셨다고 하지 않았나요?

포　　수 에이, 잘못 들었겠지. 난 갑니다. 허허허허허~

포수가 퇴장한다.

우산장수 부, 분명 돌아가셨다고 했는데… 허…거 참

우산장수도 짐을 짊어진다.

우산장수 아이고, 나도 이제 가야겠다. (깨달은 듯) 아니다. 이노무 팔리지도 않는 우산일랑은 집어치우고 이제부턴 이야기를 팔아야겠다. 그래! 좋아! 하하하하하하~어떤 이야기부터 팔까? 아! 그래! 이야기 사려~ 이야기~ 아무도 겪어보지 못한 진짜 이야기, 우산장수와 짚신장수와 포수가 거인의 뱃속에 들어갔다가 살아 돌아온 이야기. 눈물 없이는 들을 수 없는 진짜 이야기. 지금! 시작합니다!

노래. 이야기사려

이야기 사려~이야기~

이야기 쏙! 이야기~

셋이 듣다가 하나 죽어도 모르는 재밌는 이야기~

너무 재미있어 밤을 꼴딱 새는 이야기 사려~

어린아이가 시간 가는 줄 모르고 듣다가

정신을 차려보니 할아버지 돼 있다는 이야기~

눈물 콧물 쏙 빠지는 이야기 사려~

웃다가 배꼽 빠지는 이야기 사려~

이야기 사려~이야기~

이야기 쏙! 이야기~

셋이 듣다가 하나 죽어도 모르는 재밌는 이야기~

〈끝〉

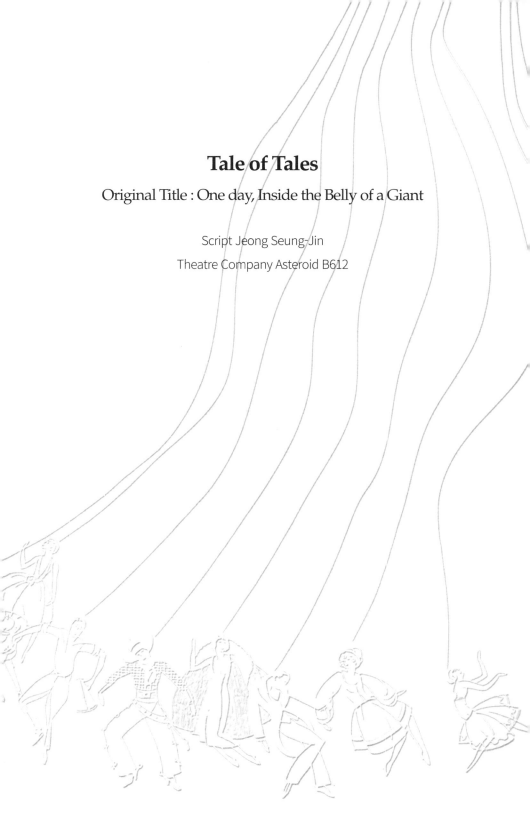

Tale of Tales

Original Title : One day, Inside the Belly of a Giant

Script Jeong Seung-Jin

Theatre Company Asteroid B612

Characters

* Umbrella peddler's story
   Umbrella peddler / his friend / Long pipe dokkaebi[1] /
   Folding Fan dokkaebi / Rubber shoes dokkaebi / bride

* Straw shoes peddler's story
   Straw shoes peddler / Father / Host

* Hunter's story
   Hunter / Mother / Tiger / Wild Boar / Deer / Giant

Stage

Marketplace
Deep in the mountains
Giant's lair
Inside the giant's stomach
Beyond the mountain pass

---

1) It is a type of mischievous mythical creature that frequently appears in
   Korean folktales, often taking the form of an animal or a human. It is said
   to possess extraordinary strength and abilities, often enchanting people or
   playing pranks and causing trouble.

Prologue

An umbrella peddler moves through the audience, selling umbrella.

Umbrella peddler Get your umbrella. Get your umbrella here. It'll rain soon. Get your umbrella. Quite a lot of people in the market today. But if nobody is buying umbrellas, what are they buying then? Did they just come to have a look around? Then they should watch. But wait, what is that? A mobile phone? Why do you have that? They said you should switch it off and watch the show. It's because this is a story about long ago. If we see it we'll get startled. So please everyone, turn off your phones and enjoy the show.

Chapter 1: A Chance Encounter

A Straw shoes peddler enters.

Straw shoes peddler Buy your straw shoes. They will definitely fit. Come and try them. Only two nyang![2]

Umbrella peddler (Pushing the straw shoes peddler away and taking over the spot) This is my spot! Get your umbrellas. A sturdy and long-lasting stylish umbrella for only two nyang!

---

2) Historical Korean currency.

Straw shoes peddler (Feeling pushed out, as if annoyed) For the kids only one nyang.

The most comfortable straw shoes in the world.

Two nyang a pair, one nyang for just one side!

Umbrella peddler Light and pretty umbrella for just two nyang⋯ no wait just one nyang!

A hunter enters, picking at his teeth.

Hunter Oh. I am stuffed.

Straw shoes peddler Mister! Come and buy some straw shoes. A pair of straw shoes made with great care, perfectly crafted to fit your feet after being soaked in water!

Umbrella peddler An umbrella soaked in oil, making the rainwater slide off smoothly!

Straw shoes peddler Straw shoes so soft that not a single thorn can prick you!

Umbrella peddler Even the flies slide right off!

Straw shoes peddler The sun is shining in the sky today!

Umbrella peddler It's going to rain today!

Song. Straw shoes and umbrella

Straw shoes, straw shoes. The world's second-best straw shoes!

(Hunter: Then who's first?)

Straw shoes, straw shoes. Straw shoes for such a sunny day!

(Umbrella peddler: I told you it's going to rain)

Soft, soft straw shoes.

Smooth, smooth straw shoes.

Straw shoes, straw shoes!

(Hunter: How much are they?)

(Straw shoes peddler: Two nyang.)

(Umbrella peddler: Two nyang thrown out the window!)

(Straw shoes peddler: Two nyang thrown out the window. What?)

Umbrella, umbrella. Light and pretty umbrella

(Hunter: Oh, it's lovely!)

Umbrella, umbrella. The dark clouds are gathering.

(Straw shoes peddler: Isn't the sun shining so brightly?)

Spinning, spinning umbrella.

Smiling, smiling umbrella.

Umbrella, Umbrella!

(Hunter: How much is it?)

(Umbrella peddler: Two nyang.)

(Straw shoes peddler: Two nyang thrown out the window.)

(Umbrella peddler: Two nyang thrown out the window. What?)

Soft, soft straw shoes.

Smooth, smooth straw shoes.

Straw shoes, straw shoes!

Umbrella, umbrella!

The sun is blazing! Kaboom! (Umbrella peddler, Straw shoes peddler at the same time)

(Hunter: Is the sun rising, or is it going to rain?)

(Straw shoe peddler: The sun is rising!)

(Umbrella peddler: It's going to rain!)

(Straw shoe peddler: The sun is rising!)

(Umbrella peddler: It's going to rain!)

The sun is rising It's going to rain The sun is rising It's going to rain The sun is rising It's going to rain The sun is raining It's going to rise The sun is raining It's going to rise The sun is raining It's going to rise The sun is raining It's going to rise The sun is raining It's going to rise.

Straw shoes, umbrella!

Hunter　　The sun is raining? It's going to rise? Are you making fun of me? Whatever! I'm not buying any!

Hunter gets off stage.

Straw shoes peddler　Mister! The sun is raining!

Umbrella peddler　It's going to rise!

Straw shoes peddler　(Pointing at the umbrella) You should have sold that, at least.

Umbrella peddler　(Pointing at the straw shoes) You should have sold a pair, at least.

Straw shoes peddler　The day is already fading.

Umbrella peddler　Give me just one straw shoe.

Straw shoes peddler　I don't need your pity.

Umbrella peddler　My shoes don't fit properly. Just give me one.

Straw shoes peddler　Really? Here.

Umbrella peddler　(Tries on the shoe.) Wow, it fits just right.

Straw shoes peddler　Perfect fit. Please give me an umbrella too.

Umbrella peddler　I don't need your pity either.

Straw shoes peddler　You said it's going to rain. Come on, give me one.

Umbrella peddler　Here.

Straw shoes peddler　Thank you.

Opens the umbrella.

Straw shoes peddler　Nice, the umbrella is quite sturdy.

Umbrella peddler　The shoe is also sturdy. I like it.

Hunter　(Watching closely, then slyly butting in) Is it sturdy..?

Straw shoes, Umbrella peddler　It's very sturdy!

Hunter　(Opening up the umbrella and trying on the shoes.) I'm heading over the mountain pass, so I guess I will need one each.

Umbrella peddler　Going beyond the mountain pass? So am I?

Straw shoes peddler　Oh? I'm also going that way. Beyond the pass is my hometown.

I'm visiting after ten years.

Umbrella peddler　So am I.

Hunter　It seems we are all from the same hometown. Shall we go together, then?

Straw shoes, Umbrella peddler　Sure!

They pack their things and leave.

Hunter　Just follow me.

Chapter 2: At the Front of the Mountain Pass

It's getting dark because it is night-time.

The Umbrella peddler, Straw shoes peddler, Hunter enter holding a lantern that illuminates their feet.

Hunter Oh! My stomach suddenly hurts so much. I'll quickly take care of things and be right back, so please wait here for a moment.

Umbrella peddler (Puts the umbrella basket down.) Then let's take a break here.

Straw shoes peddler (Puts down the jige[3].) Let's.

The umbrella peddler discovers a sign stuck between the rocks.

Umbrella peddler What is this? (Shines the light on the sign) Beware of······ What should we beware of?

Straw shoes peddler There is something written over here.
(Shines the light on the sign)
Gather in groups of ten people

Umbrella peddler There is something here too. (Shines the light on the sign) Go around.

Straw shoes peddler What in the heavens are we supposed to beware of?
A tiger maybe?

---

3) A jige is a traditional Korean carrying frame, typically used to carry heavy loads on the back, often with the help of straps.

Hunter	(Makes a tiger from the shadows) Rawr!
Umbrella peddler	Or maybe, a bandit?
Hunter	(Shines the lantern on his face) Give me all your belongings!
Umbrella peddler	I don't have any belongings!
Straw shoes peddler	I'm not tasty!
Hunter	Rawr! Give me everything you have! (Aiming the gun towards the straw shoe peddler and the umbrella peddler.) Hahaha! Gotcha!
Umbrella peddler	Oh my Godness! I thought it was a tiger.
Hunter	That's right, my presence is that scary. Hahaha!
Straw shoes peddler	I almost jumped out of my skin!
Umbrella peddler	Apparently there is something in the mountains.
Hunter	What?
Umbrella peddler	It says we should gather in groups of ten people to cross over.
Straw shoes peddler	Since we are only three right now, I suppose we cannot cross over today.
Hunter	Something living in the mountains, no matter how scary it may be, can it be worse than a tiger? So don't worry about the tiger and just follow me!
Straw shoes peddler	Sure, Sure. We'll follow you.
Umbrella peddler	Wait! Is it really ok?
Hunter	If you two are not coming, I'm going alone.
Straw shoes peddler	I'm coming. If you are scared then wait here until morning to cross over.
Umbrella peddler	Who's scared? Let's get going - go!

The three go together.

Chapter 3: A Chance Encounter with a Giant

It starts raining.

Straw shoes peddler It's raining! (Opening the umbrella) Good thing
I bought the umbrella.

Hunter (Opening the umbrella) That's right!

Umbrella peddler (Opening the umbrella) I told you it was going to
rain!

Hunter Let's go.

Straw shoes peddler I can't even see an ant - who said anything
about a tigers?

As the straw shoe peddler lights up the lantern, the giant's
eyes are reflected in the umbrella of the hunter.

Straw shoes peddler Oh? There seems to be something there!

The Umbrella peddler shines the lantern and the giant's eye
are reflected in the Straw shoes peddler's umbrella.

Umbrella peddler Eeeeeek!

Hunter What is it?

Umbrella peddler It's all black and mottled⋯ I'm too scared to go!

Hunter Is there something over there?

The hunter shines the lantern and the mouth of the giant is reflected into the Umbrella peddler's umbrella.

Hunter, Straw shoes peddler   (Both of them, noticing a shape reflected in the umbrella peddler's umbrella.) Eeeeeek! It's a monster!

Every space illuminated by the light reveals the giant's shape, appearing and disappearing.
They huddle together, trembling, and as they shine the lantern in the centre, the giant's face is reflected.
The eyes, nose, and mouth appear, then scatter.

All   Eeeeeek! It's a monster!

Everyone is shocked and panicking, running around in confusion.

Giant   Ahahaha, do you want to pass?
Umbrella and shoe peddler   Yes.
Giant   Do you want to survive?
Umbrella and shoe peddler   Yes!
Giant   Then you must pay the price!
All   Aaaaaaaaaa! Don't kill us!

The giant's shadow moves wildly back and forth.
The umbrella peddler, straw shoe peddler, and hunter run around in all directions, creating total chaos.

Chapter 4: The Hunter's Story

The giant's prison.

Giant   From now on, tell me your desperate story of why you must survive and return home. After hearing your stories, I will spare only one among you three.

Hunter   (Looking around at each other) Just one person?

Giant   (Pointing at the hunter) You there, the good-looking bloke at the front! Let's start from you.

Umbrella peddler   Go on!

Hunter   M··· Me? (Rising to his feet awkwardly) My mother, who is alone, has fallen ill.
I went to the mountains to gather herbs.

The hunter walks through the forest, gathering herbs.

Hunter   What will I find today? (Finding wild raspberries) Delicious raspberries.
Wow, so sweet. (Finding mushrooms) These mushrooms are good for your health. I should take them to my mother. Sniff sniff. What is that smell? (Pulling out some wild ginseng) I can't believe it!!

Tiger appears.

Tiger   Rawr!

Hunter   Oh no, a tiger!

Tiger	Rawr, I'm going to eat you. Yum yum!
Hunter	I'm definitely going to die now. They said that as long as I stay alert, even entering the tiger's den would be fine, right? Eh, whatever. Go for it! All or nothing

The hunter bows to the tiger.

Hunter	Oh my big brother Tiger, I finally get to meet you. I am so glad, thank you.
Tiger	Huh? You're human, but you're calling me 'brother'? Grrr!

The tiger tries to eat him.

Hunter	(Ducks) Mother always said this,
Mother	My son, your brother went to the mountains when he was young and he never came back. I thought he was killed by a tiger. But then, one night, I had a dream…
Tiger	Mother. I got lost and wandered in the mountains, thinking I would die, but by the grace of the mountain spirit, I became a tiger. With this appearance, I can't go back home. I miss you! Mother!
Mother	My son, if you ever see a tiger that resembles you in the mountains call him big brother!
Hunter	You look just like my big brother. Big brother!
Tiger	(After stopping the hunter from bowing) What part of me

looks like your brother?

Hunter	Our family has always had voices as loud as thunder.
Tiger	Oh, My voice is quite thunderous! Rawr!
Hunter	(Striking a bold pose) And this sharp gaze.
Tiger	It is quite sharp indeed!
Hunter	And these are big feet.
Tiger	(Looking at his feet) Oh, my feet are quite big.
Hunter	And you are easy to trust what others say.
Tiger	Oh, I'm so gullible.
Hunter	And not very smart.
Tiger	Right, not very smart. What did you say?
Hunter	(Hastily bows.) Oh my brother, how hard it must have been for you all this time?
Tiger	(Acknowledging the bow) Oh, oh my.

The two hug and cry.

Hunter	Mother told me I have to tell you this if I ever meet you.
Tiger	Yes, little brother. What did mother want you to say to me?
Mother	I love you, my son! I have never forgotten you for a moment and have been longing for you!
Tiger	(Deeply moved) Mother! (The tiger turns towards where the Mother is.) I want to run to you right now and cry in your arms, Mother, but⋯ (crying) I can't go. I've

become a beast like this… I'll bring you what I've hunted twice a month, so you can enjoy it, Mother. This is all I can do.

Hunter	(Hugging the tiger) Big brother!
Tiger	(While embracing each other) Little brother!

The tiger brings the prey.

Tiger	Heavy ho!
Mother	What's with the wild boar?
Hunter	Mother! It seems that big brother Tiger brought it for you.
Mother	Oh my! Is that so?
Tiger	Heavy ho!
Mother	What's with the deer?
Hunter	Big brother Tiger! Thank you very much.
Mother	My son the Tiger is very good. Thud!

Mother passes away.

Hunter	Mother!
Tiger	Rawr!
Hunter	I have to tell my big brother Tiger that I am grateful for everything and also tell him that I love him… I need to live so I can tell him this so please let me live!

Chapter 5: The Straw Shoes Peddler's Story

The shoe peddler enters, pushing the hunter aside.

Straw shoes peddler I'll be telling my story next. I'm a straw shoes peddler. My father was also a straw shoes peddler. I learnt from my father how to weave straw into shoes. One day, I became faster than him at making shoes. When he made one, I made two! When he made two, I made four! But my father said I still had much to learn and wouldn't let me sell my shoes. Angry, I went to the market and challenged him to see whose shoes are sold more.

Host From now on, we will begin the father and son shoe-making contest! In the red corner, the father's shoes, made by the master shoemaker with 50 years of experience!

Father's straw shoe enters.

Host In the blue corner, skill over experience. The son shoemaker, full of passion and determination!

Son's straw shoe enters.

Host This contest, sparked by the son's bold challenge, is about to begin! Who will emerge victorious? Let's find out!

Song. Contest

(Son straw shoe) 'I' am a straw shoe. Young and full of energy.

I make twenty a day. Fast and precise, amazingly sturdy.

(Father straw shoe) Allow me to introduce myself. I am old, but I stick to the basics. Five a day is enough. Delicate and meticulous, I think of the customers.

(Son straw shoe) Mine is the best, I am the best!

My straw shoes are the best, the very best!

Mine is the best, I am the best!

(Father straw shoe) My straw~~~shoes~~are~~~the best~~!

Host   Stop! looking at them, don't they look the same?

Son straw shoe   The same? Then my victory, I'm four times as fast as you!

Father straw shoe   Try it on first.

Host   Let's.

The host tries on both shoes.

Host   They look the same······

Son straw shoe   Clearly my win then.

Father straw shoe   Let's wait and see.

He tries on the straw shoes on both feet.

Host   I will present the winner. The straw shoes contest winner is!

Host   The father straw shoe!

The son straw shoe falls into despair.

Son straw shoe   Why? I'm four times faster than you! I just don't understand. Why⋯

Host   If you cannot distinguish between the father straw shoes and the son straw show, you are not worthy of being a master!

The umbrella peddler approaches the straw shoe maker, holding a pair of straw shoes.

Straw shoes peddler   What could be the difference?

The umbrella peddler examines them closely.

Umbrella peddler   Do you want me to tell you?

Straw shoes peddler   Yes. tell me!

Umbrella peddler   The secret lies in the roughness. Your father's shoes were carefully smoothed, making them soft and comfortable, but yours were left as they are, rough and prickly. With this, your feet will be sore and you won't be able to wear them.

Straw shoes peddler   Soft and smooth, rough and prickly. At last, I understand my father's deep intention! Father! Please forgive your unfilial child.

I must return home! I still have so much to learn and seek your forgiveness. Please let me go home!

The umbrella peddler pushes the straw shoe maker aside.

Chapter 6: The Umbrella Peddler's Story

Umbrella peddler   Now, let me tell you my story. I have loved stories since I was young. Whenever I heard an interesting story, I would write it down.

The papers with stories on them begin to pile up.

Umbrella peddler   Whenever I hear a story, I write it down.

He puts the stories into his pocket

Umbrella peddler   I wrote the stories down and put them in my pocket.

One pocket becomes three.

Umbrella peddler   I was so focused on collecting stories that I only wrote them down nd never shared them. Then, I got married.

The friend enters the stage.

Friend	Congratulations on your wedding.
Umbrella peddler	Thanks. I'll be in your care tomorrow.
Friend	Don't worry and get a good sleep. It's a long way to Mr. Kim's house beyond the hill. But what are these pockets?
Umbrella peddler	The stories I've gathered so far.
Friend	You're bringing these?
Umbrella peddler	Will they scold me for collecting useless things? I'd better leave it here for now.
Friend	Yes, you should.
Umbrella peddler	There's long way to go so let's get some sleep.
Friend	Let's.

It gets dark and night falls.

The friend wakes up from sleep.

Friend	Did I eat something wrong for dinner? Why does my stomach hurt like this?

He steps outside. At that moment, the dokkaebi begin to emerge, one by one, from the pockets.

Friend	What is that?
Long pipe	That guy trapped us there and won't let us out!.
Folding fan	Tomorrow, after he gets married beyond the hill, we'll never see him again.
Rubber shoes	I can't stand it, it's so unfair. To lock up such interesting stories like ours!

Long pipe   Is he planning to lock us up here forever?

Folding fan   Once he gets married and lives happily, will he ever think of us?

Rubber shoes   We'll become stories that will never see the light of day again, disappearing forever.

Long pipe   Let's get revenge before it's too late.

Folding fan   Let's poison him.

Rubber shoes   Let's get revenge!

Folding fan   Revenge is mine!

The dokkaebi(pl.)[4]   Revenge is ours! Revenge! Revenge! Revenge!

The dokkaebi disappear.

Friend   The stories have aged and turned into dokkaebi. What should we do now?

Morning comes.
The umbrella peddler and his friend set off for the wedding hall, while the long pipe is waiting for them.

Umbrella peddler   Come on! Let's go!

Long pipe   Here he comes. Transform into a tempting poison apple!

Umbrella peddler   Look over there! There's a very delicious-looking apple. Shall we share it?

Friend   Wait a second!

4) Refer to note 1.

209

Such a delicious-looking apple wouldn't just be lying on the ground. This is dangerous!

He steps on the apple and crushes it.

Umbrella peddler   What's wrong with you?

Friend   You can't eat something that's fallen on the ground right before the wedding!

Umbrella peddler   It looked delicious though⋯

Friend   Let's get going.

They set off again. The folding fan is lying in wait.

Folding Fan   The poison apple failed. In that case, I'll transform into a poison flower!

Umbrella peddler   A beautiful flower, one I've never seen before, has bloomed. I should take it to the bride.

Friend   Wait! Just a second. Such a beautiful flower in a place with no grass! This must be a dokkaebi's trick! (Picks the flower and throws it) Throw this away!

Umbrella peddler   Come on, what is wrong with you?

Friend   A red flower does not suit your bride.

Umbrella peddler   It was a beautiful flower. Why is he like this?

Friend   Let's go. We're going to be late.

Umbrella peddler   We're almost there. Let's go!

They take off again.

Voice	Let the wedding begin.

The bride and groom dance to the music of the Kkokdugaksi [5].

Rubber shoes	You won't be able to escape this. Transforms into a poison needle!
Voice	The bride and groom bow to each other!

The dokkaebi transforms into a poison needle, and as the bride and groom bow down, the friend appears.

Friend	Wait!

The friend pushes the groom, and the friend falls out.

Umbrella peddler	You! What the hell is wrong with you? To humiliate me three times!
Friend	That's not it. The dokkaebi living in the story pockets you collected are the ones seeking revenge, are they not?
Umbrella peddler	Am I supposed to believe that?
Friend	If you don't believe me, go ahead and dig up the spot where you were about to bow.
Umbrella peddler	Alright, let's dig. If you're lying, you'd better be ready!

---

5) 'Kkokdugaksi Noreum,' is a traditional folk puppet theatre of South Korea, and this part depicts a dance performed to traditional Korean music, illustrating the wedding ceremony of the bride and groom.

As the groom digs, a needle emerges from the ground.

Umbrella peddler   That really is a poison needle. I owe my life to you. I'll burn these damn story pockets once and for all!

The needle transforms into the dokkaebi.

Rubber shoes   Wait! Listen to what I have to say.

Umbrella peddler   Well, well, well, look who it is. What grudge do you have against me to do such a thing? Do you know how much I love stories?

Rubber shoes   You say you love stories? You just selfishly collected them for yourself and never shared them with anyone! If you truly loved stories, you should've shared them with others.

How wonderful it is when stories are passed from one person to another, how happy it makes people when their ears are tickled by them!

Umbrella peddler   That day, I was so startled by the dokkaebi that I couldn't even marry the bride. Now, I'm wandering the world, selling umbrellas.

As I drift along, I've started to long for marriage and miss my hometown. I'm on my way back now. Please, don't kill me!

Chapter 7: The Giant's Decision

Umbrella peddler Now that we've finished the stories, please spare one of us.

Giant Ahahaha! You all are really good at telling stories!

All Thank you.

Giant I also want to tell stories, but I don't have the talent. That's why, when I see people who are good at it, I get angry.

Umbrella peddler Huh? Why are you angry? Didn't you say that if we tell you a good story, you'll be spare one of us?

Straw shoes peddler Yes, exactly!

Song: The Giant's Rhapsody

You humans, you're good at telling stories.

(Everyone) We people, we love stories!

I don't like people who are good storytellers.

No matter how fun the story is, it's not fun when I tell it.

(straw shoes peddler) Then you can listen to our stories.

I was angry. I thought, where do stories come from?

They come from storytellers like you!

(Umbrella peddler) That's right! Stories come from us humans.

I've made up my mind! I'll get rid of them!

I've made up my mind! I'll get rid of the stories!

(Everyone) Save the stories! I've made up my mind! I'll get rid of them!

I've made up my mind! I'll get rid of the people!

(Everyone) Ahhh! Please, don't kill us!

The people run away, and the giant chases after them.

Umbrella peddler   This way!
Straw shoes peddler   No! That way!

Everyone is running away.

Giant   You fools!! I've caught you!
All   Aaaaaaaa! Save us!

Amidst the chaos, the people are swallowed by the giant. One by one, they slide down into the giant's stomach, starting with the hunter, then the straw shoe maker, and finally the umbrella peddler.

Hunter   Eeek! I'm going first!
Straw shoes peddler   Please take care of my father.
Umbrella peddler   Do you think stories will disappear just because of this? Stories never vanish!

The three people fall into the giant's stomach.

Hunter   Auch!
Straw shoes peddler   Oh my!
Umbrella peddler   Oh my! We almost died before being digested!
Hunter   What do we do now?

214

Straw shoes peddler We just have to wait.

Hunter Wait for what?

Straw shoes peddler Just waiting to die. I shouldn't have listened to anyone⋯ Crossing the mountain in the middle of the night, only to end up dead.

Hunter Wait a second, why is this my fault?

Straw shoes peddler You, fool, were the one who said to just follow you.

Hunter So, what? Do you have problems with that?

Straw shoes peddler Yeah, I do so. What are you going to do about it?

Umbrella peddler Stop fighting and let's think of a way to get out of here.

Straw shoes peddler There is no way of getting out. We're all dead.

Umbrella peddler Don't be like that and let's try to think of something.

Umbrella peddler Wait⋯ I think I see something there. Come here!

The three move towards something they see in the distance - it's the audience. The space is filled with people.

Umbrella peddler There are people gathered here.

Straw shoes peddler They must be all the people the giant has eaten until now.

Are you ok?

Hunter Would they be ok?

Umbrella peddler Ah! Let's join forces with those who were captured before us and find a way to escape from here!

Straw shoes peddler   Ah! Everyone, do you know a way to get out of here?

They ask the audience for ideas and listen to their suggestions.

Umbrella peddler   Let's take out everything we have. I have a bamboo umbrella here.

Straw shoes peddler   All I have are these straw shoes.

Hunter   I have a flintlock gun and flint. That's all I've got.

Umbrella peddler   Is there any good way out, everyone?

The audience suggests setting something on fire.
If the audience doesn't offer a suggestion, the straw shoe maker comes up with the idea.

Straw shoes peddler   Oh, right! We'll use the flint to set the straw shoes on fire, and⋯.

Umbrella peddler   If we burn this bamboo umbrella along with the straw shoes, we can create a big fire.

Hunter   Then, we'll be able to defeat the giant!

Umbrella peddler   That's a great idea.

Hunter   Come on, let's do it.

They gather the three items and light them. Smoke starts to rise.

Giant's voice   Ah-choo!

Epilogue   Escape

The three people are blown out of the giant's stomach by his sneeze, flying over the hill. They all land safely on the other side of the hill.

Umbrella peddler   If it hadn't been for that flint!

Hunter   If it hadn't been for those straw shoes!

Straw shoes peddler   If it hadn't been for that bamboo umbrella!

All   The fire hadn't started! Hahaha!

The straw shoe maker picks up his things.

Straw shoes peddler   I have to get going now. Stay safe.

Umbrella peddler   Are you going to meet your father?

Straw shoes peddler   My father passed away 20 years ago.

Umbrella peddler   Wait, but···, what was that story about then?

Straw shoes peddler   Eeeei~I had to make up stories to save myself. Goodbye.

The Straw shoes peddler leaves.

Umbrella peddler   R, right. That's right.

The hunter straps his gun on his shoulder.

Hunter   I also have to leave now. If i'm late my mother will start to worry.

Umbrella peddler   Wait, didn't you say your mother has passed away?

Hunter	Oh come on, you heard that wrong. I'm leaving now. Hohohohoho~

The hunter leaves.

Umbrella peddler	Bu, but he definitely said she passed away. Oh, my gosh!!

The umbrella peddler also grabs his things.

Umbrella peddler	Oh, I guess I should go now. (As if realizing something) No, forget about these umbrellas that don't even sell. From now on, I'm going to sell stories! Yes! Alright! Hahaha~ Which story should I sell first?

Ah! Yes! I'll sell a story - a real story that no one has ever experienced! The story of the umbrella peddler, the straw shoe maker, and the hunter who entered the giant's stomach and came back to tell the story. A true story that can't be heard without tears. Now! It begins!

Song. Buy a story
Stories for sale~ Stories~
A story that captivates! Stories~
A fun story that you wouldn't even know if one of us dies while listening~
So entertaining, it'll make you stay up all night listening!

218

A story where a young child, not realising time passing by, finds themselves an old man when they snap back to reality~

A story that'll make your tears and snot flow~

A story so funny, you'll laugh your belly button off~

Stories for sale~ Stories~

A story that captivates! Stories~

A fun story that you wouldn't even know if one of us dies while listening~

〈Curtain Call〉

창작자의 글 1

역할 : 작가
이름 : 정승진

"이야기 쏙! 이야기야!"는 이야기에 관한 이야기입니다.

희곡의 원래 제목은 "어느 날 거인의 뱃속에서"입니다. 산을 넘다 거인에게 잡혀 흥미로운 이야기를 들려주면 살려주겠다는 무서운 제안을 받은 사람들이 저마다 자기 이야기를 풀어내는 액자식 구성을 갖고 있습니다. 이야기 속에 또 이야기가 들어있는 셈이지요.

극 중 거인은 이야기를 만들어 낼 능력이 없어 이야기를 잘하는 인간을 질투하고, 또 욕망합니다.

인간은 거인의 위협에서 탈출하기 위해 경쟁적으로 이야기를 지어내고, 겨우 탈출한 다음에는 그 이야기를 세상에 들려주는 직업을 만들어 냅니다. 이야기로 먹고사는 것에 이릅니다.

이렇듯 우리 인간은 이야기를 통해 세상을 배우고, 문화를 만들고, 함께 살아남아 문명을 만들어 냈습니다. 이야기는 우리 사람들의 유전자에 박혀 수천, 수만 년을 살아남아 전해 내려오는 생명력과 힘이 있습니다.

그 어떤 세상이 와도 죽지 않는 이야기의 힘으로 세대를 아우르는 정서적 연대감과 재미, 감동을 전하고자 합니다.

마음껏 이야기를 만들고, 좋아하고, 즐기고, 퍼뜨리자!

창작자의 글 2

역할 : 연출, 제작자
이름 : 인정아

"이야기 쏙! 이야기야!"는 입체적이고 생동감 넘치는 그림자극을 통해 관객과 소통하고자 노력한 작품입니다. 본 작품에서는 그림자 인형과 배우가 무대 위에서 함께 오픈되어 그림자와 그림자 인형이 어우러지는 입체적인 장면을 만들어 냅니다. 배우의 신체와 오브제를 결합한 그림자 구현으로 역동성을 더하고, 무대 위에서 펼쳐지는 다양한 그림자의 변주가 관객의 상상력을 자극합니다.

이 작품이 지닌 예술적 가치는 상상력과 창의력이 춤추는 무대를 만드는 데 있습니다.
한국적인 감성을 담은 수묵 담채화 스타일의 그림자 인형들이 무대 위를 유영하는 모습은 마치 마법 같은 장면을 연출하며, 전통과 현대를 넘나드는 다채로운 그림자 연출로 관객들에게 새로운 시각적 경험을 선사합니다. 이러한 시도는 공연 예술의 가능성을 확장하는 동시에, 화려하고 자극적인 미디어에 익숙해진 어린이들에게 상상력의 소중함과 감성의 깊이를 일깨워주는 사회적 가치를 담고 있습니다.

또한, "이야기 쏙! 이야기야!"는 한국 전통의 정서를 음악적으로도 풍성하게 담아냅니다. 우리의 옛이야기를 들려주는 작품인 만큼, 전통 악기를 기반으로 창작한 음악이 이야기와 함께 흐르며 무대에 생명력을 불어넣습니다. 전통 음악과 현대적 해석이 어우러진 창작곡들은 관객들이 우리 음악에 더욱 친숙해지고, 한국적인 멋과 흥을 온전히 느낄 수 있는 소중한 시간을 선물합니다.

이 작품이 관객들에게 단순한 즐거움을 넘어, 우리의 전통과 현대적 감각이 어우러진 독창적이고 깊이 있는 예술적 경험으로 기억되기를 바랍니다. 무대 위에서 펼쳐지는 상상력의 세계 속에서, 오래된 이야기들이 새롭게 피어나고 우리의 감성이 아름답게 울려 퍼지기를 기대합니다.

The Creator's story

Role : Playwright
Name : Jung Seung-Jin

〈Tale of Tales〉 is story about tales. The original title of the play is "One Day Inside the Giant's Belly". It follows a framed narrative structure, where people, captured by a giant while crossing a mountain, are given a terrifying proposition: "Tell me an interesting story, and I will spare your life." Each person then shares their own tale, creating a story within a story.

In the play, the giant, who lacks the ability to create stories, envies and desires the ability to tell captivating stories that the humans possess.

To escape the giant's threat, humans compete to create stories. Once they finally break free, one of them turns storytelling into a profession, making a living through his tales.

in this way, we humans have learnt about the world, built cultures, and survived together through storytelling, ultimately shaping civilisation. Stories are embedded in our very DNA, carrying a life force and power that have endured for thousands, even tens of thousands of years.

No matter how the world changes, the power of stories never fades. Through this timeless force, we hope to share emotional connections, joy, and inspiration across generations.

So let's create, cherish, enjoy, and spread stories to our hearts' content!

Role : Director, Producer
Name : IN Jung-Ah

⟨Tale of Tales⟩ is a work that aims to communicate with the audience through a three-dimensional and lively shadow play. In this piece, shadow puppets and actors are revealed together on stage, creating a three-dimensional scene where shadows and shadow puppets blend. The combination of the actor's body and objects to create shadows adds dynamism, and the diverse variations of shadows unfolding on stage stimulate the audience's imagination.

The artistic value of this work lies in creating a stage where imagination and creativity dance. The shadow puppets, designed in a traditional Korean ink wash painting style, gracefully glide across the stage, creating a scene that feels almost magical. With diverse shadow effects that transcend both tradition and modernity, it offers the audience a new visual experience. This attempt not only expands the possibilities of performing arts but also carries social value by reminding children, who are accustomed to flashy and stimulating media, of the importance of imagination and the depth of emotion.

Furthermore, 『Tale of Tales』 musically captures the essence of traditional Korean emotions in a rich manner. As a work that tells our old stories, music created based on traditional instruments flows alongside the narrative, breathing life into the stage. The original compositions, which blend traditional music with modern interpretations, offer the audience a precious opportunity to become more familiar with our music and fully experience the unique beauty and excitement of Korea.

I hope that this work will be remembered by the audience as an artistic experience that goes beyond simple enjoyment, combining our tradition with a modern sensibility in a unique and profound way. In the world of imagination unfolding on stage, I expect that old stories will bloom anew and our emotions will resonate beautifully.

[이야기 쏙! 이야기야] 초연기록

· 단체명 : 극단 별 비612
· 일시/장소 : 2023년 9월 3일
· 작가/연출 : 정승진/인정아
· 출연 : 인정아, 임보람, 안재민
· 창작 스태프 : 인형 디자인_곽성희/ 제작_인정아, 곽성희, 김경미, 박은화, 임
　　　　　　 보람, 이병선/ 무대_극단 별 비612/ 음악_오동나무 헤프닝(윤
　　　　　　 혜진)/ 조명_박성헌/ 음향_김경미
· 저작물 이용 문의 : lp-b612@naver.com

주요 공연 기록

2023.09.03	춘천인형극장 코코극장 / 제35회 춘천인형극제
2023.10.14	한예극장 / 예술인형축제
2023.12.24	춘천인형극장 / 춘천인형극제 이글루 축제
2024.03.31~31	아트팩토리 봄 / 춘천문화재단 예술공간 활성화 사업
2024.05.21~28	대구학생문화센터 소극장 / 대구학생문화센터 행복愛 공연채움
2024.06.13~22	종로아이들극장 / 종로가족공연축제
2024.07.17~20	복사골 문화센터 판타지아극장 / 부천문화재단 특별상설어린이공연
2024.09.07~08	이천아트홀 / 이천아트홀 인형극페스티벌
2024.09.28~29	국립아시아문화의전당 어린이극장 / ACC공동기획 렛츠플레이
2024.10.26	통진두레문화센터 두레홀 / 2024통진두레문화센터 어린이 아트스테이지
2024.11.02,09,16,23,30	국립국악원 풍류사랑방 / 2024 토요국악동화
2025.02.04~08	강북문화예술회관 / 즐거운 졸업선물

주요 수상 기록

2023	제35회 춘천인형극제 BEST3상 수상

이야기 하루

극작 기태인

극단 나무

등장인물

하루 할아버지
인도자 1
인도자 2
인도자 3
하루 할머니
건달 1
건달 2
남자 엉터리 마술사
여자 엉터리 마술사 보조
하루 할아버지 아이들

무대 설명

무대 위엔 허름한 독거노인의 골방이 꾸며져 있다.
허름한 책장과 냉장고, 옛날식 반닫이 장과 비키니 장.
가구들 사이로 걸린 빨랫줄 위로 널린 이불 2장.
바닥엔 작은 방 크기의 채색된 바다천이 깔려있고,
왼쪽 책장엔 구겨진 소포지로 채워진 할머니 액자, 걸쳐 놓은 밥상이 놓여 있다.
방의 양 끝엔 종이상자들과 공병들이 쌓여있다.
모든 세트의(소포지로 만든 기본 위에 갈색 톤의 채색) 색감과 종이 질감들은
이곳이 현실의 공간이 아님을 나타낸다.
주 무대의 바깥 공간 하수 쪽엔 악사석이 마련되어 아코디언, 실로폰, 봉고 등이
놓여 있다.

1장. 하루 할아버지

오프닝 음악 그리고 천둥소리, 빗소리 세차게 들린다.
이어 라디오 잡음 소리가 들린다.

하루 할아버지 하수 뒤쪽으로 유모차에 종이상자를 싣고 등장.
뒤쪽 길(골목)을 가로지르며 주변에 널린 종이상자를 손전등을 비추며 줍는다.

무대는 불 꺼진 방처럼 아직 어둡다. 희미한 빛이 인물을 확인할 수 있다.
라디오 소리에 흥얼거리며 손전등을 켠 채, 방안으로 유모차를 끌고 온 할아버지.
형광등이 나간 것을 알고 손전등을 입에 문 다음,
상자의 종이들과 주운 폐품을 내려놓는다. 라디오 꺼진다.
하지만 종이상자의 무게에 내내 힘겨워한다.

폐품을 정리한 후, 모자와 장갑 두꺼운 점퍼를 벗고, 장갑으로 먼지를 터는 할아버지.
목이 마른 듯 냉장고에서 물을 꺼내 마신다.
책장에 놓인 할머니의 사진에 인사를 하는 할아버지. 그리고 액자를 떼어 밥상 위에 할머니의 액자를 놓는다.
다소 추운 듯 걸려 있던 하얀 이불을 뒤집어쓰는 할아버지.
이불을 둘러쓰고 아이들처럼 유령 흉내도 잠깐 내본다.
냉장고에서 술과 술잔을 내어 밥상 앞에 앉아 술을 한 잔 따라 마신다.
그리고 액자 속 할머니에게 한잔 따라 올린 후, 사진 속 할머니를 매만진다.

손전등을 끈 후 이불을 덮은 할아버지는 피곤한지 금세 잠이 든다.

2장. 인도자들의 등장

할아버지가 잠든 사이, 무대가 움직이며 변화한다.
신비한 윈드벨 소리에 맞춰 불빛이 등장한다.
불빛들은 모두 3개로 살아 있는 듯 움직이다가 꺼진다.
다른 빨랫줄에 널린 이불 위에 등장하는 3인의 손인형들. (검은 옷을
입은 인도자들의 축소판) 뭔가를 의논하다가 '음'하는 저음의 소리를
내면서 이불 아래로 퇴장.
이내 책장과 냉장고 사이에서 사람으로 등장하여 할아버지의 방을
돌아다닌다.

할아버지의 자는 모습을 확인한 인도자들.
할아버지의 주위를 한 바퀴 돌며 탐색하다가 곁에 앉아 뭔가 수상한
(?) 일을 시작한다.
누워있는 할아버지의 몸속에서 뭔가를 꺼내려 하는 인도자들.
두 번의 실패 끝에 이불을 걷고, 겨우 꺼내는 것에 성공한다.
할아버지는 앉은 채로 여전히 잠이든 상태다.
커다란 무형의 덩어리를 꺼낸 인도자들은 그것을 방안 사방에 뿌
린다.

어느 순간 상수 쪽의 커다란 종이상자를 주목하는 인도자들.
인도자 1의 손짓에 인도자 3이 상자를 가져오면, 모두 상자를 연다.
상자 속에서 빛이 나오면, 하얀 종이를 꺼내 젊은 시절의 할머니 모
습을 함께 만들어 낸다.
인도자 2가 할머니의 콧노래를 부르면, 잠들어 있던 할아버지 깨어

난다.

종이로 형상화된 할머니를 보고 놀라는 할아버지.

그녀의 모습에 끌려 다가가 만져보려 하지만, 이내 사라지고 만다.

가구 뒤쪽으로 들어간 3인의 인도자들.

잠시 할아버지를 바라본 후 할아버지를 과거로 인도한다.

3장. 하루 할아버지의 어린 시절

가구들(책장, 냉장고, 반닫이 장, 비키니 장)이 흔들리면서 책장이 가로로 눕혀진다.

책장과 반닫이 장은 하루 할아버지의 어린 시절 인형들의 주 무대가 된다.

인도자 2 (소리만) 하루야~, 하루야~!

반닫이 장 위로 아기 인형이 등장. (인도자 3인이 일본 분라쿠 형식으로 조종)

아기를 바라보며 과거의 자신임을 알아보고 신기해하는 할아버지.

아기의 첫걸음 시작을 같이 기뻐하고, 아장거리며 나가는 것을 흐뭇하게 바라본다.

책장과 비키니 장등 숨바꼭질하며 등장하는 어린 시절의 소포지 인형들.

어린 하루는 동무들과 숨바꼭질, 무궁화꽃이 피었습니다 등 놀이한다.

그러다가 동무들이 몰래 사라지고, 혼자 남게 된 하루.

동산(비키니 장)에 올라 산 아래 풍경을 바라본다.

그러다가 '아빠~'하고 멀리 불러도 본다. (하루 할아버지는 함께 따라 한다.)

문득 긴 끈(마임)을 발견한 하루, 그것을 힘껏 당겨 본다.

커다란 연이다. 그것을 당겨 끌어내리려 하지만 힘에 부치는 어린 하루.

보다 못한 할아버지, 자신이 다가가 연을 잡고 어린 하루에게 건네준다.

어린 하루 고맙습니다. 얏호~!

커다란 연을 타고 노는 어린 하루. 방 안을 돌아다니며 신나게 날아다닌다.

할아버지도 즐거운 마음에 이불로 뭉게구름을 만들어 같이 어울린다.

이불 구름과 연을 번갈아 타며 재밌게 노는 어린 하루.

그런데 먹구름(인도자 2)이 등장, 연을 타고 다니는 하루에게 번개를 내리며 훼방을 놓는다.

할아버지가 자신의 구름으로 먹구름과 대결해 보지만, 먹구름에겐 역부족이다.

먹구름의 심술에 할아버지와 어린 하루는 위기를 맞게 되고,

때마침 '따르릉' 자전거 벨을 울리며 자전거를 탄 아버지(인도자 3)가 구원자처럼 등장한다.

할아버지, 어린 하루 아빠~!

번개를 뿌리며 사나워지는 먹구름. 할아버지는 어린 하루를 이불로 가리며 번개를 막는다.

할아버지가 먹구름과 다시 대결하는 동안, 그사이 어린 하루를 자전

거에 태우고 도망치는 아버지.

화가 난 먹구름은 할아버지에게 번개를 내려치고, 할아버지는 유모
차로 피신한다.

하루를 놓친 먹구름은 할아버지에게 장난스런 화풀이를 한 후 퇴장.

할아버지는 어린 시절의 자신과 만나 즐거운 기분에 벙실벙실 웃지
만, 이내 불길한 사이렌 소리가 들리면서 불안감에 휩싸인다.

4장. 6.25 전쟁
(짧지만 강렬한 역사의 기억, 지나가는 장)

군홧발 소리를 내며 가구들을 옮기는 인도자들.

난리처럼 조명도 번뜩이고 전쟁 음향 소리도 요란하게 무대를 울린다.

인도자 2, 등장하여 총(종이로 만든 봉)을 유모차에 앉아 있는 할아
버지에게 억지로 안긴 후, 유모차를 끌어 하수 쪽으로 옮긴다. 마지
못해 총을 쏘는 할아버지.

인도자들은 상수에 있는 종이상자를 쌓아 참호를 만든 다음, 할아버
지와 전쟁을 한다.

전쟁의 실제 음향 소리와 다르게 이들의 전쟁은 아이들의 전쟁놀이
로 표현된다.

실제의 소품이 아닌 종이상자와 종이봉이 주는 오브제의 느낌은 이
장면이 실제의 상황이

아닌 전쟁 또한 하나의 서글픈 추억의 한판이 될 수 있음을 의미한다.

유모차를 방패 삼아 인도자들에게 소주병과 잔(수류탄)을 투척하는
할아버지.

인도자들이 대공포(종이상자)를 쏘자 놀라서 가구 뒤로 달아난다.
인도자들이 할아버지를 쫓아 전투기로 변신하여 쫓아간다.

반닫이 장문을 안에서 열고 도망 나온 할아버지.

할아버지 싫어, 싫어, 그만 해~!

상자 속에 담긴 하얀 이불을 꺼내 흔들며 전쟁의 기억에 몸서리를
친다.

5장. 연애 시절

어디선가 동요 '오빠 생각'의 허밍 음이 들린다.
젊은 시절의 아내가 종이 인형(인도자 2)으로 등장. 젊은이 하루를
기다린다.
할아버지는 다시 기억이 펼쳐지자, 마음이 안정되어 유모차에 편안
히 앉아 할머니를 본다.

젊은이 하루(인형) 등장. 두근거리는 마
음을 억지로 가라앉히며 하모니카를
분다.
자리에 앉아 자신을 바라보는 아가씨
(아내)에게 하모니카를 불어보라고 밀
어준다.
수줍게 하루의 하모니카를 불어 보는
아가씨, 하지만 잘 불어지지 않자 다시
돌려준다.

둘 사이에 일어나는 어색한 긴장.

몇 번의 눈 마주침에 더욱더 가슴은 팔딱팔딱, 얼굴은 화끈화끈.

긴장감을 못 이겨 자리를 뜨는 젊은이 하루, 그것을 안타깝고 아쉽게

생각하는 아가씨.

결국 아가씨는 하루가 돌아오기를 앉아서 기다리기로 한다.

건달1 등장. 자신의 옷에 묻은 티끌을 털다가 아가씨를 발견.

동료를 부른다. 건달 2 등장. 건달 1의 손짓에 건달 2도 아가씨를 발

견. 둘은 쿵짝이 맞는다. 아가씨에게 다가가 수작을 거는 건달 1, 2.

그것을 바라보다가 화가 난 할아버지가 기억 속으로 (종이 인형들의

무대 속으로) 들어간다.

건달 1, 2를 막아선 할아버지, 아가씨는 화가 난 할아버지를 달래며

자리를 피하려 한다.

하지만 자꾸 돌을 던지며 도발하는 건달 1, 2.

결국 건달 2가 던진 돌멩이가 할아버지의 뒤통수를 맞힌다.

자신을 달래는 아가씨를 안심시키며 건달들에게 다가간 하루 할아

버지.

잠시 그들이 딴 곳을 보게 유도한 후, 건달 2의 뒤통수를 냅다 갈긴

다음 아가씨와 도망을 간다. 이어지는 건달들과 하루 커플의 추격전

이 시작된다.

쫓고 쫓기다가 혼자 남게 된 아가씨, 이를 발견한 건달 2.

건달 2는 아가씨에게 몰래 다가가 잡으려 하지만, 의외로 아가씨에

게 된통 당한다.

아가씨   어머, 미안~!

퇴장했다가 둘 다 동시에 다시 등장.

'끼룩끼룩' 갈매기 소리. 아가씨(권법 소녀)와 건달2 간의 무술 대결.
아가씨의 놀라운 실력에 건달 2는 쓰러지고, 건달 1도 달려들다 겁을
먹고 도망간다.
고개를 흔들며 다시 일어나 덤벼드는 건달 2.
아가씨는 장풍 한방으로 건달 2를 날려 보내며 승리를 확정 짓는다.

이렇게 싸움이 다 끝나고 등장하는 하루 할아버지.
할아버지는 '미안해요~' 하는데, 아가씨는 그런 할아버지를 보고 피
식 웃으며 장난을 건다. 그들의 장난은 이내 연애 놀음으로 이어진
다. (손가락 맞추기, 나 잡아봐라 놀이)
손을 맞잡고 춤을 추며, 온갖 닭살 연애 행각을 하는 아가씨와 할아
버지.
춤추며 서로 반대쪽 뒤로 퇴장. 이내 반닫이 장 뒤로 등장한다.

6장. 결혼식 그리고 첫날 밤

이제 결혼식 장면으로 이어진다.
족두리를 쓴 아가씨와 사모 관을 쓴 할아버지.
둘은 결혼 행진을 하고, 꼭두각시 놀음을 한다.
순간 수탉(인도자 1)이 둘 사이에 등장. 아가씨와 할아버지는 서로에
게 절을 한다.
이내 할아버지에게 내쫓김을 당하는 수탉.
둘이 서로를 바라보며 뽀뽀할 때쯤, 이불(인도자 3)이 내려와 둘 사
이를 가려준다.

첫날 밤. 이불 안의 그들은 너무도 어색하다. 아내의 족두리를 벗겨
주는 할아버지.

부끄러워하는 아내, 할아버지가 다시 어색하게 아내의 옷고름을 잡으려 할 때, 장지문(왼쪽 비키니장에 위치)을 손가락으로 뚫고 들여다보는 훼방꾼.

할아버지 가, 가, 저리 가~!

장지문을 열고 등장한 건, 다름 아닌 쫓겨났던 수탉.
초조한 아내는 수탉에 신경을 쓰는 할아버지를 이불 아래로 이끈다.
이어지는 수탉의 원맨쇼. 수탉의 모든 퍼포먼스는 이불 아래의 운우지정을 뜻한다.
수탉이 사라지면 바로 들리는 아이(인도자 3)의 울음소리.

이불 위로 아이의 얼굴이 등장.
아내와 할아버지는 아이의 얼굴을 보며 놀라워하다가, 즐겁게 웃는다.
그리고 모두 퇴장.

7장. 피크닉

첫날밤의 추억에 너무도 즐거워하는 할아버지 앞에 블라인드 커튼을 메고 등장한 인도자 1.
할아버지와 관객에게 기대감을 주는 시선을 보낸 후, 책장과 냉장고 사이에 커튼을 드리운다.

아코디언 연주가 시작되면 커튼 위로 손인형들 (인도자 1, 2)의 엉터리 마술쇼가 펼쳐진다. 이 마술쇼는 옛날 가족들이 즐겨보던 천막 극장의 향수를 담고 있다.
칼 찌르기 마술쇼가 끝나고, 꽃을 동물로 변신하게 하는 마술이 이어지면, 등장하는 동물들. 그 동물들(기린, 오리, 사자)에게 쫓겨 퇴장하는 마술사(손 인형). 동물들도 모두 퇴장.

사자를 타고 나오는 하루의 아들(종이 인형).
다시 나오는 동물들 위엔 모두 가족들(아들, 아내, 젊은 하루)이 타고 있다.
이들의 움직임은 회전목마를 연상케 한다.
가족들을 바라보던 할아버지는 종이상자에서 종이우산을 꺼내 그들의 회전목마 놀이에 그림을 더한다. 가족들이 동물들과 퇴장하고도 그 기분에 취한 할아버지.

어느새 하수 반닫이 무대엔 소풍을 마치고 집으로 돌아가는 가족들의 모습이 보인다.
하수에서 가족들을 바라보는 할아버지.

그에게 다시 인도자 1이 다가와 장난을 건다. '쿵작짝, 쿵작짝!'
그리고 기대감을 주는 눈길을 보낸 후, 커튼을 걷어가 버리면 드러나는 톱니바퀴들.

그 위엔 작은 병들이 일렬로 늘어서 있다.

병들과 톱니바퀴들은 할아버지가 일하던 일터 '공장'을 상징한다.

8장. 일과 결혼 생활

톱니바퀴들을 바라보던 할아버지는 문득 종이상자에서 공장용 헬멧
과 작은 톱니바퀴를 찾아낸다. 헬멧을 쓰고 톱니바퀴를 다른 톱니들
이 장치된 세트에 다는 할아버지.

날카로운 호루라기 소리에 톱니바퀴들이 돌아가고, 할아버지는 그
시절로 들어간다.

이 장면은 세 번의 퇴근과 아이들의 등장으로 시간과 세월의 흐름을
나타낸다.

공장에서 힘들게 제품(작은 병)을 검열하는 하루 할아버지,

가족들 (하수 쪽 앞, 밥상 위에 위치, 종이 인형 아내와 두 아이)을 바
라보며 힘을 낸다.

상사(인도자 1)는 '빨리빨리!'를 외쳐대고, 할아버지는 손가락을 다쳐가며 일을 한다.

첫 번째 퇴근 – 힘들지만 서로를 아끼던 신혼 시절
돌아오는 하루 할아버지를 아내는 반갑게 반긴다.
고단한 남편의 어깨를 두드리며 안마하고, 귀여운 두 아이를 보며 즐거워한다.
출근을 재촉하는 호루라기 소리에 일어나려는 하루.
남편에게 세 번째 아이를 보여준다. 당황스럽지만 웃으며 일을 나가는 할아버지.
여전히 톱니는 돌아가고 상사는 "빨리~"를 외쳐댄다.

두 번째 퇴근 – 서로가 지긋지긋해지는 5년 차 시절.
자신이 퇴근하자마자 기다렸다는 듯 손을 내미는 아내.
그런 아내를 보고 기분이 가라앉는 하루, 아내에게 월급봉투를 건넨다.
얇은 봉투를 보고 코웃음 치며 바닥에 내려놓는 아내.
화가 나지만 다시 아내에게 봉투를 쥐여주는 하루.
다시 내려놓는 아내.
그것을 보고 할아버지가 봉투를 가져가려고 하지만, 이내 아내가 뺏어간다.
출근을 재촉하는 호루라기 소리. 일어나서 출근하려는데, 아내는 다시 아이를 내어놓는다.
점차 늘어가는 생활의 부담감에 이러지도 저러지도 못하는 하루.
그러는 하루의 앞에 아내는 다시 쌍둥이를 내어놓는다.
할아버지는 기가 막히고, 부부는 서로에게 어이없어하며 으르렁댄다.
출근을 재촉하는 호루라기에 다시 공장으로 출근하는 하루.

실직 - 오늘따라 조용한 공장. 톱니바퀴도 멈춰 있다.

헬멧을 쓰고 다시 일하려 하지만, 누군가(인도자 3)가 헬멧을 벗겨 간다.

직장 상사가 나와서 안 됐다는 듯 혀를 차고는 퇴장한다.

갑작스런 실직에 망연자실하는 하루, 아무것도 모르는 즐겁게 아이들과 시간을 보내는 아내. 그 광경을 보다가 울분을 터뜨리며 퇴장하는 하루.

퇴근길 - 술을 먹고 퇴근하는 하루. 아코디언은 '희망가'를 연주한다. 고성방가하며 등장하는 하루, 전봇대에 토악질도 하다가 잠시 기대어 슬픔을 달랜다.

가족들을 바라보는 하루, 집으로 들어간다.

9장. 부부 싸움

술에 취한 채로 엎어지며 주사를 부리는 하루.

그런 하루를 짜증이 나지만 참고 일어나게 하려는 아내.

속탈이라도 없게 하려고 저녁 밥상을 내어놓지만, 집어 던지는 하루.

드디어 터지는 아내의 폭발! 하루를 때리며 울분을 쏟는다.

서로에게 화가 쌓이는 순간, 소의 탈들(인도자 1, 3)이 등장. 두 사람은 성난 소들로 변한다.

인도자 1의 신호를 소들로 변한 두 부부의 싸움이 시작된다.

아코디언 음악은 경쾌하게 '성자의 행진'을 연주하며, 처절한 두 싸움을 하나의 이벤트로 만든다. 서너 번의 격돌 끝에 결국 지고 마는 암소(아내), 뿔이 떨어지며 상처 입은 모습으로 흐느끼며 퇴장한다. 아이들(인도자 3)도 울음을 터뜨리고, 하루는 자신의 실수를 가슴 아파한다.

퇴장하는 아이들을 보며 하루도 자신의 기억에 괴로워하며 퇴장한다.

10장. 화해, 그리고 그 이후의 쏜살같은 날들

중앙 무대에 나무와 벤치가 놓인 작은 동산(인도자 1)이 등장한다.
더 작은 종이 인형으로 등장하는 아내. 부부 싸움의 여운이 남아 속상해하는 모습이다.
미안한 듯 멋쩍게 등장하는 하루(작은 종이 인형, 인도자 1),
아내에게 화해를 청하려 연애 시절 들려줬던 하모니카를 부른다.
그런 하루에게 어이없어하는 아내, 하지만 옛일을 생각하며 이내 마음을 푼다.
나무 벤치에 앉은 두 부부. 하루가 하늘을 보며 손짓을 하자, 아내도 같은 곳을 바라본다.

세월의 흐름 – 작은 인형들로 이뤄진 에피소드 장면들이 나타났다 사라진다.
실로폰의 '러브 테마' 음악은 이 장면이 과거의 기억, 세월의 흐름을 보여준다.

자동차를 타고 놀러 가는 아이들,
아들, 딸의 대학 졸업. 자식들의 결혼,
자식들의 가정생활(아들 가족의 아침 풍경),
아이들의 이민, 스웨터를 떠 하루에게 선물하는 아내,
갑작스런 앰뷸런스와 그것을 바라보는 딸,
병원에 누운 아내와 의사의 말을 듣고 절망하는 하루,
휠체어 탄 아내를 밀고 가는 하루 할아버지, 할머니는 '오빠생각'을 허밍으로 부른다.

모든 장면들이 사라지고 음악도 사라진다.

커다란 액자틀이 등장하며 동산 앞에 설치된다.

이곳이 할머니와 할아버지가 찍은 마지막 사진이자 시간임을 암시한다.

할머니의 죽음 – 조용히 일어나는 할머니 인형(인도자 2). 잠시 벤치에 앉은 할아버지 인형을 바라보다가 조용히 하늘로 둥실둥실 뜨며 퇴장한다.

에필로그. 길 떠나는 할아버지

아코디언의 '하루의 테마' 음악과 함께 하루 할아버지의 등장.

주마등처럼 지나간 기억들과 벤치에 앉은 자신의 인형을 보며,

자신이 오늘 죽었음을 그제야 깨닫는다.

모든 기억들을 털어버렸으니 떠나고 싶어서일까?

할아버지는 자신의 인형을 날리며 즐거워한다.

그 사이 뒤의 가구들(비키니 장과 냉장고)은 할아버지가 떠난 후의 풍경처럼 재배치되어 정리된다.

그런 할아버지 앞에 나타나는 인도자 1, 3.

그들에게 자신의 인형을 건네주는 할아버지.

할아버지의 인형(육신)을 작은 꽃 관에 담는 인도자들.

그 광경을 보던 할아버지.

신나게 유모차를 타고 밀어주며 노는 할아버지와 인도자들.

그들의 앞에 혼령(커다란 흰 종이 인형. 인도자 2)으로 등장하는 아내.

아내를 만나 행복해하는 할아버지.

인도자들에게 '가자~!'라고 외친다.

앞서가는 아내를 따라 흥겹게 춤추며 길을 떠난다.

인도자 1, 3도 춤을 추며 퇴장.

커튼콜, 인사.

〈끝〉

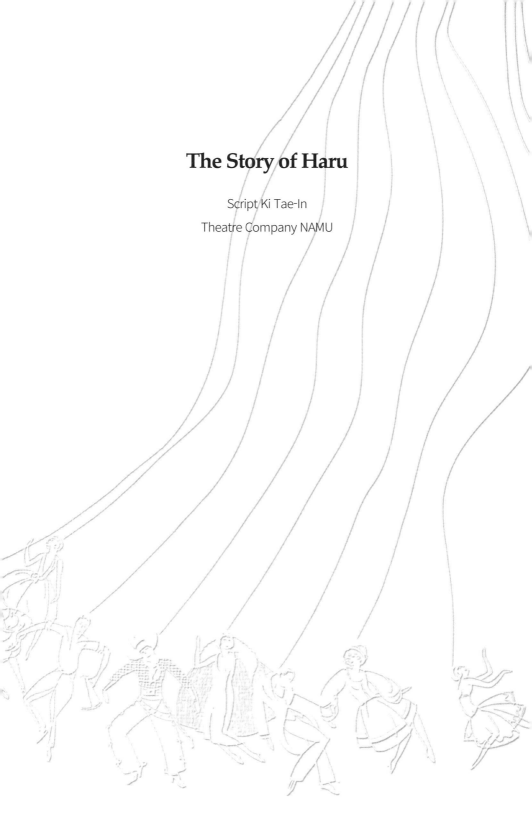

The Story of Haru

Script Ki Tae-In

Theatre Company NAMU

Characters

Grandpa Haru
Guide 1
Guide 2
Guide 3
Grandma Haru
Loafer 1
Loafer 2
Male impostor magician
Female impostor magician assistant
Grandpa Haru's Children

Stage Description

The stage is set to depict a shabby, solitary old man's room.
There is a worn-out bookshelf, a refrigerator, an old-fashioned drawer chest, and a dresser.
Two blankets are hung on a clothesline stretched between the furniture.
On the left a bookshelf, where there is a photo frame of a grandmother filled with crumpled wrapping paper, along with a table placed nearby.
At both ends of the room, stacks of cardboard boxes and empty bottles are piled up.
The colour of the all sets(with a base of crumpled paper and brown tones) and the textures of the paper indicate that this is not a real-world space.
In the outer space of the main stage, near the stage right area, a musician's place is set up with an accordion, xylophone, and bongos.

Chapter 1: Grandpa Haru

Opening music plays, followed by the sounds of thunder and heavy rain.
Then, static from a radio can be heard.

Grandpa Haru appears from the back of stage right, pushing a stroller with a cardboard box on it. He crosses the alley behind him, picking up scattered cardboard boxes, shining his flashlight on them.

The stage is still dark, like a room with the lights off. A faint light allows the figure to be seen. Humming along to the radio, Grandpa Haru pulls the stroller into the room, still holding the flashlight.
Noticing that the fluorescent light is out, he places the flashlight in his mouth,
then sets down the papers and collected scraps from the box. The radio turns off. He struggles with the weight of the cardboard box.

After sorting the scraps, Grandpa removes his hat, gloves, and thick jacket, using the gloves to dust off the furniture.
Seeming thirsty, he takes a bottle of water from the fridge and drinks it.
He greets the photo of his wife on the bookshelf, then takes the frame and places it on the dining table.
Feeling a bit cold, he wraps himself in a white blanket that

was hanging nearby.

Wrapped in the blanket, he briefly pretends to be a ghost, like a child.

He takes out alcohol and a glass from the fridge, sits at the table, pours himself a drink, and takes a sip.

He raises a glass to the photo of his wife, then gently touches the photo.

After turning off the flashlight, Grandpa, now wrapped in the blanket, falls asleep quickly, looking exhausted.

Chapter 2: The Appearance of the Guides

While Grandpa sleeps, the stage shifts and changes.

Mysterious wind chimes play, and lights begin to appear.

The three lights move as if alive before eventually fading away.

Three hand puppets(miniature versions of the guides dressed in black) appear on a different clothesline where blankets are hung. They discuss something briefly, then make a low "Hmm" sound, and then disappearing beneath the blankets.

Soon, they appear as humans between the bookshelf and the refrigerator and begin exploring Grandpa's room.

The guides check to see that Grandpa is still asleep.

They circle around him, searching, then sit beside him and begin doing something suspicious.

They attempt to pull something from inside Grandpa's body while he is lying down.

After two failed attempts, they remove the blanket and finally succeed in pulling it.

Grandpa remains sitting, still asleep.

The guides, having pulled a large, formless mass, scatter it around the room.

At some point, the guides focus on a large cardboard box near the stage left.

At Guide 1's gesture, Guide 3 brings the box over, and they all open it.

As light shines from inside the box, they pull out white paper and use it to form an image of Grandma, from her younger days.

When Guide 2 hums a tune, Grandpa, who had been asleep, wakes up.

Startled by the paper figure of Grandma.

Grandpa is drawn to her image and reaches out to touch it, but it quickly vanishes.

The three guides move behind the furniture.

After briefly watching Grandpa, they guide him into the past.

Chapter 3: Grandpa Haru's Childhood

The furniture(bookshelf, refrigerator, chest, and clothes

hanger) begins to shake, and the bookshelf tips over horizontally. The bookshelf and chest become the main stage for the childhood puppets of Haru.

Guide 2   (Voice) "Haru~, Haru~!"

A baby puppet appears on top of the chest.(The three guides operate it in the style of Japanese Bunraku puppetry.)
Grandpa recognises the baby as his younger self and is amazed.
He joyfully watches the baby take its first steps and smiles as it toddles away.

Childhood paper puppets emerge, playing hide-and-seek between the bookshelf and the dresser.
Young Haru and his friends play hide-and-seek and[1]
"Mugunghwa Kkochi Pieot-seumnida(a traditional Korean play)"
However, his friends disappear secretly, and young Haru is left alone.
He climbs the "mountain"(dresser) and gazes at the view below.
Suddenly, he calls out, "Daddy~" from a distance. (Grandpa echoes him.)
Then, young Haru finds a long rope(miming) and pulls it with all his might.

---

1) The play "Mugunghwa Kkoch-i Pieot-seumnida" is a traditional Korean folk game, similar to a game of "red light, green light."

250

It is a giant kite. He struggles to pull it down, but young Haru doesn't have enough strength.

Seeing this, Grandpa approaches, grabs the kite, and hands it over to young Haru.

Young Haru "Thank you! Yippee~!"

Young Haru joyfully plays with the giant kite, flying it around the room.

Grandpa, feeling cheerful, creates cloud-like shapes with a blanket and joins in.

They take turns flying the kite and playing with the cloud, having fun together.

But then, a dark cloud(Guide 2) appears, causing trouble by throwing lightning bolts at Haru as he rides the kite.

Grandpa tries to battle the dark cloud with his own cloud, but is no match for it.

Due to the dark cloud's mischief, Grandpa and young Haru are in danger.

Just in time, the sound of a bicycle bell rings, and Grandpa's father(Guide 3) appears as a hero.

Grandpa and Young Haru "Daddy~!"

The dark cloud grows angrier and continues throwing lightning bolts. Grandpa shields young Haru with the blanket to protect him.

While Grandpa battles the dark cloud, his father grabs young

Haru, puts him on the bicycle and escapes.

The angry dark cloud throws lightning bolts at Grandpa, and Grandpa takes refuge in a stroller

The dark cloud, having missed Haru, playfully takes out its frustration on Grandpa before leaving.

Grandpa smiles happily, enjoying the time with his younger self,

but soon, an ominous siren fills the air, and an unsettling feeling begins to overwhelm him.

Chapter 4: The Korean War

(A brief but intense memory of history, passing scene)

The guides move the furniture while army boots sounds are heard.

The lights flicker in chaos, and loud war sound effects echo across the stage.

Guide 2 enters, forcing a paper-made stick(representing a gun) into the arms of Grandpa, who is sitting in a stroller.

Reluctantly, Grandpa fires the gun, as they push the stroller.

The guides stack paper boxes on the left side of stage, to create a trench, then engage in a battle with Grandpa

Unlike the actual sounds of war, their battle is portrayed as a children's war game. The use of paper boxes and paper sticks, rather than actual props, giving the scene a quality of not being a real situation, but rather a sad memory of war, a heartbreaking recollection of a past tragedy.

Grandpa throws a bottle of soju and a glass(a grenade) at the guides, using the stroller as a shield.
When the guides fire their anti-aircraft gun(paper box), Grandpa runs behind the furniture in surprise.
The guides chase him, transforming into fighter jets.

Grandpa opens the sliding door of the chest and escapes.

Grandpa "No, no, stop it~!"

He takes out a white blanket from the box and shakes it, shuddering at the memories of war.

Chapter 5: The Days of Young Love

A humming sound of the children's song Oppa Saeng-gak(*translation: "I'm Thinking of My Brother") is heard from somewhere.
The young wife appears as a paper puppet(Guide 2). She waits for young Haru.
As the memory unfolds again, Grandpa feels calm and sits in the stroller, gazing at Grandma comfortably.

Young Haru(the puppet) appears. He tries to calm his racing heart and plays the harmonica. He sits down and encourages the lady(his wife) to try playing the harmonica.

Shyly, the lady attempts to play the harmonica but struggles, handing it back to Haru. There is an awkward tension between the two.

After a few brief stolen glances, their hearts are pounding, and their faces turn red. Unable to handle the tension, young Haru gets up and leaves. The lady, disappointed and regretful, decides to wait for him to return.

Loafer 1 enters. He brushes the dust off his clothes and spots the lady. He calls his colleague. Loafer 2 appears. They both see the lady and nod in agreement. The loafers approach her and try to flirt.

Grandpa, angered by this, enters his memory(the stage of paper puppets) and tries to block the loafers. The lady tries to calm Grandpa down and moves away.

However, the loafers provoke Grandpa, throwing stones at him. Eventually, a stone thrown by the Loafer 2 hits Grandpa on the back of his head.

Calming the lady, Grandpa walks towards the loafers. After briefly distracting them, he hits Loafer 2 on the back of the head and then escapes with the lady. A chase between the loafers and Grandpa, with the lady, begins.

While being chased, the lady is left behind. Loafer 2 notices

this, sneaks up on her but is unexpectedly outsmarted by
the lady.

Lady   Oh, I'm sorry~!

After they both exit and reenter, the sound of seagulls(kki-
ruk-kki-ruk) is heard. The lady(a martial artist) and Loafer 2
have a martial arts showdown. With her amazing skills, the
lady defeats Loafer 2. Loafer 1 also tries to join in but gets
scared and flees.
Shaking his head, Loafer 2 gets up again, ready to fight, but
the lady uses a blast of energy(like a martial arts move) to
send him flying, securing her victory.

After the fight is over, Grandpa returns to the stage and says,
'Sorry~!'. Then the lady laughs and teases him. Their playful
banter turns into a love game(a game of finger-wrestling,
'Catch me if you can'). Holding hands, they dance together,
engaging in all kinds of cute romantic gestures. They exit
dancing, moving towards opposite sides. Shortly after, they
reappear from behind the chest.

Chapter 6: The Wedding and the First Night

The scene transitions to the wedding.
The lady wears a jokduri(*ceremonial headpiece), and
grandpa wears a samo-gwan(*scholar's hat). They proceed

with the wedding march, playing the Kkokdugaksi-Noreum(*puppet game) together.

Suddenly, a Rooster(Guide 1) enters between them. The lady and Grandpa bow to each other.

The rooster is soon kicked out by Grandpa, and just as the couple is about to kiss, a blanket(Guide 3) falls down to cover them.

The first night. Inside the blanket, they are both incredibly awkward. Grandpa gently removes the lady's headpiece.

The shy woman turns her head. Grandpa awkwardly tries to adjust her garment, but just then, a meddlesome figure peeks through a hole in the wooden screen (on the left side of the sliding door)

Grandpa   "Go, go, get out of here!"

It turns out to be the same rooster, who was kicked out earlier.

Anxious, the lady leads Grandpa beneath the blanket to avoid the rooster.

What follows is a one-man show by the rooster. His antics represent the intimate relationship happening under the blanket.

When the rooster exits, the sound of a baby crying is heard.

A baby's face appears from below the blanket. Grandpa and the lady look at the baby's face, surprised, but then smile joyfully.

The scene ends as they all exit.

Chapter 7: Picnic

Grandpa, who is greatly enjoying the memories of the first night, is greeted by Guide 1, who appears tying a curtain.

After giving a glance filled with anticipation to Grandpa and the audience, Guide 1 pulls a curtain between the bookshelf and the refrigerator.

As accordion music begins, a puppet show with hand puppets(Guide 1 and 2) unfolds above the curtain. This magic show evokes the nostalgia of the old tent theaters that families used to enjoy. After a sword-throwing trick, follows a magic trick where flowers turn into animals. The magician(hand puppet) exits, chased by the animals(giraffe, duck, lion). The animals also exit.

Haru's son(a paper puppet) rides the lion. The animals return, each carrying a family members(son, wife, young Haru) on their back. Their movements resemble that of a merry-go-round. Grandpa, observing his family, takes a paper umbrella out of a box and carefully adds to the picture of the merry-go-round they are playing with. After the family and animals exit, Grandpa remains intoxicated by the mood.

Soon, on the half-closed stage(stage right), the family is seen returning home after their picnic. Grandpa watches the family from the stage.

Guide 1 approaches Grandpa again and playfully teases him. "Thunk-thunk, thunk-thunk!" After giving an expectant look, Guide 1 pulls back the curtain to reveal the cogwheel. Small bottles are arranged in a line above the cogwheel. The bottles and cogwheel symbolise the factory where Grandpa used to work.

Chapter 8: Work and Marriage Life

As Grandpa gazes at the cogwheel, he suddenly finds a factory helmet and small cogwheel in a paper box. Wearing the helmet, Grandpa attaches the cogwheel to a set with other cogwheels. At the sharp sound of a whistle, the cogwheels begin to turn, and Grandpa is transported back to that time. This scene represents the passage of time and years through three workdays and the appearance of the children.

At the factory, Grandpa struggles to inspect products(small bottles). He draws strength from looking at his family(the paper wife and two children, positioned in front of the stage right and on the table). The boss(Guide 1) yells, "Hurry up!" as Grandpa works, even injuring his fingers.

First Workday – The honeymoon years, full of mutual care despite the hard work.

When Grandpa returns home, his wife greets him warmly. She massages his tired shoulders and smiles at the cute children. A whistle blows, signalling it's time for Grandpa to go back to work. His wife shows him their third child. Although puzzled, Grandpa smiles and goes off to work. The cogwheels continue turning as the boss yells, "Hurry up!"

Second Workday – The 5th year, when they start to tire of each other.

As soon as Grandpa arrives home, his wife eagerly extends her hand. Seeing this, Grandpa's mood sours, and he hands her his paycheck. She scoffs at the thin envelope and drops it on the floor. Upset, Grandpa hands it to her again, but she drops it once more. Grandpa tries to take it back, but she snatches it away. The sound of a whistle urges him to go to work. As Grandpa gets up to leave for work, his wife hands him the child again. The burden of life has grown too much, and Grandpa is trapped in his own despair. As his wife hands him twins, both he and his wife grow angry and helpless. Grandpa goes back to the factory.

Unemployment – The factory is eerily quiet today. The cogwheels are still.

Grandpa tries to work again, but someone(Guide 3) takes off his helmet. The boss comes out, clicks his tongue in sympathy, and exits. Grandpa, stunned by the sudden unemployment, is left in despair. Meanwhile, his wife happily spends time with the children, oblivious to the situation. Grandpa, watching this, bursts into tears and leaves.

On the way home – Haru, returning home after drinking. While the accordion plays "The Song of Hope."
Haru enters loudly, gagging and leaning against a telephone pole, trying to calm his sadness. He looks at his family and heads inside.

Chapter 9: A Fight Between Husband and Wife

Drunken Haru stumbles and starts acting mischievously. His wife, frustrated but patient, tries to get him up. She sets the dinner table, trying to ease his stomach, but Haru throws it away. The wife finally explodes, hitting Haru and venting her anger.

The moment when anger builds up between them, a cow and a bull mask(Guide 1 and 3) appear, and the two of them transform into enraged cows. At the signal of Guide 1, the fight between the two begins. Accompanied by lively accordion music playing "March of the Saints" turning the brutal struggle into a performance. After several clashes, the cow(wife) eventually loses. With her horns broken and wounded, she exits crying. The children(Guide 3) also cry, and Grandpa feels regretful of his mistakes. He watches them leave and he exits, too, burdened by painful memories.

Chapter 10: Reconciliation, and the Fleeting Days

A small hill with trees and a bench(Guide 1) appears on the central stage. The wife, a smaller paper puppet, appears and looks sad, still affected by the aftermath of the fight. Haru(the small paper puppet, Guide 1), appearing awkward but sincere, approaches her with a harmonica, the same one he played during their courting days, hoping to reconcile.

The wife is initially indifferent but begins to soften, remembering the past. The two sit on the wooden bench, looking at the sky together. Haru gestures to the sky, and his wife follows his gaze.

Passage of Time – Short episodes with small puppets appear and disappear.

The music of the xylophone playing "Love Theme" signals the passage of time and memories.

The children drive off in a car for a trip.

The son and daughter graduate from university. The children marry.

The family life of the children(a morning scene with the son's family.)

The children emigrate, and the wife knits a jumper to give to Haru.

The daughter watching as an ambulance appears suddenly.

Haru hears the doctor's words and feels despair as his wife lies in the hospital.

Haru pushes his wife in a wheelchair, and Grandma hums "Oppa Saeng-gak".

All the scenes fade away as the music dies down.

A large picture frame appears and is set in front of the hill.

This symbolises the last photo they took together and their last moments together.

Grandma's Death – The Grandma puppet(Guide 2) quietly rises, gazing at Grandpa(the puppet) on the bench. She quietly floats upward and exits.

Epilogue : Grandpa's Journey

Grandpa enters to the accordion's "Haru's Theme" music.

As memories pass by like a dream, and he sees his own puppet sitting on the bench, he realises for the first time that he has died today.

Is it because he has shaken off all his memories that he now wants to leave?

Grandpa joyfully flings his puppet self away.

Behind him, the furniture(the dresser and refrigerator) is

rearranged and organized, as if the scene has changed after Grandpa's departure.

Guide 1 and Guide 3 appear before him.

Grandpa hands them his puppet self.

The guides place Grandpa's puppet(his body) into a small flower coffin.

Grandpa watches the scene.

The guides playfully push his puppet around in a stroller.

Suddenly, Grandma(as a large white paper puppet, Guide 2) appears as a spirit.

Grandpa is happy to meet her.

Grandpa exclaims, "Let's go!"

Following Grandma, they dance joyfully as they begin their journey.

Guide 1 and Guide 3 also dance and exit.

〈Curtain Call〉

창작자의 글

역할 : 작가, 연출,
        인형제작자
이름 : 기태인

〈이야기 하루〉는 인생이라는 무거운 주제를 비언어 이미지극으로 풀어낸 작품입니다. 시각적 표현을 통해 어린이에게는 꿈과 상상의 세계를, 어른들에게는 잊고 있던 내면의 감수성을 일깨워주는 따뜻한 공연입니다. 이 아름다운 이야기보따리는 연령에 상관없이 모든 관객의 마음에 감동을 전하며 특별한 경험을 선사합니다.

■ 기획 의도

이 작품은 종이라는 오브제와 아코디언 음악이 조화를 이루는 테이블 인형극입니다. 찢어지고 구겨지는 종이의 특성을 활용하여 '하루' 할아버지의 인생 여정을 표현하고자 합니다. 종이의 다양한 형태와 변화는 인생의 굴곡과 세월의 흔적을 상징적으로 보여주며, 할아버지의 따뜻한 추억의 문을 열어갑니다. 아코디언의 깊고 감성적인 음색은 회상과 향수의 감정을 더하여 이야기에 깊이를 부여합니다. 무대 위에서 펼쳐지는 종이의 환상적인 움직임과 아코디언의 선율을 통해, 인생이라는 다소 무거운 주제를 친근하고 따뜻하게 풀어내어 관객들에게 공감과 위로를 전하며 행복한 소통의 시간을 만들고자 합니다.

■ 연출 의도
구겨진 종이. 다양한 선과 그 선들을 통해 여러 굴곡이 보입니다.
굴곡은 입체적인 여러 이미지를 만들어 냅니다.
불현듯 우리의 인생과 닮았다고 생각합니다.
종이의 다양한 성질을 이용해 '하루'라는 할아버지의 인생을 표현합니다.
표정 없는 종이 인형에 삶의 희로애락이 담긴 연극, 이야기 하루.
이야기 하루는 인생의 끝에서 한 인간의 삶을 되돌아볼 수 있는 연극입니다.
기억의 단편들은 아코디언의 소리와 어우러져 관객들 앞에서 펼쳐질 것입니다.
아름다운 기억의 단편들이 다시금 재조명될 것입니다.

■ 공연 소개
하루라는 할아버지는 폐지를 줍는 일을 한다. 할아버지는 늘 많이 지쳐 있다.
어느 날 할아버지는 손수레에 잔뜩 짐을 싣고 들어온다.
폐지를 모두 정리하고 잠깐 쉰다. 그러다 깊은 잠에 빠져든다.
할아버지 기억 속으로의 여행.
다양한 종이 인물들이 나타나 할아버지의 추억 속으로 떠난다.
잊혔던 시간들이 다시 보여지며 할아버지의 소중한 기억의 단편들을 찾아간다.
할아버지는 인생의 아름답고 즐거운 마지막 여행을 즐긴다.

The Creator's story

Role : Playwright, Director, Puppet Maker

Name : Ki Tae-In

⟨The Story of Haru⟩ is reinterpreted as a non-verbal image play that makes the weighty theme of life easy to understand, unfolding a beautiful bundle of stories. For children, it leads to a world of dreams and imagination, while for adults, it is a heartwarming performance that evokes the deeply buried sensitivities within their hearts.

• Concept

We aim to create a table puppet show where the characteristics of paper and the music of the accordion blend harmoniously. Through the torn and crumpled appearance of paper, we want to capture the life of an old man named Haru. Perhaps, the various aspects of life will open a door to Haru's warm and beautiful memories through the many images of paper. Through the fantastic movements of paper and the deep sounds of the accordion on stage, we hope to share a warm and joyful communication with the audience, telling the somewhat heavy story of life.

• Directorial Concept

Crumpled paper. Through its various lines and folds, we can see different contours. These folds create three-dimensional images. Suddenly, I thought that it resembles our lives. Using the various qualities of paper, we express the life of an old man named Haru. A play, The Story of Haru, in which the joys and sorrows of life are contained within a faceless paper puppet. The Story of Haru is a play that allows us to look back on a person's life at the end of their journey. Fragments of memories will unfold before the audience, harmonizing with the sound of the accordion. Beautiful fragments of memories will be reexamined once again.

• Performance Introduction

An old man named Haru collects scrap paper for a living. He is always very tired. One day, he comes in with a cart full of items. After sorting the paper, he rests for a moment and falls into a deep sleep. A journey into the grandfather's memories begins. Various paper figures appear and travel through his memories. Forgotten times re-emerge as they search for fragments of the grandfather's precious memories. The grandfather enjoys the beautiful and joyful final journey of his life.

[이야기 하루] 초연기록

· 단체명 : 극단 나무
· 일시/장소 : 2012년 11월 6일~11일 인천수봉문화회관
· 작가/연출 : 기태인 / 기태인
· 출연 : 임효신, 이준수, 안휘준, 곽효중, 임보람
· 창작 스태프 : 연출_기태인/ 조명_박석광/ 작곡 및 아코디언 연주_임효신/ 무
　　　　대, 인형디자인_극단 나무/ 제작_극단 나무/ 음향_김성일
· 저작물 이용 문의 : chose007@hanmail.net

주요 공연 기록
2023.09.03   2012년 11월 인천문화재단 창작지원 공연 수봉문화회관
　　　　　　　〈이야기 하루〉
2013.06   부평 문화사랑방 초청공연 〈이야기 하루〉
2013.06   김포 통진 두레 문화센터 초청공연 〈이야기 하루〉
2013.07   경기 인형극제 초청공연 〈이야기 하루〉
2013.08   춘천 인형극제 참가 〈이야기 하루〉
2014.08   거창국제연극제 참가 〈이야기 하루〉
2015.08   동해 젊은 연출가전 동해문화예술회관 〈이야기 하루〉
2016.07   인천예총 문화가 있는 날 초청공연 〈이야기 하루〉
2016.07   인천 비타민 축제 초청공연 〈이야기 하루〉
2016.12   인천상주단체프로그램 레퍼토리공연 〈이야기 하루〉
2017.08   방방곡곡 문화공감사업 광주동구문화원 〈이야기 하루〉
2020.09   춘천인형극제 공식초청공연 〈이야기 하루 〉
2020.12   인천형중진예술가지원사업 〈이야기 하루〉
2021.06   양평 yp아트홀 초청공연 〈이야기 하루〉
2021.07   수봉문화회관 수봉 꿈노리 〈이야기 하루〉

주요 수상 기록
2013.05   부산국제연극제 아비뇽 off 경연 〈이야기 하루〉 - 최우수상

268

2013.08   김천 가족극 연극제 참가 〈이야기 하루〉 – 은상
2015.03   인천 항구 연극제 〈이야기 하루〉 – 연출상 수상

인형극 공연의 뿌리 다지기

오판진

연극평론가 | 서울대 강사

1. 시작하며

식물은 땅에 뿌리를 내리고 있다. 그리고 그 뿌리에는 흙이 묻어 있다. 인형극 공연 또한 희곡이라는 대지에 뿌리를 두고 있으며, 그 희곡에는 인간의 삶과 여러 관점이 묻어 있다. 물론 인형극 공연 가운데는 문자 텍스트로 기록된 희곡 대신 연행으로만 존재하는 것도 없는 것은 아니지만, 그런 연행 또한 문자로 정리하면 희곡이 되고, 말과 연기로 이루어진 텍스트가 있다. 우리나라 인형극 공연이 활성화되고 발전하려면, 인간에 관한 이해가 깊으면서도 인형극에 관해서 안목이 높은 작가가 쓴 인형극 희곡이 많이 필요하다. 이 희곡집은 이런 측면에서 마중물 역할을 할 것으로 기대한다. 더불어 우리나라 인형극 발전에 도움을 주는 든든한 뿌리가 되어, 인형극인들에게 많은 영감을 주고, 관객들에게 커다란 감동을 선사할 것으로 확신한다.

이 인형극 희곡집에는 훌륭한 인형극 공연 다섯 편의 텍스트인 인형극 희곡이 실려 있는 데 정승진의 〈이야기 쏙! 이야기야!〉, 기태인의 〈이야기 하루〉, 조현산의 〈달래 이야기〉, 배근영의 〈소금인형〉, 문재현의 〈구름이와 욜〉이 그것이다. 여기에 실린 다섯 편의 희곡을 읽어보니 다음과 같은 몇 가지 특징이 발견되었다. 첫째, 우리가 사는 이야기에 천착하여 따뜻하게 담아낸 작품들이 있었고, 둘째, 인간이란 존재의 본질이 무엇인지, 인생에서 가치관이 얼마나 중요한지에 관해 탐구한 작품도 있었으며, 셋째, 대한민국의 역사를 바탕으로 지구인 전체가 공감할 수 있는 전쟁을 반대하고 평화를 지향하는 아름답고 감동적인 작품도 있었다.

2. 우리 사는 이야기에 천착한 작품들

가. 정승진의 〈이야기 쏙! 이야기야〉

이 인형극의 희곡을 쓴 작가는 정승진이다. 정승진 작가는 관객들이 흥미롭게 관람할 수 있는 인형극 희곡과 다양한 장르의 여러 희곡을 창작하고 있어서 우리나라 연극계에서 크게 주목하고 있는 재원이다. 이 희곡집에 실린 〈이야기 쏙! 이야기야!〉는 정승진 작가가 기존 설화를 새롭게 해석함으로써 쫄깃하면서도 묵직한 인형극 희곡으로 탄생한 것이다. 그래서 서사가 매우 단단하고, 재미있으며 인형극 희곡의 힘을 제대로 느낄 수 있는 작품이라는 평가를 받고 있다. 이 인형극의 구성은 극중극 형식으로 되어 있는데, 한 공연이 또 다른 작은 이야기 세 개를 품고 있다. 구체적으로 살펴보면, 전체 이야기는 '우산장수와 짚신장수'를 바탕으로 하면서, 극중극에는 '호랑이 형님', '짚신장수 아버지와 아들', '이야기 귀신'을 배치하였다. 옛이야기를 많이 들었거나 읽은 관객이라면 이 이야기들을 알고 있을 텐데, 원래 이야기를 재구성하여 인형극 희곡으로 스펙터클하게 해석한 점이 매우 탁월하다. 학술적인 용어로 표현하자면, '상호텍스트성' 또는 '텍스트상호성'이 뛰어난 작품이라고 할 수 있다. 이 작품의 가장 큰 특징은 관련된 이야기를 서로 연결하여 메

타적인 사고를 하면서 관람하는 재미를 극대화한 데 있다. 전체 서사 가운데 압축할 수 있는 어느 대목은 과감하게 삭제하거나 줄여서 서사가 매우 긴박하고 속도감 있게 전개된다. 그리고 다른 대목에서는 원래 서사에 상상력을 더하여 더욱 풍성하게 만들어서 서사의 메시지와 작품의 정서를 더 깊이 공감할 수 있다.

이 인형극 희곡에서 창조적으로 변형시킨 대목을 구체적으로 살펴보자. 먼저 원작 '우산장수와 짚신장수'에서 두 인물은 가족이었는데, 여기서는 남남으로 관계를 재설정한 후, 여기에 괴물 이야기를 덧붙여서 더욱 흥미롭게 만들었다. 그리고 우산장수, 짚신장수, 포수라는 인물의 성격을 재해석하여 각각 '호랑이 형님'에 나오는 나무꾼, '짚신장수 아버지와 아들'의 주요 인물인 아들, '이야기 귀신'의 신랑이라고 설정한 것도 재미있고, 탁월했다. 더불어 이야기의 세부적인 사항들을 재해석하여 변경한 것들도 돋보였다. 예컨대 원작 '이야기 귀신'에서 신랑은 홍시, 물, 바늘로 공격받는데, 이 작품에서는 독 딸기, 독 꽃, 독바늘의 공격을 받았다. 같은 듯 다른 설정을 하였기에 관객들에게는 견주어보는 맛이 생긴 것이다. 이렇게 기존의 내용을 재치 있게 살짝 비틀고, 장황하고 긴 대사나 서사를 짧고 분명하게 다듬어서 새로움과 속도감을 만들어 냈다. 이를 통해 말맛이 살아있는 새로운 이야기를 만들었고, 이런 서사를 바탕으로 하여 그림자와 인형, 소품, 사람이 자연스럽게 등장하는 인형극 공연으로 이어짐으로써, 생동감과 박진감이 넘치는 멋진 작품이될 수 있었다.

나. 기태인의 〈이야기 하루〉

이 인형극의 희곡은 극단 나무의 대표인 기태인이 쓴 작품이다. 〈이야기 하루〉의 주인공은 폐지를 줍는 '하루' 할아버지이다. 도시에서 생활하면 쉽게 볼 수 있는 그런 분이다. 그는 허름한 집에서 혼자 사는 독거노인인데, 폐품이나 종이를 주운 후 집으로 돌아와 할머니 사진과 대화하며 외롭게 살고 있다. 할아버지가 피곤해서 잠들었을 때, 검은 옷을 입은 세 명의 인도자가 찾아오면서, 하루 할아버지가 어떻게 살았는지 그의 인생이 펼쳐진다.

인형극은 귀엽고 밝은 이야기만 하고, 어린이들만 관람하는 것으로 오해하는 분들이 있다. 그러나 인형극도 다른 예술처럼 인간에 대한 통찰과 사랑을 바탕으로 현실 속 인간의 모습을 탐구하여 깊이 있고 진실하게 담아내는 공연이 많다. 다소 무겁거나 어둡게 보이는 메시지나 인물일지라도 인형극인들은 관심을 두고, 인간과 인생에 대한 깊이 있는 질문을 이어가고 있기 때문이다. 인형극이란 장르적 성격에 어울리게 다양한 형식과 내용으로, 그리고 거기에 어울리는 인형을 만들어서 공연을 해 왔다. 그래서 다른 예술 작품이나 철학 서적에서 볼 수 있는 심오한 사상이나 정서를 우리 인형극 공연에서도 볼 수 있는 것은 특별한 일이 아니다. 기태인의 작품이 대표적인 사례인데, 그가 만든 〈이야기 하루〉는 인간에 관한 통찰과 사랑이 빛나는 훌륭한 작품이다.

인도자들이라는 세 명의 인형극 배우가 하얀 종이로 인형을 만들어서 젊은 시절 할머니를 표현한다. 그러면, 할아버지는 잠에서 깨어나고, 아련한 어린 시절의 추억과 마주하게 된다. 먼저, 어린 하루 인형은 동무들과 함께하는 전래놀이를 하고, 할아버지와 함께 하늘 높이 연도 날린다. 그리고 사이렌 소리와 함께 6.25 전쟁 시기로 돌아간 할아버지가 등장하는 장면에선 총을 쏘며 전쟁에 참여하지만, 이런 기억에는 몸서리를 치면서 견딜 수 없을 만큼 힘들어한다. 이어서 젊은이 하루가 등장하여 하모니카를 불면서 할머니와 만나 연애하는 달콤한 장면이 나온다. 건달들과 하루 커플의 추격전이나 권법 소녀로 변신한 할머니의 모습, 닭살 애정 행각 등도 따뜻하고 재미있게 배치되었다. 이어서 족두리를 쓴 아가씨와 사모 관을 쓴 할아버지의 결혼식을 올리는 장면이 나오고, 첫날 밤 이불을 덮는 신혼부부의 모습도 볼 수 있다. 젊은 시절 하루는 가족과 함께 아코디언 연주에 맞춰 진행되는 마술쇼를 보기도 하고, 여러 동물도 관람하며, 회전목마를 타는 등 행복하게 소풍을 다녀오는데, 하루 인생의 봄날로 보인다. 신혼 시절 하루 할아버지는 이렇게 행복하게 생활하면서 공장에서 일도 열심히 하였다. 그렇지만, 그는 회사에서 실직하게 되고, 할머니와 부부싸움도 한다. 이런 갈등을 인형들의 소싸움으로 표현한 것은 매우 창의적이고, 인상적이었다. 힘든 시절 하루 할아버지는 아내에게 화해를 청하려 연애 시절 들려줬던 하모니카를 다시 불어준다. 그리고 함께한 세월 동안 일어났던 여러 대소사가 영상 이미지로 빠르게 이어지는데, 마지막 장면에 할머니께서 하늘로 올라가신다. 그 장면에서 하루 할아버지는 벤치에 앉아 있는 인형을 보면서 자신 또한 죽었다는 사실을 깨닫고, 아내를 따라 흥겹게 춤을 추며 인도자들과 함께 먼 길을 떠난다.

우리 인형극인들이 만든 인형극의 서사에는 아주 오래된 옛날이야기나 외국 사람들의 이야기만 있는 것은 아니다. 우리 시대 할아버지, 할머니의 인생 이야기도 포함될 수 있다. 희곡이나 공연 영상 속에 나타난 인형극 미장센을 살펴보면, 여러 형태의 독창적인 인형들과 함께 할아버지가 사람으로 등장하여 무대 위에서 멋진 앙상블을 보여준다. 한 마디로 이 인형극의 구성과 연출이 매우 다채롭다. 이 작품은 2025년 현재 우리 어르신들의 인생 이야기가 흥미로우면서도 감동적인 인형극이 될 수 있다는 것을 증명하였다.

다. 조현산의 〈달래 이야기〉

이 인형극의 희곡은 예술무대 산의 조현산이 썼다. 이 작품의 배경은 봄날이 찾아온 어느 농가이고, 등장인물은 아낙과 사내이다. 이야기는 어느 초가집 마당에서 시작된다. 빨래해서 광주리에 담아 온 아낙은 그 빨래를 빨랫줄에 널려고 하고, 사내는 아낙에게 줄 꽃신을 아낙의 빨래 광주리에 몰래 넣어둔다. 진달래 동산에 나비가 날아드는 봄날, 새침한 아낙과 어수룩한 사내가 만나 예쁜 아이를 낳는데, 이름은 달래이다. 여름이 되자, 사내와 낚싯대를 든 달래는 물고기를 잡으려고 낚시질하다가 커다란 물고기를 타고 사라진다. 감이 열리고, 잠자리가 나는 가을, 달래는 엄마에게 감을 따 달라고 하고, 아빠에게는 잠자리를 잡아달라고 한다. 달이 뜨고 눈이 내린 어느 겨울, 달래는 강아지와 함께 뛰어다니고, 아빠와 함께 눈사람을 만든다. 그런데 갑자기 비행기의 공습 소리가 들리고, 탱크가 달래네 집 울타리를 부수며 지나갈 때, 아빠는 누군가에게 끌려간다. 총격전이 시작되고, 사내는 얼결에 누군가를 총으로 쏜 후, 혼란에 빠진다. 현실과 환상의 경계에 선 사내의 눈에는 달래가 보이고, 나비와 물고기도 나타났다 사라진다. 공습을 피해 도망가던 아낙은 꽃신을 떨어뜨리고 땅에 머리를 박고 숨는다. 아낙은 무서워서 바들바들 떨다가 나비가 이끌어주는 곳으로 가는데, 거기서 남편이 준 꽃신을 다시 발견한다. 아낙은 꽃신을 끌어안고, 지난 추억을 떠올린다. 달래는 흙장난을 하며 혼자 놀다가 지쳐 잠이 드는데, 달래의 강아지 인형이 살아나 달래를 찾아오고, 함께 즐겁게 논다. 달래는 상상 속에서 엄마를 만나 즐거운 추억을 회상하지만, 정신을 차려보니, 엄마는 사라지고, 강아지 인형만 달래 곁에 널브러져 있다. 강아지 인형을 꼭 끌어안은 달래 머리 위로 꽃비가 내리면서 막이 내려간다.

　이 인형극 희곡과 공연의 특징은 목가적인 농가의 풍경과 아름다운 삶의 모습을 마치 한 폭의 그림처럼 감각적으로 담아냈다는 데 있다. 희곡을 읽어보면, 인형과 소품에 관한 묘사에서 시각적인 상상력이 충분히 자극되어 희곡을 읽으면서 상상하는 즐거움을 체험할 수 있다. 사계절을 배경으로 한 농촌에서 아빠와 엄마, 딸이 함께 행복하게 사는 모습을 충분히 상상할 수 있고, 전쟁으로 인해 가족의 평화가 사라지는 모습을 어느 예술 장르보다 생생하게 느끼고 감상할 수 있다. 이 책에서 소개하는 공연 영상 링크를 찾아보면, 공연 영상을 볼 수 있을 텐데, 무대에서 연출된 인형극 미장센은 매우 한국적이면서 동시에 세계적인 수준이라고 느낄 것이다. 특히 인형들을 조종하는 능력이 뛰어나서 공연에 등장하는 인형들이 마치 살아서 숨 쉬는 것처럼 보인다. 마치 마술을 보는 것과 같은 판타지를 경험할 수 있기에 인형극을 보면서 행복하고, 본 후에는 평생 잊지 못할 가장 소중한 공연으로 기억할 것이다.

3. 존재의 본질과 자기만의 꿈을 찾는 작품들

가. 배근영의 〈소금인형〉

배근영이 쓴 이 인형극 희곡의 주인공은 소금인형이다. 이 인물은 스스로에게 질문하고 사색에 잠긴다. '나'는 누구이며, '무엇'으로부터 왔고, '어디'로 가는지를. 그러던 중 소금인형은 바람결에 들려온 '바다'라는 소리를 듣게 된다. 그래서 소금인형은 마음속에서 싹이 튼 질문의 답을 찾기 위해 바다에 가기로 결심한다. 즉, 소금인형은 자기 존재의 뿌리이자, 생명의 근원인 바다를 찾아 여행을 떠난다. 소금인형은 맨 먼저, '물'을 만난다. 그는 물을 만나 대화하면서 이 여행은 나를 찾아 떠나는 길이고, 믿음을 가지고 행복하게 가는 게 중요하며, 인내하는 마음이 필요하다는 것을 알게 된다. 그리고 소금인형은 두 번째로 강렬한 햇빛을 만나서, 잠시 쉬어 가는 것도 괜찮다는 것을 배운다. 주인공은 세 번째로 고목을 만나서 그의 품과 같은 따뜻하고 행복한 곳에 머물고 싶은 마음을 느끼지만, 들꽃이 말하는 자기 마음을 따라 자신의 길을 찾아 떠나는 길을 선택한다. 네 번째로 소금인형은 숫자를 만나서 이성과 냉정이 중요하고, 규칙과 분석에 따르면 바다로 갈 수 있다는 말을 듣게 되지만, 마음이 답답해지는 것을 느낀다. 그래서 이 인형극의 주인공은 마음이 시키는 대로 다시 길을 떠나고, 어느 길에서 소녀 인형을 만나게 된다. 소녀 인형은 소금인형에게 골치 아프게 따지지 말고, 자신과 함께하면 행복하게 해주겠다고 말한다. 그렇지만, 소금인형은 그 말을 듣고 자기 마음이 텅 빈 것만 같았기에 바다로 가는 길을 뚜벅 뚜벅 다시 걷기 시작한다. 그 길에서 소금인형은 사라져 버릴 것 같은 고통을 주는 비를 뿌리는 먹구름을 만나서 바다로 가는 것이 아무 의미도 없다는 말을 듣게 된다. 심지어, 먹구름은 소금인형에게 건방지다는 말까지 하자, 소금인형은 누군가를 만나는 것이 두려워지기 시작했다. 그렇지만, 소금인형은 다시 한번 바다를 향해 떠나기로 마음을 굳게 먹는다. 바다로 가는 여행의 마지막 관문에서 만난 이는 얼음이다. 그는 모든 것을 자기 곁에 머물게 하려고 꽁꽁 얼려서 가두어 두는 인물이었다. 그런 얼음을 벗어나면서, 마침내 소금인형은 바다를 만난다. 아름답게 빛나는 거대한 바다를 보자, 소금인형은 자기가 처음부터 바다와 한 몸이었다는 것을 깨닫게 된다. 공연은 소금인형과 바다는 서로 몸이 닿고, 하나가 되면서 막을 내린다.

이 인형극은 인간이 정체성을 형성할 때 갖는 의문을, 구도자가 깨달음을 추구하듯 주인공이 바다를 향해 가는 여행의 과정으로 무대 위에서 아름답고 환상적으로 표현한다. 마치 생텍쥐페리의 〈어린왕자〉처럼 주인공이 다양한 인물들을 만나는 여정을 통해서, 인간이란 어떤 삶을 살아야 하는지에 관한 메시지를 상징적으로 전달한다. 즉, 비유와 상징을 통해 다양한 성격의 인물이나 가치관을 탐색한다. 인형극 공연 영상을 살펴보면, 배근영 작가는 소금인형이 어떤 장소에서 어떤 인물을 만나는 모습을 통해 삶의 의미에 관해 상징적이고 신비하게 표현한다. 즉, 지구상의 모든 존재가 연결되어 있고, 함께한다는 깨달음을, 바다를 찾아가는 소금인형의 여정으로 형상화하였다. 철학적인 깊이가 상당한 인형극 작품이라고 평가한다.

나. 문재현의 〈구름이와 욜〉
이 인형극의 희곡은 오미경이 쓴 동화 〈꿈꾸는 꼬마돼지 욜〉을 인형극단 아토의 아토, 문재현이 인형극 대본으로 각색한 작품이다. 이 희곡의 주인공 꼬마돼지 욜은 막내 돼지인데, 다른 돼지들과 달랐다. 꿀꿀꿀 우는 소리도 마음에 들지 않아서 적당한 소리를 찾다가 욜욜욜을 찾아낸다. 그래서 자기 이름을 욜이라고 짓는다. 다른 돼지들은 밥을 먹는 것이나 돼지우리 안에 머무는 것을 좋아하지만, 욜은 꽃향기를 맡으며 산책하는 것을 좋아했고, 세상에 관한 호기심도 강했다. 욜은 어느 날 우연히 만난 '구름'이라는 염소를 통해 하늘이라는 존재를 알게 된다. 그는 자기 머리 바로 위에 있는 하늘을 보지 못하는 것이 속상해서, 자기 두 눈으로 하늘을 직접 보고 싶다는 꿈을 꾸게 된다. 그러나 돼지들은 목이 굳어서 고개를 들 수가 없었고, 욜도 하늘을 보는 것이 쉽지 않았다. 하지만, 막내 돼지 욜은 날마다 고개 드는 운동을 열심히 하면서 하늘을 보려고 노력한다. 비록 쉽게 성공하지 못했지만, 운동을 멈추지 않던 어느 날, 가시덤불을 건너뛰다가 언덕에서 구르게 된다. 욜은 언덕 아래까지 굴러떨어진 후 누워서 생전 처음으로 하늘을 보게 된다. 욜은 숨이 막힐 듯 눈부시게 파란 하늘을 보면서 다음과 같이 생각한다.

"쓰러져 모든 게 다 끝났다고 생각했을 때, 신기하게도 길이 보였습니다. 지금까지 몰랐던 전혀 다른 길."

그런데 욜은 친구인 염소 구름에게 그동안 끝없이 갈망하던 하늘을 본 것보다 구름이와 친구가 된 것이 더 기쁘다고 말한다. 그는 꿈을 찾는 과정에서 만난 진정한 친구의 소중함을 깨달은 것이다. 〈구름이와 욜〉에는 사람들이 각자 원하는 꿈을 선택하고, 꿈을 이루기 위해 노력하며 살아가기를 바라는 작가와 각색자의 마음이 담겨 있다. 그리고 꿈꿀 때 혼자만이 아니라 친구나 가족과 함께하는 것이 중요하다는 메시지도 발견할 수 있다.

이 인형극의 공연 영상을 살펴보면, 다양한 크기의 목각인형을 사용하는 것과 여러 형태로 유연하게 변형되는 테이블 인형극 무대를 볼 수 있다. 거기에서 기존의 인형극 스타일에 안주하지 않고,

인형극 희곡의 메시지를 잘 드러내기 위해 고민한 흔적을 발견할 수 있다. 인형극 배우 문재현은 공연하는 가운데 욜 목각인형을 들고, 인형극 무대에서 벗어나 객석으로 들어가기도 했다. 관객과 더욱 가까이에서 만나는 연출 기법을 활용하여 관객이 공연에 빠져들거나 더 깊은 관계를 맺을 수 있도록 하기 위해서였다. 이 인형극은 배우 한 명이 공연하는 1인극이어서 일인다역을 해야 하는 부담이 있었다. 특히 야외무대에서 하는 공연이어서 소음이 많고 관객이 공연에 집중하는 것이 쉽지 않았지만, 원활하게 공연을 진행하였다. 아마도 공연자인 문재현 작가의 풍부한 연기 경험과 역량이 뒷받침되었기에 가능했을 것이다. 다른 공연과 마찬가지로 이 인형극 공연 또한 현장에서 만나는 생생한 경험을 하게 되면 인형극 희곡을 보는 즐거움이 매우 크게 확대될 수 있다.

4. 전쟁 반대 메시지를 담은 작품들

지금도 세계 여러 나라에서는 크고 작은 전쟁이 끊이지 않고 있다. 가령, 러시아-우크라이나 전쟁과 이스라엘-팔레스타인 전쟁이 대표적이다. 여기에서는 총과 칼, 포탄, 생필품 부족 등으로 인해 많은 사람들이 죽거나 다치고, 관련된 사람들의 마음에도 말로 표현할 수 없는 상처가 생기고 있다. 지구적인 차원에서 일어나고 있는 이런 비극적인 전쟁은 당장 끝나야 하고, 다시는 일어나지 말아야 한다는 주장에 동의하지 않을 사람은 없을 것이다. 우리 땅에서 벌어진 전쟁의 상처를 주요 사건으로 다룬 인형극 〈달래 이야기〉와 〈이야기 하루〉 또한 전쟁 이야기를 다룸으로써 반전과 평화의 메시지를 강렬하게 담아냈다.

가. 조현산의 〈달래 이야기〉

행복하게 살고 있던 달래 가족에게 다가온 결정적인 사건은 전쟁이었다. 사계절 행복하게 살던 달래 가족은 전쟁이 일어나자, 가족의 잘못이나, 희망, 뜻과는 무관하게 고난에 처한다. 작가가 굳이 6.25 전쟁이라고 구체적으로 밝히지는 않았지만, 1950년 한국전쟁이 떠올랐다. 그 전쟁에서도 그랬겠지만, 이 희곡의 주요 인물인 달래 아빠도 전쟁에 참여하는 것을 원하지 않았다. 그렇지만, 강제로 끌려가서 총을 들어야만 했고, 어쩌다 보니 사람을 죽이게 된다. 그래서 그 상처로 인해 달래 아빠는 회복할 수 없게 되었다. 달래 엄마 또한, 남편이 전쟁에 끌려가고, 딸은 공습으로 인해 사라지자 정신을 차릴 수 없었다. 전쟁으로 인해 어른들의 삶만 무너지는 게 아니었다. 어린 달래 또한 엄마와 아빠를 잃고, 고아가 되는 모습이 가슴 아프게 묘사되고 서술된다. 전쟁에는 승자가 없고, 패자만 남는다는 메시지가 아주 생생하고 가슴 먹먹하게 잘 표현되었다. 그래서 이 인형극 또한 주제와 표현 측면에서 모두 매우 가치 있고, 수준 높은 희곡이라고 말할 수 있다.

인형극 공연이나 그 영상을 보면, 배우가 실물 크기의 총을 직접 사용한다든지, 남편이 끌려가는 대목을 그림자극으로 표현한 장면을 볼 수 있다. 이런 인형극 미장센은 관객이 느끼는 생동감을 극대화하고, 관객 스스로 상상하는 여백이 더 많아진다. 이런 장치를 통해 인형극 희곡에서 전하고자 하는 작가의 메시지나 정서가 관객에게 훨씬 더 전달될 수 있었다.

나. 기태인의 〈이야기 하루〉

조현산의 〈달래 이야기〉가 전쟁으로 인한 피해가 너무 커서 회복하기 어려운 지경에 이른 인물들을 다루었다면, 기태인의 〈이야기 하루〉는 전쟁으로 인한 상처가 그보다 덜한 인물을 다루었다. 〈이야기 하루〉의 주인공은 달래 가족처럼 전쟁으로 인해 풍비박산이 나거나, 회복이 불가능한 전쟁 피해자는 아니다. 그렇지만, 그는 총을 들고 싸우면서 정신적인 상처를 크게 당한 참전용사이다. 인물 측면에서 하루 할아버지의 성격을 분석하면, 대한민국에서 1920년대부터 40년대 사이에 태어난 한국 남자들을 상징하는 것으로 보였다. 이 시기에 태어나 1950년 한국전쟁과 1960~1980년대 산업화를 겪으면서 힘들게 살아온 사람들이 떠올랐다. 제목에서 상상할 수 있는 것처럼, 먼 미래까지 생각할 겨를도 없이 '하루하루' 어찌어찌 힘들게 살아온 우리 어르신들을 주인공으로 삼은 것이다.

그리고 이 인형극의 희곡에서는 전쟁이 중심 사건이긴 하지만, 주인공이 젊은 시절 다니던 직장에서 실직당했던 경험 또한 가볍게 다루지 않았다. 물론, 전쟁에 비교할 수는 없겠지만, 실직 또한 우리 인생에 커다란 상처를 남기는 큰 사건이기 때문이다. 그리고 노년에 가족이나 국가의 돌봄을 받지 못하고, 하루하루 폐품을 모아 팔면서 힘들게 살다가 쓸쓸하게 고독사하는 모습을 가슴 찡하게 그렸다. 우리나라 노인의 빈곤율이 높고, 노인의 자살률이 심각하다는 것은 어제오늘의 이야기가 아니다. 그래서 국가 차원에서는 갈수록 심해지는 사회 양극화 문제와 빈곤한 노인들의 삶에 관심을 두고 더 많은 대책을 마련해야 한다. 그리고 개인이나 민간 차원에서도 하루 할아버지와 같은 분들에게 도움이 되는 대책을 궁리하고, 사회적인 이슈로 공론화하는 일을 멈추지 말아야 한다는 것이 이 작품의 메시지로 보였다.

5. 마무리하며

인형극 희곡을 읽어보면, 대사와 지문들을 통해서 인형극 무대를 상상하고, 등장하는 인형들의 모습과 움직임을 떠올릴 수 있다. 이런 활동은 새로운 즐거움을 느끼게 해주면서 동시에 독특한 경험이다. 특히 어린 독자들에게는 상상력이 풍부해지고, 언어적 감수성이 증진된다. 그래서 학생들은 여럿이 모여서 함께 이 책의 인형극 희곡을 낭독해 보길 추천한다. 그리고 만약 기회가 된다면, 인형극 희곡에서 특정한 대목을 골라서, 거기에 등장하는 인형을 만들어보고, 인형의 움직임도 연구하여 다른 사람 앞에서 보여주는 경험을 하길 추천한다. 분명히 평생 잊지 못할 행복한 추억이 될 것이다.

인형극이 재미있고, 활성화되려면 여러 가지 요소가 충족되어야 한다. 그 가운데 중요한 요소로 거론할 수 있는 것은 문자로 기록된 훌륭한 인형극 희곡이 풍부해져야 한다는 점이다. 단단한 인형극 희곡이 뒷받침된 인형극 공연이라면 더 감동적이고 아름다운 인형극 공연이 될 수 있기 때문이다. 그러나 우리나라에서는 인형극 희곡을 출판하는 일이 쉽지 않았다. 출판 시장에서 특히 희곡 분야의 책이 대중의 관심에서 멀리 떨어져 있었기 때문이다. 그러나 지금부터라도 재미있으면서 의미 있는 인형극 희곡들이 책으로 출판되어 대중의 사랑을 많이 받아야 한다. 인형극 공연의 뿌리는 인형극 희곡이기 때문이다.

Strengthen the Roots of Puppet Theatre

Oh Pan–Jin

Theatre Critic | Lecturer at Seoul National University

1. Introduction

Plants take root in the soil, and their roots are covered in earth. Likewise, puppet theatre performances are rooted in the foundation of scripts, which carry traces of human life and diverse perspectives. Of course, some puppet theatre performances exist solely as live enactments rather than as written scripts, but when they are recorded in writing, they also become scripts, forming a script of words and actions. For puppet theatre in Korea to thrive and develop, there must be a rich collection of puppet play scripts crafted by playwrights with profound insight into human nature and a deep appreciation for the art of puppetry. This anthology is expected to serve as a catalyst in this regard. Furthermore, it will provide a solid foundation for the advancement of Korean puppet theatre, inspiring puppeteers and deeply moving audiences alike.

This anthology of puppet play scripts contains the texts of five outstanding puppet theatre performances: 〈Tale of Tales〉 by Jeong Seung-Jin, 〈The Story of Haru〉 by Ki Tae-In, 〈Dallae Story〉 by Jo Hyun-San, 〈Salt Doll〉 by Bae Geun-Young, and 〈Guroom and Yol〉 by Moon Jae-Hyun. Upon reading these five scripts, several distinct characteristics emerge. First, some works warmly portray the stories of everyday life. Second, some explore the essence of human existence and the significance of values in life. Third, some are deeply moving and beautiful, based on Korea's history, opposing war, and advocating peace in a way that resonates with people around the world.

2. Works deeply immersed in the stories of our lives

A. "Tale of Tales" by Jeung Seung-Jin

The playwright behind this puppet theatre script is Jeong Seung-Jin. He is a notable person in the Korean theatre scene, recognized for his talent for creating engaging puppet play scripts and other works across various genres. The play "Tale of Tales" featured in this anthology, is a reinterpretation of traditional folktales by him, transforming them into gripping yet profound puppet play scripts. Therefore, it has been praised for its solid narrative, engaging storytelling, and ability to express the full power of puppet play scripts. This puppet theatre is structured in a play-within-a-play format, in which one overarching performance encompasses three smaller stories. Specifically, the main narrative is based on The Umbrella peddler and the Straw Shoes peddler, while the embedded stories include "The Tiger Brother", "The Straw Shoes peddler and His Son", and "The Story of Dokkaebi". Audiences familiar with traditional tales may recognize these narratives, but Jeong Seung-Jin's spectacular reinterpretation transforms them into a dynamic and visually engaging puppet theatre. In academic terms, it can be said to be a work with excellent "intertextuality" or "textual interconnectedness". One of its most remarkable features is the way it interconnects related stories, encouraging a metacognitive viewing experience, which in turn enhances audience engagement. The script strategically condenses certain sections to maintain a fast-paced and suspenseful progression, while at other times, it expands on the original narratives with imaginative elements, enriching the emotional depth and thematic resonance of the play.

Let's examine in detail the creative modifications made in this puppet play script. In the original work The Umbrella Peddler and the Straw Shoes Peddler, the two characters were family members, but in this version, their relationship has been redefined as strangers, and a monster story has been added to make it more engaging. Moreover, the personalities of the umbrella peddler, the straw shoes peddler, and the hunter have been reinterpreted and set as the woodcutter from The Tiger Brother, the son from The Straw Shoes Peddler's Father and Son, and the groom from The Story of Dokkaebi, which is both interesting and remarkable. Additionally, modifications made by reinterpreting specific details of the story stand out. For example, in the original The Story of Dokkaebi, the groom is attacked with a ripe persimmon, water, and a needle, whereas in this version, he is attacked with a poisonous apple, a poisonous flower, and a poisoned needle. By incorporating elements that are both familiar and distinct, the performance enables the audience to recognise and appreciate the differences. The original content was cleverly and subtly altered, and long, verbose dialogues and narratives were refined into shorter, clearer forms, enhancing freshness and pacing. This process created a new story with a lively rhythm, which then translated into a puppet performance where shadows, puppets, props, and actors seamlessly appeared, resulting in a dynamic and immersive production.

B. "The Story of Haru" by Ki Tae-In

The script for this puppet play was written by Ki Tae-In, the head of the theatre company Namu. "The Story of Haru" follows the life of its protagonist, Grandpa Haru, a man who collects discarded paper. He is a familiar figure in the city - an elderly man living alone in a shabby house. Every day, he gathers recyclables and returns home to his small dwelling, where he speaks to a photograph of his late wife and spends his days in solitude. One day, as he falls asleep from exhaustion, three mysterious guides in black appear, and his life story begins to unfold before him.

Some people mistakenly believe that puppet theatre only tells cute and cheerful stories and is meant solely for children. However, like other forms of art, many puppet performances deeply and truthfully explore the human experience, grounded in insight and love for humanity. This is because puppeteers engage with even seemingly heavy or dark themes and characters, continually posing profound questions about human nature and life. To align with the characteristics of the puppet theatre genre, performances have been created in diverse forms and narratives, accompanied by puppets crafted to match each story. As a result, it is not unusual to encounter profound ideas and emotions in puppet theatre, just as one would in other works of art or philosophical literature. A prime example is the work of Ki Tae-In, his play The Story of Haru is an exceptional piece that beautifully reflects deep insight into and love for humanity.

Three puppeteers, acting as guides, craft a puppet from white paper to depict the grandmother in her youth. At that moment, the grandfather awakens and finds himself reliving distant memories of his childhood. First, the young Haru puppet plays traditional games with his friends and flies a kite high into the sky alongside Granda Haru. Then, as sirens wail, the scene shifts to the Korean War era, where the grandfather appears as a soldier, firing a gun in the midst of battle. However, as these memories resurface, he shudders and recoils, unable to endure their painful weight. And young adult Haru appears, playing the harmonica as he meets the grandmother, unfolding a tender romance. Scenes like a chase between Haru and the Loafers, the grandmother transforming into a martial arts girl-fighter, and their affectionate moments are presented with warmth and humor. Then, a wedding scene unfolds, where the bride wears a jokduri(*ceremonial headpiece), and the groom dons a samo-gwan(*scholar's hat).[1] The newlyweds are then seen on their wedding night, lying together under the blanket. During his youth, Haru enjoys a joyful outing with his family. Accompanied by the sounds of an accordion, they watch a magic show, observe various animals, and ride a carousel - moments that symbolise the springtime of his life. In his early married years, Haru lives happily while diligently working in a factory. But, he eventually loses his job and begins to have conflicts with his wife. This marital strife is creatively and symbolically depicted as a puppet bullfight, making for a striking and memorable scene. During these difficult times, Haru tries to reconcile with his wife by playing the harmonica - the same tune he played for her during their courtship. As the years they spent together flash by in a rapid sequence of visual images, the final scene shows his wife ascending to the sky. At that moment, Haru, seeing a puppet of himself sitting on a bench, realises that he has passed away, too. Accepting this, he joyfully dances and follows his wife, departing on a long journey alongside the guides.

The narratives of the puppet plays created by our puppeteers

---

1) In traditional Korean weddings, it is customary for the bride to wear a jokduri(ceremonial headpiece) and the groom to wear a samo-gwan(scholar's hat).

are not limited to old folktales or stories from foreign cultures. The life stories of grandparents in our time can also be explored. A close examination of the mise-en-scène in the script and performance recordings reveals a remarkable ensemble on stage, where a human actor portraying the grandfather interacts seamlessly with a variety of uniquely crafted puppets. In short, the composition and direction of this puppet play are exceptionally diverse. As of 2025, this work serves as clear evidence that the life stories of today's elderly can become a compelling and deeply moving puppet theatre experience.

C. ⟨Dallae Story⟩ by Jo Hyun-San

The script for this puppet theatre was written by Jo Hyun-San of ArtstageSAN. The setting of this work is a farmhouse in spring, and the characters include a woman and a man. The story begins in the yard of a thatched-roof house. The woman, who has finished doing the laundry and placed it in a basket, prepares to hang the clothes on a drying line. Meanwhile, the man secretly places a pair of floral shoes for the woman inside her laundry basket. On a spring day, as butterflies flutter over the azalea-covered hill, the shy woman and the naive man come together and have a beautiful child named Dallae. When summer arrives, the man and Dallae, holding a fishing rod, attempt to catch fish, but they suddenly disappear while riding on a large fish. As autumn comes, with persimmons ripening and dragonflies darting through the air, Dallae asks her mother to pick persimmons for her and her father to catch dragonflies. On a winter night, under the bright moonlight and falling snow, Dallae runs around with her puppy and builds a snowman with her father. However, the sudden sound of an air raid shatters the peaceful moment. A tank crashes through the fence of their home, and the father is taken away. Gunfire erupts, and in the chaos, the man instinctively fires a gun at someone, leaving him in shock and confusion. As he stands on the boundary between reality and illusion, he sees Dallae, along with butterflies and fish that appear and vanish like fleeting memories. Fleeing from the air raid, the woman drops the floral shoes and hides with her head pressed to the ground. Trembling in fear, she follows the path guided by a butterfly and eventually finds the floral shoes her husband had given her. Holding them tightly, she recalls their past memories. Meanwhile, exhausted from playing alone in the dirt, Dallae drifts into sleep. Her stuffed puppy comes to life and finds her, and they play joyfully together. In her imagination, Dallae reunites with her mother and reminisces about their happy times. However, when she comes to her senses, her mother has disappeared, leaving only the lifeless puppy beside her. As Dallae clings tightly to the stuffed puppy, flower petals rain down upon her, marking the curtain's descent.

The defining characteristic of this puppet theatre script and performance lies in its vivid portrayal of a pastoral farmhouse setting and the beauty of life, rendered with the sensibility of a painted scene. Reading the script stimulates visual imagination through detailed descriptions of the puppets and props, allowing readers to experience the joy of envisioning the story as they read. The depiction of a rural family - a father, a mother, and their daughter - living happily through the four seasons is brought to life with remarkable clarity. The depiction of the loss of familial peace due to war can be felt and appreciated more vividly than in any other art form. If you search for the performance video links provided in this book, you will be able to watch the performance. The mise-en-scène of the puppet theatre stage feels both deeply Korean and of a world-class standard. Especially, the amazing manipulation of the puppets is particularly outstanding, making them appear as if they are truly alive and breathing. Watching the puppet theatre feels like experiencing a magical fantasy, bringing happiness, and it will be remembered as one of the most treasured performances, unforgettable for a lifetime.

3. Works exploring the essence of existence and searching for one's own dreams.

A. 〈Salt Doll〉 by Bae Geun-Young

The main character of the puppet theatre written by Bae Geun-Young is the Salt Doll. This character questions itself and becomes lost in contemplation, wondering who they are, where they come from, and where they are going. In the midst of this, the Salt Doll hears the sound of the "sea" carried by the wind. Then, the Salt Doll decides to journey to the sea to find the answer to the question that has sprouted in its heart. In other words, the Salt Doll embarks on a journey to find the sea, which is the root of its existence and the source of life. The Salt Doll first encounters "Water." Through its conversation with Water, it learns that this journey is a path of self-discovery, emphasising the importance of travelling with faith and happiness, while also requiring patience. And, the Salt Doll meets intense sunlight and learns that it is okay to take a rest along the way. Then, Salt Doll meets an old tree, where it feels a desire to stay in the warm and happy place like the tree's embrace. However, following the words of wildflowers, it chooses to continue on its path, searching for its own way. Furthermore, the Salt Doll meets Number, which tells it that reason and calmness are important, and that by following rules and analysis, one can reach the sea. However, the Salt Doll feels overwhelmed by this and decides to follow its heart once more. On its journey, it meets a girl, who tells the Salt Doll not to be troubled by details and promises happiness if it stays with her. However, the Salt Doll, feeling emptiness after hearing these words, begins walking towards the sea once again. Along the way, it meets a dark cloud that brings down a pain-inducing rain and tells the Salt Doll that going to the sea is meaningless. The cloud even calls the Salt Doll rude, causing it to become fearful of meeting anyone. Nevertheless, the Salt Doll firmly resolves to continue towards the sea. At the final obstacle in its journey to the sea, the Salt Doll meets Ice, a figure who locks everything in place to keep it near. Breaking free from the ice, the Salt Doll finally reaches the sea. Seeing the vast sea shining beautifully, the Salt Doll realises that it has been one with the sea from the beginning. The performance ends as the Salt Doll and the sea meet and merge into one.

This puppet theatre beautifully portrays the questions humans face in forming their identity, depicting the Salt Doll's journey to the sea as a quest for enlightenment, much like a seeker on a spiritual path. Similar to Antoine de Saint-Exupéry's "The Little Prince", the protagonist's journey, through encounters with various characters, symbolically expresses a message about the kind of life one should live. That is, it explores different characters and values through metaphors and symbols. When watching the performance video, playwright Bae Geun-Young symbolically and mysteriously expresses the meaning of life through the scenes where the Salt Doll meets various characters in different places. The Salt Doll's journey in search of the sea embodies the realization that all beings on Earth are interconnected and exist together. This work is regarded as a puppet theatre with considerable philosophical depth.

B. ⟨Guroom and Yol⟩ by Moon Jae-Hyun

The script of this puppet theatre is an adaptation of the fairy tale ⟨The Dreaming Little Pig Yol⟩ by Oh Mi-Kyung, reworked into a puppet play by Ato(Moon Jae-Hyun), the puppeteer and adapter. The protagonist of this script, Little Pig "Yol", is the youngest pig and is different from the others. He didn't like the usual "oink" sounds made by the other pigs, so he searched for the right sound and found "Yol Yol Yol." Thus, he named himself Yol. While the other pigs enjoyed eating and staying in their pigsty, Yol loved taking walks and smelling the flowers, and he was also very curious about the world around him. One day, Yol met a goat named "Guroom" by chance and learnt about the existence of the sky. Feeling frustrated that he couldn't see the sky right above his head, Yol dreamt of seeing it with his own eyes. However, the pigs had stiff necks and couldn't lift their heads, and Yol found it difficult to see the sky as well. Still, Little Pig Yol diligently practised neck exercises every day, determined to look at the sky. Although he didn't succeed right away, one day, as he jumped over a thorn bush, he rolled down a hill. After tumbling all the way down, Yol lay down and saw the sky for the first time in his life. Looking at the dazzlingly blue sky, Yol thought to himself.

"Just when Yol thought everything was over after falling, miraculously, a new path appeared. A completely different path that he had never noticed before."

However, Yol tells his friend, the goat Guroom, that he is happier about having become friends with Guroom than about seeing the sky which he had longed for. Through the process of searching for his dream, he realized the value of a true friend. ⟨Guroom and Yol⟩ contains the writer and adapter's wish for people to choose their own dreams and live their lives striving to achieve them. In addition, a message can also be found that it is important to dream not alone, but with friends or family.

When watching the video of this puppet theatre, one can

observe the use of puppets in various sizes and a table puppet stage that can be flexibly transformed into different shapes. In this, we can find traces of careful thought and effort to avoid relying on traditional puppet theatre styles and to effectively convey the message of the script. During the performance, puppeteer Moon Jae-Hyun not only held the wooden Yol puppet but also stepped out of the stage and into the audience. This directing technique was used to bring the actor closer to the audience, allowing them to immerse themselves in the performance or form a deeper connection. This puppet theatre is a solo performance, so the performer had the responsibility of playing multiple roles. In particular, it was a performance on an outdoor stage, where there was much noise, making it difficult for the audience to focus on the performance, but it was carried out smoothly. This was likely possible because of the rich acting experience and skill of the performer, Moon Jae-Hyun. Like any other performance, when experiencing the puppet theatre live, the joy of reading the puppet play script can be greatly enhanced.

4. Works that carry a message against war

Large and small wars continue to persist in various countries around the world. For example, the Russia-Ukraine war and the Israel-Palestine war are representative of these conflicts. In these wars, many people are killed or injured due to guns, knives, artillery, and shortages of daily necessities.

Those involved also carry emotional wounds that cannot be expressed in words. No one would disagree with the argument that these tragic wars, taking place on a global scale, must end immediately and should never happen again. Puppet theatre such as "Dallae Story" and "The Story of Haru" which focus on the scars of war on our land, strongly deliver messages of anti-war and peace through their stories about war.

A. ⟨Dallae Story⟩ by Jo Hyun-San

The decisive event that befell Dallae's family, who had been living happily, was war. Despite having spent all four seasons in happiness, Dallae's family was thrown into hardship due to war, regardless of their faults, hopes, or intentions. The author does not explicitly specify the Korean War, but the 1950 Korean War naturally comes to mind. As in that war, Dallae's father, one of the main characters in this script, did not want to participate in the war. However, he was forcibly taken and had to wield a gun, and eventually, he ended up killing someone. This inflicted an irreparable wound upon him. Likewise, Dallae's mother could not compose herself after her husband was taken away to war and her daughter vanished due to an air raid. It was not only the lives of the adults that were destroyed by war. Young Dallae is also heartbreakingly depicted and described as she loses her parents and becomes an orphan. The message that war leaves no victors but only losers is expressed in a deeply moving and realistic manner. Therefore, this puppet theatre is highly valuable and sophisticated in both its themes and its expression.

Watching the puppet performance or its video, one can see scenes where the actor directly uses a life-sized gun or where the moment the husband is taken away is described through shadow play. Such mise-en-scène elements in the puppet theatre maximise the audience's sense of immersion and allow for greater imaginative space. Through these devices, the playwright's intended message and emotions were effectively delivered to the audience, enhancing the impact of the play.

B. The Story of Haru by Ki Tae-in

While Dallae's Story by Jo Hyun-san depicts characters who have suffered irreparable damage due to war, The Story of Haru by Ki Tae-in portrays a character whose wounds from war are somewhat less severe. Unlike Dallae's family, whose lives were completely devastated and left beyond recovery, the protagonist of The Story of Haru is not a war victim to such an extreme degree. However, he is a war veteran who has suffered deep psychological scars from fighting on the battlefield. Analysing Grandpa Haru's character, he seems to symbolise Korean men born between the 1920s and 1940s. This generation endured the Korean War of 1950 and the industrialisation of the 1960s to 1980s, struggling through hardship. As suggested by the title, the play focuses on elderly people who have lived their lives just trying to survive day by day, without the luxury of thinking far into the future.

Although war is the central event of this puppet play, Haru's experience of being laid off from his job in his youth is also treated with weight. Of course, losing one's job cannot be compared to war, but unemployment is still a major life event that leaves lasting scars. The script also describes, in a heart-wrenching manner, Haru's lonely old age - where he struggles to survive by collecting and selling scrap materials, only to eventually pass away in solitude. The high poverty rate and severe suicide rates among the elderly in Korea are long-standing issues. On a national level, more attention should be given to elderly poverty, particularly in the context of growing social polarisation, and more comprehensive measures should be implemented. On an individual and community level, efforts should be made to help those like Grandpa Haru, ensuring that discussions about elderly welfare remain an active social issue. This seems to be the message of this work.

5. Conclusion

Reading puppet theatre scripts allows readers to imagine the puppet theatre stage, visualise the puppets, and picture their movements through the dialogue and stage directions. This activity not only provides a new kind of enjoyment but also offers a unique experience. Especially for young readers, it helps enhance their imagination and develop their linguistic sensitivity. Therefore, it is highly recommended that students gather together and take turns reading the scripts aloud. If possible, they should also select a specific scene from the script, create the corresponding puppets, study their movements, and perform in front of others. This experience will undoubtedly become a cherished and unforgettable memory.

For puppet theater to be both entertaining and widely embraced, several key factors must be met. Among them, having a rich collection of well-written puppet theatre scripts is essential. A puppet theatre supported by a strong script will naturally lead to a more moving and visually captivating performance. However, in Korea, publishing puppet theatre scripts has been challenging, as scripts, in general, have received little public interest in the publishing market. Nevertheless, from now on, entertaining and meaningful puppet theatre scripts should be published as books and gain greater popularity among audiences. The foundation of any puppet performance lies in its script.

극작가이며 배우이고 연출가이다. 1995년 문화일보 하계문예 단막희곡 〈중독자들〉이 당선되며 등단했고 창작마을 희곡문학상, 한국희곡 신인문학상, 대산창작기금 등을 받았으며 2018년에는 〈대한민국 극작가상〉을 수상했다. 사단법인 한국극작가협회 이사장, 재단법인 강원도립극단 초대 예술감독을 역임했다. 2019년부터 2024년까지 춘천인형극제 예술감독으로 재직했다.

저서

1998	〈절대사절〉, 도서출판 창작마을/희곡뱅크 창간호 단막 〈절대사절〉 수록
2000	〈양파〉, 도서출판 창작마을/한국극작워크샵 8기 희곡집 〈악몽〉 수록
2001	〈2001 한국대표희곡선〉, 집문당/한국연극협회 펴냄/〈고추 말리기〉 수록
2003	선욱현 희곡집1 〈피카소 돈년 두보〉, 도서출판 모시는사람들
2005	〈문학시간에 희곡 읽기1〉, 도서출판 나라말/〈의자는 잘못 없다〉 수록
2008	선욱현 희곡집2 〈거주자 우선 주차구역〉, 도서출판 모시는사람들
2011	선욱현 희곡집3 〈해를 쏜 소년〉, 도서출판 모시는사람들
2015	선욱현 희곡집4 〈돌아온다〉, 도서출판 모시는사람들
2015	선욱현 시집 〈만취〉, 도서출판 모시는사람들
2019	선욱현 희곡 〈허난설헌〉, 도서출판 평민사
2020	〈카모마일과 비빔면〉, 창작 2인극 선집2/월드2인극페스티벌 20주년 기념집 수록/지만지 출판
2023	〈한국단막극1〉, 평민사/우산(엄브렐러) 수록/한국, 러시아 어판 합본
2023	선욱현 희곡집5 〈아버지 이가 하얗다〉, 도서출판 모시는사람들

주요 발표작

- 연극 : 〈돌아온다〉, 〈의자는 잘못 없다〉, 〈절대사절〉, 〈황야의

물고기〉 등 다수
- 인형극/오브제/야외극: 〈물싸움_너무 오래된 전쟁〉, 〈오리대
  왕〉, 〈파롱이〉 등

Editor : Sun Wook-Hyun

He is a playwright, an actor, and a director. He made his
debut in 1995 when his one-act play 〈Addicts〉 won the
Summer Literary Contest of the Munhwa Newspaper. He
has received the Changjakmaeul Playwriting Award, the
Korean Playwrights Newcomer Award, and the Daesan
Creative Fund, and in 2018, he was awarded the 〈South
Korea Playwright Award〉. He served as the President of the
Korean Playwrights Association and the inaugural Artistic
Director of the Gangwon State Theater Company. From
2019 to 2024, he served as the Artistic Director of the
Chuncheon Puppet Festival.

소개 | 서평_오판진

약력

서울교육대학교 학사 졸업
서울교육대학교 석사 졸업
서울대학교 박사 졸업

주요 논문 및 저서

가면극 연행 체험 교육 연구(박사), 교육연극을 통한 동화교육 방법 연구(석사), 아동극 창작과 교육(저서), 연극에서 감정은 어떻게 작용하는가?(공역), 내 맘대로 할거야(아동극집) 외 다수

주요 경력

한국교육연극학회 이사, 한국아동문학학회 이사, 교사연극모임 '소꿉놀이' 회장, 공연과이론을위한모임 회원 외 다수

감수_김주연

약력

서울교육대학교 초등교육 전공 학사
영국 Birmingham City University Drama in Education MA
영국 Birmingham City university Ph.D

주요 논문 및 저서

How to embrace culturally different voices: a search to produce a new educational drama practice in Korea

주요 경력

영국 Birmingham City University Drama in Education MA Thesis with Distinction
한국초등국어교육연구소 봄하늘 우수 학술상
"2015 개정 교육과정 국어과 '연극'단원의 구성 방향: 드라마(drama)와 씨어터(theatre)의 통합에 기반을 둔 드라마 예술 형식"